THE DEATHGUARDS

THE DEATHGUARDS

PHYLLIS ANN KARR

A Reformed States of America Romance

WILDSIDE PRESS

Published by Wildside Press LLC.
www.wildsidebooks.com

INTRODUCTORY NOTES

The Reformed States of America exist in a timeline parallel to our own. The major split seems to have occurred about the year 1868. Since then, an indefinable tension has sought to realign the alternates, so that in some ways they are almost identical, in others startlingly different. The R.S.A. has been on metric since the 1880s; thus, temperatures are given in Celsius. "Wraparound" is their idiom for "weekend."

This is no attempt to depict actual university life in our U.S.A. time-line today. I have extrapolated backward from my own college experience of some decades ago and tried to adjust for the R.S.A. in its 1950s.

They say that nothing is impossible; but I'd guess it would be as nearly impossible to find an unused combination of Greek letters, as to populate a story in any setting resembling our own with characters none of whose names appear in any of our telephone books. The Greek houses in this novel are as fictitious as the characters, and any resemblance to actual ones past, present, or future is purely coincidental.

As in most tales of fiction, the opinions of the characters do not always match those of the author.

PRELUDE

OCTOBER 14, 1940

Songs and legends sprang up quickly about the fire that destroyed the original Hellmouth Amusement Park, up in the state of Minnemagantic, closest village the hamlet of Udder Bliss. It was the kind of disaster that inspired folklore, especially coming as it did the year after the curtain went up in Eurasia on Act II of the Last Great War. Many people—especially the pickets who had formed an ever-present circle around the park throughout its history—called the catastrophe another indicator that the R.S.A. would get into the Second Act fighting a lot sooner than it had into the First, back in the Nineteen Teens.

Hellmouth Amusement Park had first been erected in the wild 1920's, when Americans coped with horrifically runaway worldwide inflation by minting, printing, carving, and otherwise manufacturing their own bootleg media of exchange. Five elongated stories tall, Hellmouth towered above a field artistically strewn with black cinders. Its shape was that of a simianly canine head with fiery eyes above a huge, gaping mouth that served as the general entrance. A red-carpeted pathway led like a lolling tongue into a ground floor entrance maze of movie-projected flames and distorting mirrors. The middle floors comprised various restaurants and adult entertainment areas. The top floor, filled with more or less traditional amusement-park rides given a Dantesque look—for instance, the merry-go-rounds featured various gargoyles, dragons, and demons, alongside coal-black nightmares with blood-red eyes and blaze-crimson manes. Glass panels in the back of this top-floor cranium suggested the rides to be the visible inner workings of the monstrous brain. The lower floors being open only to people of sixteen years and older, the ears were outside elevators in which families with younger children could ride directly to and from the top floor. The entrance fee for sixteen- to twenty-five-year olds was twice that for adults twenty-five and older, but few people of either age group seemed to read the signs closely enough to notice.

Whatever went on in the fabled subbasement "dungeons" below Hellmouth Park was spoken of sometimes in boasts and oftener in whispers by people who claimed to have enjoyed—or suffered—visits down there, and survived.

Prominent in the folklore of the disastrous fire was a man in the bedraggled remnants of a cheap Dracula costume who ran through the park raising the alarm. Many songs and legends gave him a companion, usually a costumed dog, occasionally a costumed human being, the costume generally suggesting green scales and gold glitter. Almost everybody had a friend or relation, or knew of the friend of a relation or the relation of a friend of a friend, whom this man, with or without his companion, had helped escape the conflagration. One opinion held strongly that he was an angel. The contrary opinion asked, reasonably enough, what an angel would be doing clad in the rags of a cheap vampire costume.

Whoever or whatever this hero in the shredded costume and his equally heroic companion may have been, he or they never came forward after the disaster. It was generally assumed that, if not actually supernatural beings or else the stuff of pure folklore, he or they must have perished heroically in the blazing collapse of the demonic head.

The following year, Hellmouth Park was rebuilt on the original site, to reopen on the same day the R.S.A. entered the war. This was anything but coincidence, according to the pickets, who were already regrouping as soon as the new construction began. Others, however, claimed that a visit to Hellmouth Amusement Park was an excellent way to escape for a few hours the worse horror of the war raging over two thirds of the world, across the Atlantic east over Eurasia and much of the Pacific.

PROLOGUE

TUESDAY, AUG. 14, 1945

V-P Day—Victory in the Pacific—and Hodag Crossing was delirious with celebration. No doubt like the whole of Minnemagantic, and every other state and territory in these Reformed States of America, not to mention every other country on the victors' side. But he didn't even like to think what was going on in finally-defeated Japan. He wondered if they were going to find the kind of death camps in Nipponese territory that the liberating troops had reported in Russia under Stalin and India under the Kali Party's Sign of the Svastika.

Of more immediate concern to him, the near-total euphoria had infected even the hospital. Most of the staff acted as if they'd been sneaking champagne, which made it easy for a fifteen-year-old vampire to sneak inside. And just like any other growing boy and, by what he had seen, growing girl, fifteen-year-old vampires were always hungry.

Watch out! *This* nurse didn't look slaphappy. She looked nervous, scared. He flattened himself against the wall and got ready to shoot the hypnotic stare, but she never even turned her head his way, just fast-stepped right on by.

He slid into the room she'd just left. Two beds, one occupied. By a boy maybe two or three years younger than himself. A boy red-faced and shivering, gasping and nose-bleeding. Unconscious, or as good as.

From the nose or not, the blood smelled good. Handy thing they were safe in an Upper Midwest general hospital and not in some crowded military infirmary where all the beds would be occupied. Still, he had to hurry. That nurse looked as if she was heading for help as quickly as she could. He hoped the mad celebrating—you could hear it even in here—would slow her down enough for his snack.

The boy's blood tasted as good as it smelled. Basically type O, with the flavors he thought of—like a wine connoisseur, simply to have labels for them—as chocolate, peach, and raspberry. And the tang he liked to call "sharp." Only…not really sharp. Seemed a lot weaker than usual. Not much more than a hint. A *soupçon*, as the French said.

He paused, lifted his mouth from the boy's face, smacked his lips in concentration. The sharp was diluted, very much diluted. That was it.

The few people who didn't have the sharp naturally, didn't have it at all. He guessed it was something like A and B. Could this mean…

Maybe they'd given this boy a transfusion of the wrong kind of blood! A type that could kill him—that'd be why the nurse was running scared.

Could he…would it save this boy if…as Irina had done for him…he bent, bit a vein, and started sucking again, sucking as fast as he could, sucking for all that he was worth…and then, when his victim was bled white and his stomach full to bursting, he bit open the vein in his own wrist, bent over, forced it to the patient's mouth, and reached around with his other hand to pinch his nostrils, *making* him drink, unconscious or not.

From what Irina had told him—his mother in blood, who'd been staked—as *he* was probably going to be staked if he didn't hurry—a vampire's digestion purified any blood, making it safe for any other vampire to drink, whatever its owner's health, whatever its type. Types didn't matter for blood as food. Not A or B or O or any of all those other flavors medicine didn't seem to know about yet.

He let the boy get a breath, pinched his nostrils again, kept doing it, breath and swallows, breath and swallows, until color was coming back into the bled-white face. When the patient's body was drained and fighting desperately to stay alive, vampire blood went from stomach to circulation almost as fast as by direct transfusion into an artery. He knew by his own experience, when Irina did it to him. He'd never wanted or expected to do it to anybody else. Ever.

The boy opened his eyes, looked up, said, "Huh," and shut his eyes again. Hearing footsteps near the door, the vampire slid behind the empty bed, to crouch there and listen.

"This is the patient?"—a man's voice. He recognized it. The Muslim doctor, the refugee from what India had been doing during the War.

"He looks—he looks better now!"—a woman's. He thought he recognized her voice, too. M. Wanamaker, the nurse.

"Transfusion reaction, you thought?"

"Acute. Fever, chills, racing heart, shortness of breath, hemorrhage…"

A rustling of paper.

"I didn't take time to fill in his chart," Nurse Wanamaker apologized. (Yes, he was sure it was her.) "It seemed more important to get a doctor right away. And with everyone…you know…"

"Yes." Dr. al Shammari's voice didn't sound approving. "I wonder if the army medics celebrate themselves like this today. Can you remember—"

"Temperature up to 39.5—heart rate 95, respiration uneven but—"

"Chest or back pains?"

"I don't know, doctor. He was unresponsive when I came in."

"Then we will not wake him to ask now when he appears so comfortable…breathing easily…a good and natural sleep. Skin a little pale, but not clammy."

"But if it wasn't hemolytic transfusion reaction…"

"Could it have perhaps corrected itself? There is so much about these things we do not yet— What is this?"

"I don't know. Could something have bitten him in the water? Before they fished him out?"

"Whoever was his emergency team, they failed to make a note of it on his chart. Who were they?"

"Let me see…Dr. Blakely and Ken Sondergaard. Oh, my!" The nurse made a strange little sound—a laugh? "Can you think what that math professor over at the university would say?"

"What professor?"

"Professor Fairchild. Matthew, I think. My oldest daughter had him last semester. According to her, there's a campus rumor that says he's teaching math because he's too far out for the Parapsychology and that new Psychomystical or whatever they call it Department—*they* won't have him! *He'd* probably call this the mark of a vampire!"

"Would he? Let us hope that Dr. Matthew Fairchild does not see what we saw to happen in India. What they find there at last, the liberators, all this summer. This would give your vampire-fearing professor something actual to worry his mind. For now, we will bandage the boy's neck, and whenever Blakely or Sondergaard see fit to rejoin the sober, we will question them."

"He still seems very pale. Maybe it's just because he was so flushed earlier, but… Do you think we should try another transfusion? I believe we still have enough Type O on hand."

The vampire hiding behind one of the far beds held his breath and thought at them, hard, *"No! No! No!"* He was still giddy from his own loss of blood, his stomach was still protesting, his huge last meal hadn't made it through into his own veins yet—a "victim's" blood didn't go into a vampire's system as quickly as the other way, it took almost as long as for anyone else to digest a regular food meal—another complete exchange was beyond him right now, even if he could hope to be alone with the boy long enough…

"No, I think not," said Dr. al Shammari. *(Thank God! Maybe this power of suggestion even works at a distance.)* "I think that I remember Landsteiner has done further work in this field, found new evidence… I will try to find his newest article again tonight. Meanwhile, as long as—let me see, Clement Black—seems to sleep so comfortably, I do not want to risk another transfusion, even with Type O. There was maybe some confusion the first time. But also, there can be factors we do not yet understand. And what you say sounds like transfusion reaction. So for now, we will simply keep young M. Black under close observation. When he wakes of himself, feed him a nice steak, very rare, and one glass of red wine."

"He's underage."

"I will write a prescription for the wine. Also the steak, if it must be purchased, and we will hope to find a butcher sober today."

Their footsteps left the room. "Close observation" had to leave time for checking on any other patients who hadn't gotten up, well enough or not, and joined most of the staff in celebrating V-P Day.

As soon as the vampire felt sure they were gone, he pulled himself up from behind the bed. He might not have much time to make his exit, but now he could always act drunk and pretend he'd been celebrating, too, and wasn't entirely sure what place it was he was stumbling around in.

So. Professor Matthew Fairchild, Math Department, University of Minnemagantic, here in town. Hadn't he heard that name before? In connection with one of the Greek houses?

That was where they'd found Irina Kiripovna's body, over in Greek Town. Sheriff Nurmi's investigation had been worth roughly as much as a sodden tissue. A prostitute—and a Russky one at that, never mind that Irina had left the old country well before Russia invaded Poland in 1939— A Russky hooker daring to let her body be found contaminating good, clean, wholesome Greek Town. Never mind about the fence post through her heart. That only went to prove it had been some sort of freak accident.

And now he had done what he'd promised himself he would never do— Bitten someone else and passed it along. A boy who would very likely have died otherwise, but still… He made himself another promise as he wove his way out of the hospital, acting drunk in case anyone saw him: I will be there for this boy. The way Irina couldn't be there for me.

I will be there, whether I can watch over him close at hand or must do it from a distance.

INTERLUDE: 1947-'48

In the early post-War flush of peace and prosperity, Hellmouth Amusement Park got a neighbor. Roughly twice the length of a football field away, in what had been—and remained—a large green pasture complete with cows—rose Heavengate Amusement Park: seven soaring stories of white marble and sparkling glass, every window arch suggesting Age of Faith cathedrals, flowering greenery on every balcony suggesting a redeemed version of the Hanging Gardens of Babylon. The windows of even-numbered stories were clear glass for a light and airy effect; of odd-numbered, stained glass to rival Chartres. A very straight and narrow flagstone walk led to the lofty entrance gate of delicate gilt wirework, before which sat a desk clerk costumed as St. Peter, who made a show of consulting an impressive tome before accepting any visitor's entrance fee. Very occasionally he refused admittance to some obviously rowdy, inebriated, insulting, or publicly notorious individual, with a melancholy nod of his white head toward the rival park across the way (which admitted anyone at all who was at least sixteen and paid); occasionally, also, he let someone—not always famously distinguished for good works—pass free of charge through the mother-of-pearl gates; but for most, he deposited their entrance fee in a drawer below his white marble desktop. On the desktop itself could be seen nothing but the massive, gilt-edged book, a pair of showy gold keys, and sometimes a crystal goblet from which the saint sipped innocent refreshment.

Although Heavengate's entrance fee for adults over twenty-one was half what Hellmouth charged for sixteen- to twenty-five-year olds, nominal for juveniles, and nothing for children younger than seven—all of whom were allowed free access to the entire park—Heavengate got noticeably less custom than Hellmouth. Curiously enough, it attracted almost as many pickets. There was a widely believed rumor to the effect that both parks were backed by the same owners and management, and that at least some of the pickets were secretly in the parks' own employ.

PART I
FALL

CHAPTER 1

FRIDAY, OCT. 6

"I was born," said Pater Fairchild, "the same year this university was founded, 1884. Pi Rho has been a presence here since the following term, and never in those sixty-five years has this fraternity nor, to the best of my knowledge, any other in Hodag Crossing, welcomed a practicing vampire among its members."

"Question," Ramon Mendoza said calmly, from his vantage point as a junior. "Does our own mixed diet make us 'practicing' omnivores?"

"A question of mere semantics, Mendoza."

"But, Pater Fairchild, sir," Spud said, frowning in concentration, "aren't semantics supposed to be pretty important? Shaping the way people think and all?"

"Perhaps I ought to have said, 'an openly self-acknowledged' vampire." The fraternity house father sounded impatient.

Ramon smiled. "I see. Clement Czarny would better meet your moral criteria if he pretended to be other than what he is. If he…well, let us suppose, instead of provisioning himself from friendly butchers and carrying about with him a needle to beg from the kindness of friends and strangers the few drops of human he requires to make the lunch in his thermos complete nutrition for him, acquired all his nourishment on the sly, perhaps even bit a few necks now and then at midnight?"

"How do we know he doesn't?" Fred asked. "I'll bet that cute little Keiko Kato would love to let him take a little bite out of her neck every so often."

"Fletcher," Pater Fairchild told Fred sternly, "that will be enough. Whatever his…shall we say, nutritional disadvantages? I have never heard Czarny speak disrespectfully of the complementary gender or any member thereof."

"Exactly, Pater. Never in your hearing."

"Neither have I, Fletcher," said Mendoza. "Have you?"

Fred answered, "And how much chance have we had to chat that stuff over with him, during Rushtide and all?"

"As for the biting of necks," Ramon went on almost like Fred hadn't spoken at all, "I, for one, incline to believe our young vampire's integrity in this and other matters."

"Oh, sure!" Fred kept it up. "Here and now you do. But how would you like to be out alone in the same tent with him?"

The junior looked down his nose at Fred. "Better him than you, Fletcher."

"That is enough, men!" said Pater Fairchild. "Very well. Knowing nothing against Czarny aside from his openly self-acknowledged vampirism, shall we put it to the vote?"

They were sitting around the heavy old pine table in the basement Meeting Room of the Pi Rho House, discussing which of this year's hopeful rushees they were going to drop in on Sunday night with the word, "Okay, lower life forms, Hell Week starts tomorrow!" Like they did it to Spud last year—he guessed he probably wasn't ever going to forget the mix of elation and butterflies, like getting dumped into a barrel of beer like some floater in a Shakespeare play, wasn't it? and rolled around inside happily sloshing. And now here he was on this year's Pledge Committee, with Pater Fairchild, House Prexy Carl Avosso, the super-aristocratic junior Ramon Mendoza, Spud's fellow sophomore Fred Fletcher, and a list of ten promising candidates.

"I vote Nay on Czarny," Fred said right away.

"And I vote, Aye," Mendoza said quietly.

"Aye," said Carl. "That is, Yes. Affirmative."

Then they all looked at Spud.

Between double bedrooms, singles, and two triples, the Pi Rho house slept forty brothers and the house father. 'Way back when, they'd started with the idea that every June ten would graduate and every fall ten more would get brought in to fill those beds back up. It didn't work out that neat and tidy. Sometimes a brother liked living in the house so much that he stayed on as a grad student. Sometimes there were more than ten pledglings and they all stuck right through Hell Week. Sometimes, for one reason or another, somebody left early—they said a lot of that had happened during the War. But brothers who couldn't get a bed in the house right away could always ask to go on the waiting list. This committee didn't really have to weed anybody off the list this year, none of the rushees who'd made it this far.

But now, even with a list of just the right number, Pater Fairchild was questioning Clemmie.

If Spud voted with the upperclassmen, that'd settle it. It'd be three to one, and Clement would be in. If Spud voted with his good buddy Fred, that'd probably settle it, too. It'd be a tie vote, and go to the house father for a tie-breaker, and unless Pater Fairchild did a sudden about-face, or had just been testing them or something, Clemmie would be out, without even his chance to face Hell Week.

So what did Spud do? All he really had to go on were just the other guys' arguments, and the pater's. If it'd been a football game, it'd be easy. Just do what your quarterback says, as far as the field lets you. But this thinking for himself... How'd I ever land on a real committee, anyway? Sure, sure, "just the honor of it," Fred had said. "Nothing to do, not really."

For a guy's good buddy, Fred Fletcher could be kind of a jerk.

Clemmie's a good kid. Maybe a little too good, maybe that's how come he lets on to being a vampire. I like Clemmie. He's okay. Never hurt me, never hurt anybody I ever heard of.

But the pater doesn't want him in. And the pater's voice, that goes for a lot. Unless Pater Fairchild's just testing us...

Thing was, if they dropped Clem, didn't they have to drop somebody else, too? The Purple Rose always wanted to go into Hell Week with an even number. Buddy System. Hoping the right roommates would find each other. The rest of the ideal scheme might get ragged, but so far as Spud knew they'd always managed to start Hell Week with an even number. And that'd leave it just eight this year...

Oh, Hell, Spud Bartlett, just do what feels right to your own conscience!

"I vote Aye," said the football player. "Yes."

The other nine names passed okay. Thank the Lord. If any other young floater had gotten questioned...but nobody else did. Pater Fairchild just read 'em off, name by name, and name by name, everybody murmured assent. Just once—on Carse Nugent, Fred muttered, "The Nougat's a piece of candy." But Mendoza said, "Then how did you let his name get this far?" and Avosso added, "If he is, Saturday night will weed him out, assuming he lasts that long."

Spud thought Mendoza's eyebrow went up when the prexy mentioned Saturday night, but he didn't say anything right then. Saturday night had always been the capper to Hell Week, the six-hour Midnight Haze, 1800 to 0200, when everybody who had lasted it out got a sponge bath, a good rubdown, a brotherly hug, and a soft bed to sleep it off till the painless formal Initiation Ceremony Sunday evening.

When all ten were passed, Mendoza brought it up again. "Concerning Saturday night. I believe we are overdue to bring our Midnight Haze into line with the new national protocol."

"Do you, Mendoza?" said Pater Fairchild. "Explain."

"The idea that penitential suffering on the home front ever did them any good on the war front was always mere theoretical philosophy, and better left to religious affiliations in any case. And the War has been over for five years. Our sister house went to the sorority version of the new national Midnight Haze in 1947."

"Chi Rho Epsilon still has something like it," said Avosso.

"Should we keep up with Chi Rho Epsilon?" Mendoza returned. "Shouldn't Chi Rho Epsilon be trying to keep up with us?"

"If you feel this way, Mendoza," said Pater Fairchild, "why did you join Pi Rho?"

Mendoza sat and looked back at the house father almost—not quite—long enough for it to come across as a staring contest. Finally he answered, "For the prestige, of course."

"And loyalty—to goals and ideals, as well as to brothers—is much of what gives our house its prestige," said the professor. "We swore five years ago that we would keep our tradition here at the University of Minnemagantic alive and well until the last deathguard was brought to justice."

"You may have sworn that in 1945," Mendoza returned. "Not having joined until three years later, I neither swore it, nor have I ever been given the choice to swear or refuse."

"That choice could have been yours had you opted to join the Inner Circle."

Again Mendoza returned Pater Fairchild's look. "And if I should exercise that option now?"

"It remains open to you."

"Perhaps I may. But only if, and when, we adopt the national Pi Rho protocol for the Midnight Haze."

All this time, they had been staring at each other. Now, at last, Pater Fairchild turned his eyes to the rest of the Committee. "Well, men, shall we vote on it?"

Fred said, "I vote, let's keep our own chapter's tradition in all its messy glory, and let the 'national protocol' look out for itself."

"I vote No," Spud said quickly, before he found himself the last one to vote again. "Let's go national."

Fred looked at him. "Hey, *we* had to go through it all last year, and we survived."

Yeah, thought Spud, and you've been looking forward ever since to doing it to other floaters, haven't you? "I still vote, let's go the national way," he said aloud, wondering how far it was worth the effort to go on being best buddies with Fred Fletcher. Well, the way Avosso had brought up Chi Rho Epsilon, he figured there'd be another vote for their U. of

M. tradition, and that'd throw it to Pater Fairchild, and nothing would change.

But Carl Avosso surprised him by voting with Mendoza, making it another three to one.

Pater Fairchild sighed. "So be it. Well, let us hope…"

"We have not voted the Inner Circle itself out of existence, Pater," Mendoza told him, sounding more man-to-man than student-to-mentor. "Indeed, you have tonight gained one more member."

CHAPTER 2

A WEEK LATER: SATURDAY, OCT. 14

Hell Week had been…well, beside the Inferno as pictured by Dante and other theological authorities, misnamed. "Boot Camp Week" might be a better name for it. All the same, Clement felt very grateful it was almost over. Only a few more hours…only the Midnight Haze…then the formal initiation tomorrow evening, and after that, full brotherhood in the most prestigious Greek House at the University of Minnemagantic, ties of fraternity brotherhood that'd open doors for him all the rest of his life, and, more important for right now, the chance to get back to combing the books and hope he could catch up on his studies in time to justify his full scholarship. At least he hadn't missed a single class. That would've been against Hell Week's own rules. But he was so far behind in homework and library hours… And in a pretty constant ache. They were all allowed just two asprik a day, at bedtime. Some of the floaters snuck more—one night even Solly swallowed an extra one at about oh three hundred hours. Clement hadn't taken his permitted two oftener than a couple of nights. It was plenty tricky keeping his conscience clean enough for normal living around the Hell Week activities. Made him feel, sometimes, like a renegade demon, so maybe it was a good name for it, after all. Tuesday, when Fred Fletcher and Evan Sterkel ordered Clement to steal them a Mae West blue-back from the newsstand, he'd actually stood up and refused, slave to master or not, explained that stealing condemned smut would be outright sinning on two counts, and he wouldn't be able to face sunlight, or so much as the shadow of a cross, might even have trouble handling silver coins. Fletcher said in that case, after he'd stolen the eight-pager he could just polish the Pi Rho silverware, when Ramon Mendoza came along and dragged the first two aside. The brothers never dressed each other down in front of the pledglings, but whatever was said in that exalted full-brother conference, the rules got relaxed just enough in Clement's case to exempt him from anything that might feel to him like a mortal sin.

At least being a vampire did him that much good. All the more important not to cheat on the little things, like sneaking more asprik than permitted. He wasn't sure how much good asprik did him, anyway.

Of course, if he hadn't been a vampire, he wouldn't have needed those exemptions. Ordinary people could still function normally even with all kinds of junk on their consciences.

It was like having to get a tooth pulled, he guessed. He hadn't been sick or had any tooth decay since getting turned into a vampire, but he had sometimes wondered if it'd do any good to get his fangs pulled. Dentists nor anybody else couldn't seem to see them as fangs, but they could see longish dog-teeth. But maybe the doggone clumsy things would just grow back. Like they did after that one dentist who agreed yes, they were kind of long, finally filed them down a little for him. Anyway. He could remember one time before the accident, when he needed a *lot* of drilling for a filling: sitting there dreading the next couple hours, comforting himself by thinking how good it was going to feel once they were over! That was the dentist who a year or so later had tried filing his fangs down.

Like Purgatory, maybe.

At the dorm room's other desk, Solly shut his book with a bang and said, "Guess we'd better get down to supper. The ladies might be waiting for us."

"Give 'em my best. I thought I'd skip supper tonight."

"Better not. They told us to make sure and eat something, keep our strength up."

"You know nothing but blood does that for me."

"Okay, come on down and drink your dinner. What else'll they do with it?"

Dr. al Shammari had authorized the dorm kitchen to keep a supply of butcher's blood on hand for Clement. They didn't keep much at a time. As far as anyone knew, Clement Czarny was the only vampire in town.

The men's dormitory and the women's were joined in the middle by a common dining room where the genders could mix socially for meals. Keiko was with Theda Jones, waiting for them beside the end of the line. "So," said Keiko, "think you floaters are really going through with it?"

"Be a lot of work for nothing," said Clement, "if we backed out now, with only a few more hours to go."

Theda said, "It'll be a few hours till we eat, if we don't actually get in line now the fellas are here."

"Maybe for the last time," Keiko said as they got in line. "Have you floaters thought about that?"

Clement swallowed. "There are lots of nights the Purple Rose opens its dinner table to women guests. And Sunday supper, always."

"And we can come get lunches here lots of days," Solly added. "Closer to classes."

Keiko shook her head. "I'll take whatever we can get, but it won't be the same."

Theda said brightly, "Y'know, I think maybe I'll pledge the sister house next time they rush. Pi Psi, the Purple Sigh."

"Yeah, that'd solve the problem, all right," said Solly. "How about you, Cake-o? Why don't you paddle up that stream, too?"

She shook her head. "I'm an Independent. I've always been an Independent, and I'll always be an Independent. Momma, this kitten don't join *anything*."

"'S okay," said Solly. "We'll still invite you over, guest evenings."

"Yeah, 'f you two lunk-heads really go through with it all the way."

"Sure, no question," Solly said with more confidence than Clement felt. "What's going to stop us now?"

"At this point," the vampire said, "I'm not sure we could back out even if we wanted to."

* * * *

An hour and a half later, they lay bound wrists and ankles, gagged, blindfolded, and folded up two to a trunk, being driven in a rattletrap old pre-War car over rough, rocky roads to an unknown destination. It seemed like the ride was taking forever. Clement guessed, but wasn't quite a hundred percent sure, that his trunkmate was Solly. It would've been nice to be able to talk. To Solly or whoever else it could be. Instead, he occupied his mind with figuring out what he'd do if this was a real kidnapping and not a freewill thing to get into Pi Rho fraternity. Surely being a vampire should give him some kind of edge in any really desperate kind of situation? He guessed he could probably chew through his gag if he tried—dang fangs had to be good for *something!*—but then what? Hands behind him, so he couldn't chew them free. Would there be enough room in here to wiggle through and get his wrists in front? Well, air was getting into the trunk—maybe they'd drilled a few tiny holes somewhere—and if air was getting in, sound should get out. But if this was for real, he'd have to wait till they were parked somewhere he could hear strangers who might come and help right away. Not a very vampirish piece of heroics. Or if he and his trunkmate (he was about ninety-five percent sure it was Solly) were lying back to back instead of forehead to forehead, they could maybe get at each other's ropes with their fingers, which he kept wiggling to keep the circulation going. If he bit his gag off, he could explain it all to the other floater, maybe they could get themselves turned around back to back… Quite a few of the books and novels and things—that he'd combed right after it happened to him. When he was as a kid, the Phantom of the Opera had been his big favorite. He'd guessed Dracula mainly appealed to girls for some reason…maybe, deep down where he only about half glimpsed it himself, that was partly why he'd made up his mind to go with the Dracula uniform, because he'd just been figuring out why girls might go for that stuff… Anyway, a bunch of the stuff said vampires had superhuman strength. That'd be nice. Come in handy at times like this…if they'd really been in any danger. Not that Clement was any weakling, in a plain, healthy young male human way…but Superman, he wasn't. Even bigger in the vampire lore was the thing about the hypnotic powers it was supposed to give you, make people do what you wanted. Maybe he shouldn't have given up on that one, but it just hadn't fit with being good enough to get along with crosses and sunshine and stuff. Hypnotizing ladies into…that'd sure make the crosses and stuff hard on him! Hypnosis as self-defense, now that should be plenty virtuous, his conscience should be perfectly okay with that. Only, how did you practice? When you were spending all day, almost every day, with pretty good people, and almost never met any really bad ones. Hypnosis as a martial arts class for vampires? Not enough of us around! Far as I know, I haven't ever met another one, except that one who did it to me, whoever it was and wherever he or she is by now. Anyway, the time to use hypnosis or any of that stuff would've been before they got you all tied up like a… like a Thanksgiving turkey. Now, the only thing that'd do it would be superhuman strength, which we've already established is a lot of hooey. Like vampiric immortality, he hoped. He didn't want to end up staked, but better even that than living on and on forever… Well, there'd always be the End of the World to look forward to. Wonder how it'd be, seeing the End of the World start while you were still one of the live ones? If it hadn't been full fraternity brothers, you can bet he'd never have let them tie him up like this, not just two of them. It'd take a lot more than two, if he'd put up any kind of fight. Well, what he'd seen of life, mostly you seemed to have to pay for the good things later—old age and sickness after love and marriage…kind of a good deal, for once paying first—getting hazed and all—and then getting the good stuff, getting into the best Greek house at the U. of M. Did vampires get old and gray? I grew up okay, but will I keep on aging? Or do all vampires get staked young because they never get old? Clement sighed.

Solly—or whoever the other floater was, but he was pretty sure it was Solly—gave two little grunts, like a question. Could have been "Clement?" Does he know who I am? Or could have been "What's wrong?" or "Okay?" or almost anything.

Clement returned three answering grunts, for "I'm okay," or whatever Solly (or whoever) made of it. How the heck did the "Children of the Night," the wolves and bats and things, communicate with just howls and yips and squeaks? He was a vampire, for jiminy's sake, he was supposed to be able to order the Children of the Night around, summon them to his assistance and all that. *How?* Sure be handy if he knew. Too bad nobody ever taught him their language. Where's Dr. Dolittle when you need him? And there was another thing that'd come in very handy—this business about vampires being able to turn themselves into bats or even fog—in some movies, pretty well any time they wanted. *HOW?* Not that a bat could fly around very well inside a car trunk, no matter how roomy…for a car trunk…but he wouldn't have to fly, just change—ropes drop right off—change back, *voila!* untied and free. Yeah, handiest trick of all. Too bad nobody had ever hinted how you did it. In fact, far as he could see, he hadn't gotten a single doggone advantage out of being a vampire—if you didn't count still being alive—except maybe never getting sick, unless that was just coincidence. And getting all the raw blood he needed in his diet could get tricky sometimes. Good thing he only needed just a few drops of human mixed in with any kind of animal blood, good thing Dr. al Shammari was always willing to renew his prescription. And an extra lot of trouble staying good enough not to be bothered by crosses and stuff. Thank God for family and friends. Good family, good friends. Soon going to include a whole frat house, lots of social prestige, brothers in positions to open up all kinds of doors for him later on in life… If he turned into either a bat or a little swirl of fog, all his clothes would come off along with the ropes and gag and blindfold. Then when he turned back into himself…the movies always just slid over that part, BUT. He imagined trying to get dressed again in the car trunk here, cramped up with Solly, or whoever. And couldn't help laughing a little.

"Mmpf?" Solly, or whoever, grunted again.

"Mmm mmm mm-mmm." Tell you later, or however he heard it.

The car finally stopped somewhere, the trunk was opened, its passengers dragged out. Clement and Solly were never to be sure whether or not they had ridden together. Probably every pair of the pledges per trunkful had grunted at each other. Meanwhile, Clement found himself carried over somebody's shoulder about a dozen steps, then stood up, his arms—not his legs—unbound and then rebound around a tree. From car trunk to tree trunk in…how many minutes?

"Okay, dog dung, listen up!" Fred Fletcher's voice. "You've got an hour to get yourselves untied. Every man for himself. No helping anybody else. Once you've got your arms and legs loose, take off your blindfold. Leave your gag in place. Repeat. Leave your gag alone, on pain of disqualification. But blindfold off, so you can see the campfire. Head for it. When you get there, kneel and bow your head to the Lord High Pooh-Bah and await further developments. Patiently. Oh, and, Czarny. No cheating and turning yourself into a bat. We'll have a cross ready to test your conscience."

A few more general insults, which didn't mean anything, not really, all just part of the hazing. And then, as far as Clement could tell, he was alone. He guessed his fellow pledglings were tied to other trees not too far away. He heard some of them grunting.

He stretched his fingers and concentrated. They'd really chosen this tree for size. He could just…find…the knot at each wrist with the fingers of the other hand.

There was a poem they'd had in high school English Lit, about an innkeeper's daughter who loved a highwayman, and the redcoat soldiers set an ambush for him, bound her up somehow "with a musket beneath her breast," and she worked away until she could just touch the trigger with one finger, and shoot the musket off in time to warn her lover "with her death." Clement had always had a very hard time trying to picture that, exactly. They'd tied her hands "behind her"—yes, the poem said it just that way, he was sure—and she could work one of her hands far enough around to get hold of the trigger…and no farther? Seems like she'd just about have to get them loose completely. And then, why didn't the bullet just blow off her breast on its way to the ceiling. Would that actually have *killed* her? Right away, as opposed to bleeding to death? Come to that, why had the darn stupid redcoats even loaded that doggone musket? Those old muskets were pretty hard to load, weren't they? Complicated, wadding things in and ramming them down. Why go through all that when the musket was just for…show, he guessed. And then, didn't they have to be cocked every time? How did she cock it? Why did they tie her up with it in the first place? Well, it was still a darn good story, just hard to…visualize…

Seemed to be plain old square knots. Pretty tight, but… Be easier if he *could* turn himself into a bat for a minute—he grinned in his mind at Fletcher's crack…but…sure…he could do this in an hour, easy. Less than an hour.…

…Less than an hour later—maybe even less than half an hour—he was kicking out of his loosened ankle ropes and pulling off his blindfold. Then the gag…a lot more carefully, because that one had to go back on before he headed for the campfire. There was just one other floater within easy sight of his tree…the other guys had to be scattered around farther away…and the light was bad and the blindfold and gag acted like a mask, but yeah, he figured it just about had to be Solly. By the height and weight, and the nose and chin—what he could see of them in the flicker from the campfire over yonder. And probably the clothes, though inside-out sweatshirts and jeans were pretty anonymous.

Ramon had told Clement "in confidence" that the older brothers really liked their pledglings to kick back against orders sometimes, to show some good, healthy spirit of rebellion. That was why he figured it wasn't cheating to take his gag off for a few minutes and go help Solly get his hands untied. He'd still be okay with that test cross of Fred Fletcher's. And why else had they tied Solly and Clement to trees so close together? Probably the guys were buddied up like this all around the campfire.

Clement went up to him and whispered, "Solly?"

Solly nodded. He knew everything Clement's special "big brother" had told him the way Clem—Solly insisted on calling him "Clem," and Clement had given up trying to change him, because you had to put up with a few things from best friends—knew everything Solly's special "big brother," Joe Achinua, had told Solly. Sharing secrets.

In five minutes the vampire had his best buddy's hands loose and blindfold off. Then they exchanged a knuckle handshake and Clement carefully tied his gag back in place and headed for the campfire, leaving Solly to get his own legs untied.

The ground was pretty clear between trees, and reaching the campfire was easy. Brothers were sitting around it laughing and singing, drinking beer and roasting wieners. The Lord High Pooh-Bah was easy to spot, over there on the far side of the fire, his face all war-painted with wild designs in reds and oranges, highlight dabs of blue and green, some kind of colorful blanket around his shoulders, and a kitchen colander turned upside down and stuck over with strawflowers for a crown. He was sitting up above everybody else, on a thronelike thing that was probably a folding chair draped with a blanket or curtain, and standing on boards or something to elevate it.

Clement did a quick nose count. A bunch of guys must've beaten him to the campfire. Andy Stebbens and Randy Lundquist and "Vibes" Bhumiratana and...everyone else he who he could recognize in the flickering light and shadows was a full brother. Fourteen here already, he made number fifteen—an odd number, so the Lord High Pooh-Bah had to be an extra.

All the time he was counting and considering, Clement was making his way around the fire to the cleared space in front of the Lord High Pooh-Bah—who he guessed was probably Spud Bartlett underneath all that warpaint and the flowered colander. When he got there, as per command, he put on his big show of meekness, knelt, bowed his head, and waited.

"Well, well, well, another little one," rumbled the Lord High. Yep, sounded like Spud, all right. "Rise," he went on, "turn around and present your infant face to the circle."

Clement obeyed.

"Does anybody here present among us claim this infant?" Spud sounded like he was reading from a script.

"I do." That was Ramon—Ramon Mendoza! He must've been one of the ones in heavy shadow. Clement was flattered. Even proud. Yeah, Ramon was officially his "big brother," but he was also a junior, and upperclass brothers didn't usually take that much part in the hazing ceremonies, left it to the sophomores, mostly just saved their own exalted presences for the actual Solemn Initiation on Sunday evening when the initiates were all purged and proven.

"You know what to do, O brave one," Spud recited.

Ramon came over, turned Clement back around facing the throne, and took off his gag. Ramon was the only Pi Rho taller than Clement, by a couple of centimeters.

At the Lord High's elbow, Fred Fletcher was holding a penlight in his teeth while riffling through some sheets of paper. He found the one he wanted and passed it up to Spud with a big show of reverence, the penlight still in his mouth making it look a little ridiculous.

Spud took the paper, looked at it, and handed it regally to Clement. "Okay, lowly-but-aspiring pledgling, sing!"

Holding the paper to the light, Clement studied the words. The tune was obvious:

> *"Oh, what a beautiful evening,*
> *Oh, what a beautiful night!*
> *I've got a beautiful feeling—*
> *Gonna find me a good neck to bite."*

So they'd tailored it to him specifically. Maybe they had a special set of lyrics for every individual one of the pledges. The new last line had a few more syllables than the actual lyric, so he took a second to sing it through in his head before opening his mouth and giving it his best:

> *"Oh, what a beautiful..."*

Turned out that figuring out how to sing the last line was a waste. By the time he got to "evening," the whole group—even his fellow pledges—were booing, hissing, catcalling, and howling. Huh? thought Clement, trying to project his baritone above the ruckus. I'm a music major, for gosh sakes, majoring in voice! Even after Father O'Flynn decided

I shouldn't be an altar boy any more on account of turning into a vampire—okay, he said I was getting a little old for it, but we all know—they still let me sing in the choir! I had the lead in the high school operetta three years in a row, and Professor Sharma says I've got a good shot for Papageno when they hold the opera try-outs next week.

He'd made it to the second "beautiful" when just at the edge of his line of sight the Lord High held one hand out with the thumb pointed down, and Ramon slapped the gag back over the singer's mouth. He looked around, and his big brother gave him a wink.

All the others were singing the old limerick about the radio crooner whose singing was so bad they shot him at once if not sooner, but it was okay. Ramon's wink had confirmed Clement's suspicion that this was all part of the joke—the last of the ribbing, he hoped and prayed, seeing how Andy and Randy and Vibes looked like they were blending right in with the brothers now. So he just stood and waited till they were finished, and Ramon took his gag off again and tossed it on the fire. They didn't toss all the gags on the fire, even though what they really were, were big old folded neckerchiefs. Clement guessed it was sort of like Ramon had drunk a toast and then broken the glass. So the vampire grinned and told them all, quite truthfully, "Oh, yeah? Well, you floaters had better not plan on entering any singing competitions any time soon, yourselves. Where're those wieners?"

About then Solly made it to the campfire, knelt to the Lord High, had his gag removed by Tim Nurmi the sheriff's nephew, and got his sheet of paper from Fred. He studied it a minute, his lips moving silently, before starting to sing,

> "In a dorm room at midnight a poor little frosh,
> Sang homework, oh homework, oh—"

That was the farthest he got before they drowned him out and the Lord High gave his thumbs-down. Clement didn't join in the hooting or bad radio crooner song, and they didn't make him. Even for a joke, he could only go so far in putting anybody else down before the old vampire taboos started prickling, and even if Fred hadn't said anything more about using that cross to make sure he hadn't cheated somewhere, he probably still had it ready in his pocket.

In fact, Fred never did pull it out, all evening. It wasn't until the celebration after the solemn and painless formal Initiation the following evening that he told the new brothers, while they laughed over their Hell Week ordeals, "All the same, you young floaters had it easy compared with what we went through last year. Especially the Saturday night stuff."

CHAPTER 3

A FEW DAYS LATER: TUESDAY, OCT. 17

"It was a most interesting case," said Dr. Rabar al Shammari. "One of the most interesting I have witnessed. Five years ago it was now, on V-P Day, which makes it simple to remember the date."

"There is no chance," Dr. Pundarit Sharma asked, "that this nurse could not have been…confused, a little…on that particular date?"

Dr. al Shammari shook his head. "To my own thought, no. Others might always question, in light of that date, and so I wait to publish. For myself, I would say that M. Dolores Wanamaker and I were—I will not say the *only* two who refused even one drop of celebration—but certainly that our heads were two of the clearest in this hospital that day, and if she saw symptoms of transfusion reaction, I believe that she saw some undiagnosed condition which mimicks it very closely, or else a spontaneous remission. I do not know of any other spontaneous remissions."

"This is the young man who is currently a favorite student of my wife," Dr. Sharma verified. "Clement Czarny, who believes that he was made into a vampire that day."

"A very devout belief." Again Dr. al Shammari nodded, this time in affirmation. "Yes, there must be a strong psychomystical element—as they call it—in this phenomenon. His last name at that time was Black."

"And he changed it to 'Czarny'? Which is, I think, the Russian word for 'Black'?"

"In any case, Slavic. I think it was the family name of his grandparents, which they changed when they came here to America."

"And Clement had it changed back, at the same time when outrage was running so high against the Russians as well as the Hindu? The lad has courage," Dr. Sharma said admiringly.

"This 'psychomystique' is a strange and a powerful dimension. He may have felt that these two things—vampire and Russian—would balance each other out, that somehow people would accept a Slavic vampire more easily than they would one completely American."

"His usual dress is that of the movie Dracula."

"Yes. I see him regularly, to renew his prescription. That is the most interesting thing, perhaps, of all," the Muslim doctor went on. "In this one way, he seems indeed to be a 'vampire.' He must consume raw blood, and a few drops of it at least must be human. If this is purely of the psychomystique, it is so deep that it should interest those who specialize in studies of the mind and the spirit. Even with monkey blood substituted for human, he quickly develops symptoms of malnutrition. He must have these few drops of human to mix every day with the blood of ducks and cows—forgive me, my brother—which one can obtain from friendly butchers."

"The way Westerners treat cattle no longer enrages or oversets me," the Hindu doctor replied. "One adjusts when one must. Perhaps you could publish a study of this personal perception of dietary need, without going into too great detail of that day's celebrations at this hospital, which were a thing that happened everywhere in the victors' world on that day."

"Yes, I plan to publish a careful account of his vampirism, when I have been able to watch it a few years longer." The Muslim doctor sighed. "One wonders how much relevant data there might be in those records of research done in the Kali Camps of India and the Eugenics Farms of Russia during the War."

"One should not wonder that!" Dr. Sharma shook his head violently. "One should never wonder that! These data are forever tainted. They should be destroyed, and a final end put to the debate."

"I do not see that," Dr. al Shammari answered thoughtfully. "To use this research might bring perhaps a little benefit from the terrible tragedy."

"It would be to dishonor the memory of all those dead," the Hindu doctor said firmly. "And to open once again the wounds of those who survived. It would be to approve what was done in those evil places. To make our research from the suffering of those millions."

After a moment, the Muslim doctor argued, "But all medical research is based on the suffering of its subjects, is it not? That is its essential nature. How else will we understand how to cure and heal our patients in the future, if we do not study those whom we have at present?"

"When sickness and accident come unasked, uninvited by those who suffer, that is what I think you would call Mystery—Brahman, God, or perhaps the Will of Allah." Dr. Sharma had never renounced his birthright religion, though this was equivalent to young Clement Black reclaiming his Slavic surname, now that the Kali Camps had put Hinduism in so much disfavor here in the lands of the victors. "But when these evils are imposed by wicked persons on unwilling fellow creatures, it is for the world to offer compassion, not to exploit."

"I think," Dr. al Shammari answered soberly, "that if Fariza and I had been sent to such a place—although I praise Allah each day that she was killed first, when we escaped—the thought that our suffering might some day help others, would give us some comfort... I think that we might have felt it would be to honor our memory.... But did I exploit my patient then, when I tested his dietary need?"

"You tested how real his need was. Was this not for the young man's own health?"

"I repeated the test," Dr. al Shammari mused. "The first time, he was fully aware of it, and eager to try it with me. The second time, when he had not been told, he returned to tell me that he could taste it was not human. Three drops of monkey's blood in two deciliters from chickens! He threatened to find another doctor. Sooner than lose my subject, I will not for a third time repeat the experiment."

"He can drink any type of human blood?"

"And even, it seems, taste the difference—A or B, O..."

"And yet he showed the symptoms, by the account your nurse gave you, of transfusion reaction."

"He digests any type, swallowed orally. With intravenous transfusions, I presume—though he has not again needed a transfusion since that date—that it must be O. And perhaps even O has its dangers, unless someone that day made some error we cannot trace." Dr. al Shammari sighed. "It may perhaps involve this D antigen, or the LW factor if they are the same. Young M. Czarny claims to taste other differences beyond A and B and their absence, which is O. But one does not do transfusions to experiment! Not, at least, in a free and a sane world. Who knows what they did in—"

"And who would want to know?" Dr. Sharma cut him off. "We will learn all these things in Shiva's good time."

CHAPTER 4

A FEW DAYS LATER: FRIDAY, OCT. 20

Professor Sharma's try-outs for the operas were a School of Music legend. A recent legend, but assimilating how recent it was took a frosh brain some time and effort. Professor Sharma had only started teaching at the University of Minnemagantic the same year Clement had been a ninth grader—high school frosh—1946-'47. When he had still been adjusting to being a vampire, while the country as a whole was busy adjusting to being at peace, and the first War Crimes Trial at Geneva was the big thing in world news.

General try-outs for the male parts on a Wednesday evening, female parts Thursday, and everyone who was being seriously considered, both genders, called back for Friday finals—anyone who didn't want to give up that Friday evening wasn't serious enough about the show anyway.

Clement had made it to Friday, just like Professor Sharma thought he would. How many frosh could say that their first semester? So much for that hazing business, making out he couldn't sing!

At that thought, he bent over a little and, trying to look like he was just scratching his forehead with his thumb, traced a little cross. Sure enough, it throbbed. Not badly, but definitely. Why? Vainglory? Yeah, Czarny, stop patting your own back, pay attention to what you've got to do, and get ready to congratulate whoever ends up getting the part.

But he hoped they'd be congratulating *him*.

One of the best roles ever for a baritone—Papageno—yeah, those were the two numbers Professor Sharma had handed him Wednesday to study for tonight, all right! Who remembered the tenor of this opera? It was the earthy, Jacky Average bird-man they remembered. A role that'd give Clement Czarny, the gottabe saint, a chance to make-believe wallow in all the faults he had to be so doggone careful to avoid in ordinary, everyday living, just to keep it ordinary and everyday. G…olly, but he wanted to get this part! And him only a frosh, too! Though chances were he'd be lucky to get Speaker of the Temple and not just land in the Chorus. Only…

He touched the cross at his neck. Still cool. Hopes and dreams and ambitions were still safe enough, just so long as he could keep vanity and vainglory out of them. He sat back in the old theater chair, shut his eyes, and reminded himself all over again that Professor Sharma had to cast for the good of the show as a whole, the best stage pictures and ensemble. So if—better make that 'when'—he didn't get the part, that maybe wouldn't necessarily mean he wasn't good enough—he had to be pretty good, to make it to the Friday finals, but maybe Professor Sharma just felt she couldn't *not* bring him back here this evening, after what she'd said to him after voice class, or maybe she was just testing how serious he was about this, for the future… When he didn't get the part, that might just mean that somebody else… Paul Engelbreit of Chi Rho Epsilon over there, or what's-his-name the short pudgy floater in the front row…would make a better stage picture with whoever she cast in the rest of the roles. Or maybe fit the costumes better? No—ouch!— watch it—that thought came close to snotty. Anyway. Whoever. Just be ready to congratulate him honestly, and it's okay to hope you'll be the one on the—

"Hi!" A girl sat down in the aisle seat, the seat next to him. A beautiful, what he thought they called, strawberry blond. "I'm April Greenhill. You?"

"Uh… My name's Clement. Czarny. Clement Czarny."

Ignoring the vampire cape and uniform, just like he had been dressed the same as any other male floater on campus, she craned her neck for a look at his music. "Oh! You've got 'Pa-Pa-Pa'? So do I!"

"You're…uh…Professor Sharma has you in mind, maybe, for Papagena?" (Why throw that 'maybe' in right there, you dummkopf?)

"Or it was just the handiest. I think all us sopranos got either this or something for Pamina. I'll probably end up as one of the Three Ladies. If I even make it out of the Chorus. I'm only a frosh."

Gol, he though, how perfect! How natural this modesty business comes to her! (Careful, Czarny, now you're close to envy… No, not *envy,* not of *her.* Jealousy, maybe…) Aloud, he said, "Green—that should be an easy name to remember. Goes with your eyes."

"Only it's Green*hill*." But she said it so gently, and with such a warm smile, it almost took away his self-reproach at muffing that attempt at a smooth compliment.

* * * *

Combing the books wasn't much fun on a Friday night. Keiko only did it because it was even less fun fitting it into a last-minute rush on Sunday night, and because she was alone tonight, hoping Clement would stop by on his way back to Greek Town and let her know how those try-outs had gone. She'd toyed with the fantasy of sitting in on them herself, over at Wedderburn Hall; but she had all this studying to do.

If she'd had any kind of a singing voice, she could maybe have tried out for the Chorus. Tied it in somehow with a history or lit course. Chances were it wouldn't have gotten her into this evening's creme de la creme auditions, but it might have gotten her into the same production with him. And all the chances that could offer backstage and around. She wondered if maybe she could volunteer for working lights or props or costumes or something—anything but make-up. She couldn't even make her own face up, just a little lipstick on formal occasions. She was lucky to live in a time and place where make-up as an obligation for women had gone out with Susan B. Anthony's administration, or maybe never got started after being frowned on by the respectable and the righteous. She was shaky on the history of clothing styles and make-up. Better fit a good social history course or two into her class load one of these years.

It was just after 2200 hours when her phone chimed.

Answer it casually, Ko-Ko girl."'Lo?"

"Hi, Ko-Ko! Say, can you pop out to Wraps for a few minutes?"

"Clement! How'd it go?"

"Wraps?"

"Be right down."

So he didn't want to tell her over the phone, but he sounded happy, and that was good. She was overdue for a break anyway, and undergrad curfew wasn't till 2330 on Fridays and Saturdays. In five minutes, they were on their way to Wraps—more formally, "Wraparound Every Day," but nobody ever used its formal name—the venerably cozy little fountain and grill grandfathered in on a peninsula of commercially zoned town land jutting into the campus midway between Thelwell Hall and Wedderburn Hall. And Clement was gushing. Yeah, gushing.

"Pa-Pa-Pa-Papageno!" Not a stutter. A lyric he was singing. "I got it! Professor Sharma didn't announce the full cast tonight, it'll be posted tomorrow on the bulletin board, but she told a bunch of us tonight, the ones she's already sure about."

"That's the lead?"

"One of the leads! There's six leads in this opera. Professor Sharma likes to say that *every* role is a leading role." That was keeping himself modest. His tone of voice told Keiko that for all intents and purposes, it was *the* leading role as far as he was concerned.

"Well, then, good for you, my boy! Think you'll be up to it?"

"Professor Sharma thinks I will, anyway." The way he'd been talking all semester about Professor Sharma of the School of Music, Keiko could almost have felt jealous, if it wasn't so obviously plain hero-worship, like he might as well have felt for an elderly male professor. One old enough to be his parent. And if he hadn't been Clement Czarny Who Had To Keep Pure In Mind And Conscience so crosses and stuff wouldn't bother him.

They were sipping chocolate sodas in one of the comfortably shabby back booths when he burst out, "They always say it comes in three's! Not only bad things—good things, too."

"Papageno, one. What're the others?"

"Getting into Pi Rho! That was the first one."

"Oh." Pi Rho was the "first" one? Not…some new friend he'd made here at the U. of M.? "So, what's number three? Or should I say, number two?"

"My Papagena—Papageno's love interest. April Greenhill. Oh, Ko-Ko, wait'll you see her—Professor Sharma says we'll make a wonderful stage presence, singing our big duet together—vocally and visually both! She says our looks will complement each other as well as our voices do."

Keiko sighed and quoted softly from the operetta where she got her favorite nickname, the one Clement had always used ever since she said it was her favorite, not like Solly who insisted on sticking with Cake-o. "'Very glad to hear my opinion backed by a competent authority.'"

He sobered. "Only…is it going too good right now? Do you think three bad things are getting ready to happen?"

"And balance it out?" She pondered. A good thing for one person could be a bad thing for someone else—case in point, this April Green-hill he was so enthusiastic about—and wasn't that a kind of balance? But she wasn't about to tell him that…

"Ouch!" he said suddenly. "Dang fangs. Even eating *ice cream,* for jiminy's sake, I bite my lip!"

"There you have it," Keiko jumped in. "Number one of the bad things. May numbers two and three be no worse than that."

He grinned and reached across the table to put his hand on hers for a few heartbeats. "Thanks, Ko-Ko."

"Any time, Clement."

"Not really all that much, is it, as bad things go?" he added thought-fully. "Nothing like what the Sharmas went through, getting out of India and over here, through the end of the War. Or Dr. al Shammari, even losing his wife while they were trying to get away. And so many other people."

After a sober moment, Keiko tried to pick the mood up again. "So? Expect you're going to have to pay for getting into a fancy fraternity, getting a dandy part in an opera, and maybe meeting the Love of Your Life by having to face death or dismemberment three times?"

He grinned. "Hit a balance, Ko-Ko! Flunking out of Italian, my lute getting broken, stuff like that… The lute alone should count for two of the bad things, maybe all three."

"Keep it in reserve. Last resort only." She dug into her ice cream and chocolate foam.

"Well, anyway," he said, "the world as a whole oughta be in for a lot of good stuff now."

"You mean because of the War? It's been over five years and counting. Maybe, as a world, we've already used up the good stuff owing from that."

He shook his head. "Seven million—at a rough estimate—killed in India's Kali Camps, and another two or three million in Stalin's Eugenics Farms? It'll be a long time before the world sees enough good things to balance *that* out." After a moment, he went on, "Part of me wishes I could have fought in it, helped liberate those places."

"Lot of floaters our age saying, 'If it had only lasted just a few more years, till I got old enough…"

"Not me. I'd never have wanted it to last a minute longer. But I was thirteen when it ended."

"Me, too."

"If I'd been born just four years sooner, I'd've been old enough to enlist and get in a year of fighting."

"And ended it sooner, all by yourself?" But that wasn't fair, was it? She knew some other floaters who talked as if that was the way they felt, but not Clement. "Or maybe gotten killed in your first battle," she added more realistically.

"And maybe never had that silly diving accident and landed in the hospital and gotten turned into a darned vampire."

* * * *

Stale's heart beat high. His first time with the I. C., out in the Pi Rho hunting cabin in the woods, and he'd made it just fine. He could take it! He really could, just as well as the big junior. By what he'd overheard Pater Fairchild telling Fred Fletcher, he guessed it was Mendoza's first time, too, class of '52 or not.

That made it two seniors, three juniors, two sophs, and just one frosh—Stallion "Stale" Drinkwater himself. Maybe try recruiting someone else from his own pledge group. Just a few little hints about what Important Stuff they were doing here. As much as Fred had whispered to him beforehand, maybe just a little bit more. Nothing to break the Inner

Circle Oath of Secrecy. Not even the rest of the brothers knew everything that went on at I. C. meetings.

You'd think every member of the I. C. would make it to every meeting. But two had begged off tonight—like welcoming a couple new confreres was less important than taking a couple of Pi Psi sisters over to Galop de Vache to see some touring Broadway show. Jack Hollinger and John Rogers—whose family's real original name was Rogaski, only they'd gotten it Americanized—but Polish, for chrissake, you'd think he'd be doubly interested in putting the I. C. above everything else, all the Poles who'd died in Stalin's Eugenics Farms. And then there was Gale Hartwick, who never took part in the activity, but dropped in afterward for the planning sessions, and they let him get away with it on account of his big birth brother Lance being in FIDO-WC.

So here they sat, seven of them, eight counting Pater Fairchild. Who must've been sitting on his righteous wrath all during the active part of the meeting, but was getting ready to let it out now they were resting and strategizing.

"John Imani begs to inform us that in his judgment it looks very far from evident—'very far from evident'!—that Francis Krajewski is in fact Feodor Karpovsky the Fiend of Gadansk, and that in any case the Imani circle will no longer attempt either to trace him, now that he has moved out of Indiana, nor to alert any other circle in these Reformed States of America or elsewhere to his suspected identity. I think," the pater went on with a quiver in his voice, "that remaining in communication with Imani's circle would be a royal waste of time."

Buck Shepkowski said, "You'd think they'd at least wait a full seven years."

"Which will expire," said Mendoza, "year after next. Not that the statute of limitation applies."

"It does not!" cried the pater. "We are dealing with mass murder on a scale undreamed of until the present century!"

"And there is no statue of limitations," Mendoza said softly, "on even a single murder."

Stale didn't want to sit like a lump, so he put in, "Give you any excuse? That Forest Green circle just folding up?"

"They 'will continue' their 'efforts for the good of the world in general,' but for no specific causes," Pater Fairchild answered. He sounded sarcastic. "In other words, they will exert themselves passively, but not actively."

Fred Fletcher grinner. "More than a lot of other circles are doing. A lot of 'em just shuttin' up shop like crazy, now the War's been over five years."

Mendoza commented, "Nor would I be quick to call their general efforts 'passive.'" Almost like a cat, he stretched his long, lean muscles. If Stale hadn't liked his own muscles so much, he could've envied Mendoza's.

"The point," Pater Fairchild cut in, "is that *we* are far from 'shutting up shop.' Not until the last deathguard, Indian *or* Russian, stands in the dock. M. Imani fails to mention where Karpovsky, hiding under his Krajewski alias, has relocated. This *may* of course be mere oversight on Imani's part, but from the general tenor of his letter I doubt that my direct query will bring us any clearer information. Hartwick, alert your brother accordingly."

CHAPTER 5

NEXT DAY: SATURDAY, OCT. 21

This was the real deal, Clement figured, not just puppy love, even if he had just met Her last night. After making it through half the night, whenever his hormones let him—good grief, he'd thought they were powerful back in high school, but that was just a thunderstorm to last night's tornado, which was another reason he figured it for True Love this time… How the heck had Jesus handled it when He was this age, "like us in everything but sin…" Didn't that mean "like us in being tempted"? Or what was the whole point of the Temptation in the Desert story?

Anyway. He'd heard good things about this new place that opened up this fall on Fillmore, the street of shops grandfathered into the edge of Greek Town. This B & Z: Good Games & Fine Jewelry.

Interesting combination. The games were displayed on one side and down the middle aisle, the jewelry cases were all neatly arranged along the other side. Boxed games took up more space than brooches and bracelets and stuff.

"Well, hello," said the one floater in the shop—a medium-plump man with glasses, salt and pepper hair going bald on top, and a hesitant attitude, like he was determined to be friendly. Since the day was chilly and he wasn't dressed to go out in it, Clement guessed he could be the owner himself, either B or Z. "Getting a head start on Hallowe'en?" he went on.

"Not exactly. Afraid I'm a real vampire—but friendly."

"Oh, yes! We heard there was one in town—at the university, right?" The older man grinned and held out his hand. "Pleased to make the acquaintance of a friendly vampire. Bradley's my name."

He seemed to be forcing it a little, but Clement was used to just about every kind of first reaction there was. "Thanks," he answered, shaking hands. "Mine's Czarny."

"Pleased to meet you, M. Czarny," the shopman repeated, releasing Clement's hand after the polite half a breath. "Mind if I ask… Is that a *cross* you're wearing?"

"Antique silver." Clement felt free to boast about his cross because it had been a gift. "My cousin Donna gave it to me the birthday after I got turned into a vampire."

"And it doesn't...? I mean, you obviously look okay with it?"

"As long as I behave myself."

"Interesting! Well..." M. Bradley seemed to be relaxing, getting back into his stride. "Anything in particular, or did you just stop in to browse?"

"Actually...uh...this cross was a good enough Jiminy Cricket while I was in high school, but now I'm a college man, and a fraternity broth-er—Pi Rho—I was hoping to get something even...uh...a little stronger, to help it out. Something in the way of jewelry?"

"That's my wife's side of the shop. She just stepped out for her morning coffee break—"

"I can wait," Clement said quickly. "It's...uh... This won't be any major sale for you, I'm afraid. I'm here on a scholarship...have to watch the old budget..."

M. Bradley nodded. "Lot of that always going around. So-called 'post-War boom' or not. We understand. If you have any questions, just ask, and I'll answer what I can."

Clement browsed the jewelry side slowly, until he came to the dia-mond rings. They were wonderful. He noticed a wide range of prices on all the other kinds of jewelry...but it looked like every last diamond ring was at the high end of the price range. He spotted the one he'd like to buy for April...he stood there daydreaming about how he'd offer it to her, how she'd cry, "Yes, Clement, oh, yes!" and take it with a radiant smile...his vampire sensitivities only let him get away with a few of the wilder daydreams if he was careful to put them in marriage wrappings... but he looked at the price label, and turned to the games side of the shop, to try and stop that particular daydream.

"What are these?" he asked, seeing some low-priced little pyramids and other odd-shaped things spotted like dice.

"Those are gameruler dice for rolegames."

"Rolegames?"

"Something new. There were enough groups starting up in Galop de Vache, that we thought it might take off here in a college town, espe-cially around Hallowe'en time. Some rolegame circles like to gather in costume. In fact, I thought you might be a rolegamer when you came in."

"Nope. Just your plain, everyday vampire. Sell costumes, too?" Clement looked around.

"Not enough room for them in here. Besides..." M. Bradley hesi-tated. "My wife and I were in the original Hellmouth Amusement Park the night it burned down. Two of the lucky survivors. I, uh, happened to be in costume myself that night. A really cheap vampire costume, not like yours. I'd even taken the fangs out almost as soon as putting them in. And the whole experience… Anyway, I went through quite a bit of psychotherapy afterward."

"Wow! I'm not bothering you, am I?"

M. Bradley waved his hand. "Oh, no, no, you're benign. Fangs and all."

"Hey, you can see 'em? Most people can't. I'm not sure I could even see anyone else's—never met any other real vampires, 's far as I know, never even got a look at the one who got me." Clement sighed. "Wish *I* could just take these doggone fangs out."

"They're real?"

"And worse than useless. I wouldn't even know how to bite any-body's vein, and I'm afraid they'll give me trouble with wind instru-ments, embouchure—music's my major. We found a dentist willing to file 'em down, a year or so after it happened, but the dang things just calmly grew back! But, wow!" Clement repeated. "So you survived the Hellmouth Park fire! Was it as horrific as they say?"

"Worse. We wouldn't go near the place again, no matter how many safety features they say they put in when they rebuilt." Then M. Bradley turned the conversation to more traditional games like checkers, cards, and Environopoly.

He was showing Clement some of his collectors' chess sets—there was one with pieces that looked just like the famous illustrations for *Through the Looking-Glass*—when his wife the jeweler, M. Zimmer-man, got back from her coffee break. She was a tallish, plumpish lady with darkish skin and dark red hair shot through with silver. They were interesting people. Their escape from the 1940 Hellmouth Park fire had left them both with the equivalent of shell shock, so when the R.S.A. entered Act II of the Last Great War, the most that the military let them do was civilian-support office work. After the War, they had spent a few years working in other people's stores in Galop de Vache before finding this little shop for sale in Hodag Crossing and setting up in business for themselves.

When Clement explained what he had in mind, M. Zimmerman found almost the perfect thing right on hand: a tiny crucifix charm in white gold—the vampire explained how his conscience was really more sensitive to gold than silver, he guessed because gold was even more highly prized for sacred objects and sacramental purposes. M. Bradley said, "Interesting," and then took his turn for a coffee break while M. Zimmerman pierced Clement's ear and gave him a plain stud, promising to have the crucifix charm refashioned by 1630 hours Monday. The whole thing—charm and turning it into an earring—would cost him just a tridollar more than he'd hoped to budget for it, and M. Zimmerman threw the piercing in as part of the price, which encouraged him to ask,

"Oh, one more thing. When I get my frat ring—" Seeing the way her head perked up, he hurried to add, "Sorry, it's already ordered—Pi Rho's used Cavorelli's exclusively ever since 1887—they send the order in for the whole initiation group at once... But when it comes in, what would your rate be for engraving a few symbols and things inside the band?"

"'Symbols and things'?"

"Yeah, like a cross, maybe a God triangle symbol...star of David, crescent..."

"Star of David and crescent?"

"My best friend—" (Wait? What about Keiko?) "—my best same-gender buddy, roomie and frat brother, is Jewish. And just about any religious symbol makes a Jiminy Cricket for me. Especially if the religion has a lot of martyrs. Like, you know, Muslims in the Kali Camps."

"What about the svastika?" the jeweler asked curiously.

"Oh, no, I don't want that one! Not after what the Kali Party did with it! I know it's a really ancient holy symbol and used to be a very good one, for thousands of years. Professor Sharma has a lovely one in gold, that she never wears any more, not after the Kali Camps and stuff. She just can't bear to get rid of it, one of the last little things they were able to hang onto, getting out of India when they did, and it's got sentimental value for her. But that doggone svastika burns me even when I'm being as good as I can—when I don't have anything at all on my conscience. It gets me both ways."

"I could probably refashion it into a plain cross for her, if she'd like. Well, make me a list of what you most want. Bring me diagrams, if you like. Or we can go through my pattern books." Then she named rates that sounded plenty reasonable, so he promised her that piece of business too, and was just leaving, feeling like he'd made a couple of new friends, as M. Bradley got back from his break.

* * * *

"Interesting lad," October Bradley repeated to his wife as they watched their latest customer leave to get on about his Saturday.

"Yes. He seems to have found an original way to make his fantasy benign."

"Are you sure it's a fantasy, Aurie? You couldn't see his fangs?"

"His canines? Well, of course, they're a little on the longish side. Maybe that's what gave him the idea?"

October shook his head. "More than 'longish.' Long. Also, sharp. He let me feel one. Though he did say that rather few people can really see them for what they are."

"Well, love," Aurea said quietly, "in that area, you may have an advantage over the rest of us."

CHAPTER 6

ABOUT TWO WEEKS LATER: FRIDAY, NOV. 3

2200 hours in the Pi Rho hunting cabin. Professor Matthew Fairchild looked around at tonight's group, who were relaxing after their evening's more physically strenuous exertions before bundling up the equipment and storing it away.

Only five participants this week. Hollinger and Rogers had returned to demonstrate a will that went far to compensate for their absence two weeks ago, but tonight Shepkowski had bowed out pleading press of studies, and both of the sophomore members, Shin and Fletcher, had excused themselves on grounds of bad head colds. Fairchild caught his brow puckering. Shin's symptoms might be authentic enough—though Fairchild had some doubts how long Nathaniel Shin would choose to remain active with the Inner Circle—but Fletcher found reasons to absent himself from three quarters of those sessions in which his part was to have been passive. No matter how just and pressing the need, some circles would not have tolerated such a member, despite any degree of enthusiasm for the active role. At least Shepkowski was a reasonably faithful, if less than enthusiastic, participant in both roles; and young Hartwick had had the honesty to bow out of participation completely after two sessions, though not only keeping the Inner Circle's secrets, but continuing to attend its strategy sessions, especially when he had something to contribute. Fairchild was willing to accommodate the birth brother of an alum who had graduated from here into the War Crimes Division of the Federal Investigative Departmental Office.

During the War itself, Pi Rho and its sister house had shared Inner Circle home-front activities. Fairchild sometimes regretted that House Mother Grayling's first official action following V-P Day had been to withdraw Pi Psi from the effort completely. He doubted that any of the young women in the sorority today so much as suspected there ever had been such efforts, let alone that a select few of their Greek brothers were set to keep them up faithfully until the last deathguard was brought to justice.

Matthew Fairchild's Inner Circle had, of the Class of '51, Shepkowski, Hollinger, and Avosso. Of the Class of '52, Rogers—who was less reliable than one might have expected of a man whose mother's name had been Rogaski—and now Mendoza. Of the Class of '53, Shin and the less than optimally desirable Fletcher. Of the Class of '54, thus far, only Drinkwater. This did not bode well for the changeover to the national protocol for the Midnight ordeal; but give it at least one more year. Better keep Mendoza in the Inner Circle as long as possible than antagonize him prematurely. They might yet find another from among the new boys.

A pity that the most seemingly idealistic of the Class of '54 was a vampire. Czarny seemed in other respects a good, high-minded lad. But Matthew Fairchild had always grounded his own standards in the very highest available to the human race. Czarny's special dietary requirement could not but render him untrustworthy in certain areas of life. No, they might have overruled their house father on Czarny's admittance to the fraternity, but Fairchild retained absolute sayso on the membership of its Inner Circle.

If Czarny dated the episode that had made him a vampire to a bit earlier than he did, Fairchild would have suspected that Kiripovna…but no, she would have been months in her grave. Unless she had risen thanks to removal of that fortunate fence post coupled with some failure in the embalming… More probably, there was some intermediate vampire in the chain, as yet unknown and possibly having, like the greater fiend Karposky *alias* Krajewski, moved on…there were nights when Matthew Fairchild needed an hour's escape into his avocation of mathematical artwork before slumber could find him.

Giving his own muscles a comforting stretch and shake, Rogers said, "I wonder how long it'll be before our newbie is trying out for the Met?"

"One step at a time," said Avosso, who was massaging his friend Mendoza. "I'll be content to find out how he did tonight."

"Whether he meets with triumph or disaster," murmured Mendoza, "he will learn, if he must, how to treat those two imposters equally as they deserve."

"At least he's sure of a place in Sharma's Chorus," remarked Hollinger.

Fairchild decided to call the discussion to its chief purpose. "Speaking of imposters, I do not entirely trust Professor Kastha Sharma. I have seen her wearing a neck scarf on which the svastika was quite plainly visible. Among a multitude of other symbols, true, and no more prominent than any of the rest of them. Nevertheless, visible."

Mendoza inquired lazily, "Shall we suspect everyone who happens to own Kipling's works in the Svastika Edition?"

"Maybe it was like that one I saw at Auntie Cue's Antiques and Collectibles," Rogers suggested. "Souvenir of the 1936 Bombay Olympics."

"The Sharmas could've gotten their souvenirs right at those Olympics," Avosso observed. "And worn them to help ward off Kali Party suspicion during their escape from India."

Fairchild cleared his throat. "Such a ruse could equally have wakened suspicions among the liberating Allied forces. In any case, why preserve such a keepsake once safe in Allied territory?"

"Why keep any keepsake?" said Mendoza.

"Lance still keeps both the paddles his little pledge brothers made him when he was here," the younger Hartwick brother offered.

"And why continue to wear it here?" Fairchild persisted.

"Doesn't the mere fact of wearing it here and now," argued Shepkowski, "suggest that she doesn't feel the need to hide anything?"

"In that," Fairchild acknowledged, inclining his head, "you may, perhaps, be right. Well, Hartwick, what have you for us this evening?"

"Two summaries from the Novgorod Eugenics Farm," Gale Hartwick answered proudly, bringing them forth from his briefcase, each already mounted on its sheet of black cardboard and covered with heavy cellophane. He handed them to Fairchild. "Straight from big brother Lance. Feodor Blazhenov and Kosya Petrovka, the Demon Doktors."

"We've got descriptions of them already," Drinkwater boasted. His house father nodded, pleased with the diligence he showed in studying the Inner Circle's dossier.

"These replace those. We only had descriptions before. Now we've got photos and possible fingerprints."

Fairchild had of course seen the new documents before the meeting, but now he scrutinized them again. "Old, small, and somewhat grainy photographs," he observed, "but certainly better than nothing. How likely are the fingerprints to belong to Blazhenov and Petrovka?"

"FIDO judges forty-five percent probability on her, thirty percent on him."

"But certainly better than nothing," Mendoza echoed the pater.

Hearing an ironic note in Mendoza's comment, Fairchild coughed. "Obviously, these fingerprints are to be used circumspectly and as supplementary evidence only."

"Then we need not dust all of Hodag Crossing for prints?" Mendoza went on. "Only, I presume, the office, residence, and workplace of anyone who too closely resembles our old, small, and somewhat grainy new photographs."

Fairchild passed Blazhenov's summary sheet to the man on his left, Petrovka's to the man on his right. Hand to hand, the sheets circled the room, each man in turn giving a small shake of his head. Drinkwater frowned the longest at each document, but apparently in the effort of committing the likenesses to his memory rather than in recognition.

When both sheets had made the circuit back to Fairchild, he shuffled them neatly into his own briefcase, for insertion in the permanent dossier which resided on a shelf in the small outer office of his suite in the Pi Rho House. Where few ever consulted it except members of the Inner Circle, and even they, rarely enough, and ever more rarely with the passing years and short university generations. Copies of the photos would, of course, go as usual to the student and town newspapers, *The Hodag's Yawp* and *Hodag Crossing Currents,* where, the professor emeritus sadly suspected, they served much the same purpose as did fillers, and had yet to bring results. He could only hope that was thanks, not to public indifference, but to no deathguards having yet come near Hodag Crossing, which would have been nothing but the merest flyspeck on the map of the Upper Midwest, had the founders not chosen it, back in 1883, over Galop de Vache for the site of the University of Minnemagantic.

Mendoza drawled, "Of course, our venerable and highly competent sheriff's office has its own copies of this new data?"

"You think maybe FIDO doesn't send its data out to every law office in the R.S.A.?" Hartwick shot back. Mendoza spread his hand in languid acknowledgment.

"No doubt Sheriff Nurmi receives them," said Fairchild. "And to all appearances proceeds, like all too many other law enforcers today, to bury them where they rarely if ever again see the light of day."

Avosso said, "It can even happen with local crimes."

"Putting all the more burden on us," Fairchild told his men, "the private citizens concerned for justice and right, to hold ourselves alert and to hope that, when the time comes and we can thrust hard evidence in their very faces, our ever-vigilant sheriff may deign to lend his assistance."

"As in the case of the so-called 'Hallowe'en Hooker' some years ago." Mendoza spoke almost as if he had been ignoring his house father's words, though Fairchild guessed from experience that were the lad asked, he could recite them back verbatim.

"Just one of those campus myths, wasn't she?" Drinkwater asked.

"No, unfortunately, she was quite real," Fairchild informed the frosh member of his Circle.

Hartwick volunteered eagerly, "It actually happened when my brother was living here in the Pi Rho house."

"Irina Kiripovna was indeed a local prostitute, They are, alas, everywhere," Fairchild continued. That she was also a vampire had no place in the present discourse. He went on, "And her body was indeed found in Greek Town, in a condition only slightly less morbid than described in the last version I have heard of the somewhat folklorized account. There is, however, no real evidence that it was anything other than Sheriff Nurmi ruled it: a freak accident."

"How much evidence," Avosso asked rhetorically, "does he ever uncover about anything?"

"Especially," Mendoza added, "about the death of a Russian prostitute during a war against, among other nations, 'Mother Russia'?"

Fairchild was forced to agree, however mildly. "I have always regretted that they closed that case—in effect—as prematurely as they did. Finding a solution might have helped quell the local legends, if nothing else."

"It happened when my brother Lance was here," Hartwick repeated happily. "And, say, Pater, all we've got to do is get them word in time, and FIDO will have somebody here. Probably Lance himself. So we don't need to worry about trying to get the local sheriff in on the kill at all."

Mendoza murmured something. Fairchild thought it sounded like, "In on the kill," but was not entirely sure. Nor was he entirely sure that Mendoza was so fine an acquisition for the Inner Circle as he had once believed.

CHAPTER 7

ABOUT TWO WEEKS LATER: THURSDAY, NOV. 16

Opening Night of 1950's School of Music opera. Excitement was running high in Wedderburn Auditorium when they took their seats. Keiko had managed to get Theda here almost twenty minutes before curtain time.

"A first for us!" Theda breathed. "Our first opera here at the U. of M.!"

"Actually," said Keiko, "the first grand opera I've ever seen." Clement said it wasn't really a 'grand' opera, but to her, what wasn't operetta was grand opera.

"Really?" Theda acted hoity a moment before confessing, "Mine, too. But I had leading roles in two of my high school musicals."

"I *saw* all my high school musicals. And *The Mikado* one summer when we were visiting cousins near Interlochen."

"Ooh! Were any of them *in* it?"

"My cousin Ryuu played Pish-Tush."

"You have family all over, don't you?"

"Just like Clement."

"And all of yours are Ethnic Purebloods?"

"My Uncle Taro married a Cinnamon. The rest of the family doesn't hold it against him. Too much." Keiko added in her thoughts, And, Jesus, Buddha, and Goddess willing, I plan on marrying a real Heinz 59. I'd want him even if he was another Ethnic Pureblood—any flavor but Butterscotch—but with that stew of Melting Pot genes, wow!

Theda asked, "Did any of you take advantage of the Camps during the War?"

"A bunch of the ones who lived on the West Coast. My mom and dad talked about it, but we were lucky enough to have really good neighbors in Galop de Vache. Who knew what good R.S.A. citizens my folks had been for going on half a century. Good thing our Camps were voluntary refuges for people 'of involuntary blood links with the enemy,'" Keiko added. "Not like those Kali Camps and Eugenics Farms over There."

"It's good to live in a Melting Pot nation," Theda said comfortably. Then—like she was afraid she might have offended Keiko somehow— "And it's good to keep up the old Ethnic Pureblood heritages, too!"

"Yeah. Like living, breathing museum pieces walking around at large." Keiko Kato *so* didn't want to be an Ethnic Pureblood. Especially Ethnic Pureblood Nipponese. Good as her family's relations had been during and after the War with everyone who got to know them personally... At least there hadn't been anything like Kali Camps or Eugenics Farms in Japan or any of the other enemy nations besides Russia and India, only POW camps, bad enough, but...the only worse ethnicity to be right now was Russian or East Indian Hindu. She couldn't help but admire Professor Sharma for keeping up her own heritage as much as she did. And Clement, for freely choosing to wear his surname in Slavic...

She made a big show of opening her program and sticking her nose in it, hoping Theda would take the hint and let her linger on Clement's entry a few minutes in peace.

The Chorus members were listed alphabetically by their own names, but the Cast was alphabetical by the names of their characters... Here he was:

"PAPAGENO. Clement Czarny, Class of '54. Major: Music (Vocal), minor: Education. Member: Pi Rho Fraternity, Minnesingers, University Glee Club, Hodag Thespians, Swim Team. Clement hopes to justify his full scholarship to the U. of M. by turning his talents, if not to performing professionally, to instructing future generations of aspiring artists."

Theda was looking around admiring the auditorium and the gathering audience, but politely keeping silent. Keiko darted her epicanthic eyes to the entry right above Clement's. The Rival, as she thought of her:

"PAPAGENA. April Greenhill, Class of '54. Major: Music (Vocal), minor: World Literature. Member: Minnesingers, Chess Club, Pickwick Club, G&S Society. April calls landing the role of Papagena a dream come true, especially opposite her tall Papageno. She hopes one day to pen the Great American Vampire Novel."

Keiko did a double-take and stared at those last few lines again.

They had drafted their own paragraphs. He'd even been all through his with Keiko before turning it over to the Program Committee. Who might've edited a few things out here and there, and rearranged some of the data so everyone's would be consistent, but wouldn't take it on themselves to add anything the biographees hadn't provided them. And not one word about it in *his* paragraph! But *hers*—Holy Trio, what was this Greenhill floater trying to do, hang up a "No Trespassing" sign on him *already?*

Yeah, well, lady, you may be his Papagena, but I'm his study buddy. I'm the one who remembers how he said that everybody around campus and most of town knows already, after him flapping around all fall in his Lugosi uniform of formal black suit and high-collared cape, and it really not having anything to do with this opera, or his singing, or swimming, or scholarship, or… Well, for me, I'm not so sure about Pi Rho, can't help wondering if they maybe took him in for a mascot, their own pet dracula, not that I'd ever hint that to *him,* or that maybe they're secretly subsidizing the dues and meal fees and stuff and not letting on that the dorm turning his room and board money over to the fratty house may not really take care of the whole expense…but his condition isn't relevant to any of the rest of it, anyway.

But *you*—if he ever told you he didn't want it in this Program tonight, you must've very conveniently—

"Oh, look!" Theda exclaimed suddenly. "Here come the Pies!"

Keiko looked around and back. Sure enough, the rows right behind her and Theda were filling up with brothers of the Purple Rose and sisters of the Purple Sigh. She recognized quite a few of them from invitational meals and stuff in one house or the other. Theda having signaled an inclination to pledge Pi Psi next time she could, and both Clement and Solly remembering their promise to keep Keiko in their loop and inviting her pretty often. Clement especially…but of course, the vampire was trying to keep up with every friendship he had ever made. As well as with his family members. And he had a lot of both, so with everything else it kept him hopping.

"So, Solly," Keiko accosted him. "Here in force to claque your fratty brother on?"

"What's 'clack' mean in that context?"

"'S what they call a gang of people planted in the audience to make sure some performer or other gets a lot of applause."

"Oh. Well, Clem won't need us to make sure he gets plenty of applause. We've heard him practicing these numbers around the house."

"Previews of coming attractions." Keiko nodded. Maybe the Greenhill had gotten to rehearse those songs with him, but look at the happy hours "Ko-Ko" had spent helping him with his spoken lines. You may be singing romantic duets with him on stage, Greenhill, but I'm the one who's been coaching him through his dialogue. You may be promising him some kind of immortality with your "Great American Vampire Novel," but I'm still his good ol' study buddy away from Greek Town, that he nicknames because she likes it, even if he prefers to give other people their full formal names and titles. So there!

They were using the English version by Parker-Osborne and Steiner. Professor Sharma had chosen it because it smoothed away the controversial misogyny of the 18th century original, and also offered the option of presenting the Queen of the Night as having been in on the testing-the-lovers plot from the beginning. As being privately hand in glove with Sarastro all along, because the world needs night as well as day. It was an interpretation her vampire could get along with very well. And they were doing it with Classical Mythology sets and costumes. Clement had told Keiko how Holly Sendak wanted to give the stage dressing a Hindu feel, costumes and forehead bindi and all, in honor of Professor Sharma; but the professor herself had nixed that. "Some years from now, perhaps, this wonderful, tolerant country will perhaps be ready for such a thing. But not yet now, not so soon after the War, not with the dreadful Kali Camps—which we were so fortunate to escape, my dear husband and I—still so much present to the mind's eye of all you good people." So, the Classical dress.

The amusing thing to Keiko was that the tenor playing this supposedly pure and idealistic hero Tamino was one of the raunchiest seniors on campus. He made a pass at everything even tenuously qualified to wear a skirt. He'd even made a pass at Keiko herself! About the only male floater on campus who had tried that since she got here. She'd just looked back at him and said, "Yo, Charlie, feeling that desperate?" At which he had grinned and said, "Just trying to make a little Nip sweetie feel good." Which made it also about the only time she'd run into that particular attitude since grade school, when the War was still on. And she'd heard he partied so hard, it was a wonder he could keep in training long enough to do the operas. But he sounded good, and he looked good up there on that stage, somehow managing to appear male-chaste and innocent even in a Classical tunic, with his curly golden head and big blue eyes and not-quite-rugged physique, and anyone who hadn't ever brushed up against him in person offstage would probably have been taken in.

And there was Clement, who really *was* pure in mind and body— who didn't dare *not* be pure—all clean living and high ideals and hard work offstage, even in a Greek house, hamming it up on the stage like a freebooter in a costume that made you think of Pan. As long as it was acting and make-believe, he had told Keiko, he was free to revel in everything that could have made even sunlight a problem for him in real life. As long as he was just doing the best job he could of acting, he kept his tiny crucifix conscience earring tight in his left earlobe. You couldn't see it from the audience, not even a glint—they'd dulled it over with a dab of make-up—but she knew it was there. That jeweler at B & Z had made a nice job of it.

Professor Sharma herself was the Queen of the Night, costumed as Juno or Hera—since all the Classical part was in the costumes and sets, not the lyrics or dialogue, it didn't really matter whether they were supposed to be Grecian or Roman. That was another reason she had nixed going with Hindu, which would almost surely have suggested Kali for the Queen of the Night. Clement had quoted her there, too: "In twenty years, perhaps thirty... But now, so soon... Even in India, we who grew up to know Kali as the force also of new life born from death and destruction—even we shudder at this terrible image of the 'Kali Party' and what it did to our beautiful way of life." M. Richard Ives, another prof in the School of Music, was doing Sarastro, costumed like Jupiter-Zeus. If it looked like a problem when this Classical Father of the Gods invoked Isis and Osiris, well, the Egyptian pantheon had the Greeks and Romans beat by a couple thousand years, and hadn't the Greeks borrowed the Sphinx from the Egyptians? even if they had turned it into a menacing female.

Everyone else in the Cast was a student. Most of the Chorus was students, too, though with a couple of faculty members and one woman who worked at a shop in town. They were trying to get more community people to come out for the Chorus and Orchestra, in a bid for good town and gown relations.

Clement wouldn't have needed a claque. The Pies clapped loud and long, but not that much louder and longer than everybody else. Greenhill could've had her little claque planted somewhere, but all the applause for Clement's entrance solo belonged to him alone, and when the Queen of the Night's ladies put a big prop padlock on his mouth, it brought a groan of disapproval from the audience, even though every operagoer must have known the lock would be off again pretty darn quick. And even Keiko had to admit they made a very pretty stage picture, dark Clement and strawberry blond Greenhill, glowing at each other through that doggone "Pa-Pa-Pa-Pa" duet, which otherwise Keiko would probably have liked.

She thought, at the curtain calls, the longest and loudest applause was for Clement. Though it was a little hard to tell, with her clapping so hard herself, and cheers from the Pies behind her—and from other places in the house as well, but the Pies were right in her ears. And, of course, Papageno and Papagena had to take their bows together, no matter how much smaller her part actually was, so if she had her own little claque, too... The next loudest and longest applause was probably for the Queen of the Night and Sarastro, who took their bow together, underscoring that Jupiter and Juno were cozy with each other, day and night, darkness and light, and all was right as right... Sharma was a popular prof, and she really had sung that famous aria well enough for anybody to enjoy, whether they liked opera or not.

* * * *

The Opening Night Reception after the performance was set up in Wedderburn Lobby, with punch and cookies on three long tables, and volunteers Keiko thought were School of Music students and professors' spouses—she'd heard the "Board" had something to do with it—ladling the punch into glass cups. She made a mental note that another time when all the backstage crew places were already full up, this might be a way to get involved with a School of Music show. But not a very good way of getting closer to Clement, which was the whole idea. For that, she was just as well off waiting in line to congratulate the performers.

The Purple Pies, both the Rose men and the Sigh women, were crowding up so thick and fast around the operatic pride of their Greek family, that she saw it could be a little while until her part of the line reached him. She might almost as well go over and get her cookies and punch... But that'd cost her her place in the congratulating line, such as it was with all those fratty and sassy Pies cutting in. And she might even miss him if the Cast itself cut away early to their dressing rooms, as it looked like a lot of the Chorus had done already. Worst case scenario: hands full of cookies and cup whenever she finally got up to him, and how would she...

Look! Wasn't that Solly? there with the rest of the Pies, but looking less interested in Clement—they roomed together in the Pi Rho House, just like they had in Thelwell Hall—than he was interested in Clement's Papage*na*. All *right!* Keiko's heart went into a hopeful beat.

By the time the Pies broke it up and cleared away, some of the other people in line had moved around them to congratulate the players on the far side, so it wasn't too terribly much longer before Keiko stood face to face with Clement.

"Sang it pretty good there, study buddy! Didn't flub a single spoken line, either."

"Thanks to you, Ko-Ko." Sometimes, when he was happy, he grinned like he had forgotten the fangs nobody else noticed. "See the difference between 'grand opera' and 'singspiel' yet?"

"Not really, no. I thought this one had plenty of pageantry."

"Well, maybe if you ever get a chance to see *Aida.*"

A handshake, held long enough to add a few more words without looking too rude to the line behind her. "Going to get some refreshments yourself?"

"Going to get out of this costume and make-up first."

"I'll wait for you."

"Don't want to hold you up."

"Well, I'd better stop holding up this line. Other people want to shake Papageno's hand. See you soon!" And she moved on.

Solly was still congratulating Papagena. Glad of the excuse not to face April Greenhill herself, though she guessed she'd have to be getting into their social circle sooner or later, Keiko quietly eddied around them to the tenor, who accepted her "Sounded good up there, Charlie," with a nod that told her he'd probably forgotten ever making a failed pass at her—she guessed he thought making passes was just polite condescension from him to the everyone of the complementary gender he met. Her congratulations to Prof Ives and especially Prof Sharma were sincere. You couldn't help but admire the M.'s Sharma, making it out of war-torn India the way they had, coming all the way here to the Upper Midwest R.S.A. and building new lives for themselves from scratch. They hadn't even been able to bring their vital documents with them, had had to go through an achievement testing and recertification process just in order to get their positions, and Keiko guessed M. Kastha Sharma's title "Professor" was more or less honorary. Even with the special postwar provisions for refugees in their situation, it all had to be a lot of red tape, and a good thing for them the University of Minnemagantic had an opening it was eager to fill with her, and the Hodag Crossing General Hospital was grateful to get such a well qualified doctor as her husband proved himself to be.

Solly, once finished shaking the Greenhill's hand, got through the congratulating line right after Keiko. "Now," he announced with a glow, "for a little nourishment!"

"You go ahead, fratty man," said Keiko. "I'm going to wait for Clement."

"I'll maybe have seconds whenever he comes out for his firsts. Watching opera's even hungrier work than watching football."

Solly went off to the refreshments line, and Keiko found a corner to lean against and keep an eye on things. The last of the congratulaters got through, and the Cast were heading back to the dressing rooms just about the time Solly rejoined her, balancing his cup of punch in the middle of his plate of cookies.

"Jiminy criminy," she observed, "did you leave any for anybody else?"

"Plenty. These School of Music people know how to supply the front lines. Take one." He held his plate out at her. "Tide yourself over."

"What put you in a generous mood this evening?" she asked, like he wasn't always in a generous mood, and helped herself to a small macaroon. "Mozart's great music?"

"To be precise, that bee-eau-ti-ful Pa-Papagena. Isn't she just everything Clem's been saying, and a little more besides?" Beaming, Solly took a swallow of punch.

"'F you say so."

"Oh. 'S right, might be harder for same-gender people to see things like that."

Well. So he had remembered Keiko was female. She almost had mixed feelings about that.

"Cake-o," he added, "as another woman, just how hard and fast would you say 'first dibs' are in cases like this?"

She hesitated, hit all at once by a vision of them all as just the college frosh they were—almost kindergartners, really—playing around with all these grown-up emotions. "Well, fratty man," she said, "for all I know about it, the bee-eau-ti-ful M. April Papagena Greenhill's already got two or three in the wings somewhere, so I'd say it isn't first dibs that counts, it's last dibs." There! That seemed like furthering Keiko's own interests without being too unfair to anyone involved. Could Clement himself have faulted her for putting it like that?

FROM THE NEXT DAY'S REVIEWS, FRIDAY, NOV. 17:

Hodag Crossing Currents:

The Local Arts:

"While clearly in no league with the Met, nor even with the Galop de Vache Opera, the U. of M.'s School of Music can on occasion produce a piece not totally unworthy the attention of opera lovers unhappily unable to travel. This year's *Magic Flute* proves respectably amusing in its presumption...

"Director Kastha Sharma's performance is in itself sufficiently respectable to justify her choice of this particular piece, presumably in order to present us with her interpretation of Mozart's Queen of the Night. In New York she would be assured of a place in the Chorus; in San Francisco, she could very well understudy Meltani's understudy....

"Among the more nearly promising student faces are the Papageno and Papagena, Clement Czarny and April Greenhill, she with a light little voice almost as pretty as her face, he with a reasonably robust baritone for his youth and a rather brash sense of comedy, both of which may develop well once he learns to modulate their excesses. These two young performers both being frosh, local theater-goers may look forward to several years of watching their stage presences mature....

"All in all, one could find less pleasant ways of spending a wraparound evening or long Sunday afternoon."

(For Frank Bashaw, regular critic and columnist for the twice-weekly Currents, *this constituted glowing praise.)*

* * * *

John Carpenter's Quick Pick:

"If you see just one show this year on campus, make it this one. Plaudits to all involved, from the profs to the frosh."

* * * *

The Hodag's Yawp:

"Mozart's *Magic Flute* as Greek myth? Yet, under the able direction of 'Hera as Queen of the Night' Professor Sharma of the wonderful coloratura voice, it works. The one jarring note in the interpretation being 'Zeus as Sarastro' invoking, in Professor Ives' dark smooth bass, Isis and Osiris. If they'd gone with Egyptian mythology instead of Greek, he might have invoked himself! On the other hand, the vision of the Bird-Man Papageno as Pan, brought ably to life by our own campus vampire, would have been enough in itself to justify the Classical treatment....

"...Tamino (Charlie Wilcox) and Pamina (Rita Hoffman) showed almost as much romantic chemistry onstage as Papageno (Clement Czarny) and Papagena (April Greenhill)..."

(The in-depth reviewer for the college paper had signed simply "Pundita" for so long it had become clear that the byline must be passed along from student journalist to student journalist.)

* * * *

"8 stars: one for each of the principals and one for Holly Sendak's costume and stage sets. Attaboy, Charlie 'Tamino' Wilcox—you almost had us believing! And an extra cheer for the new singing pride of the Purple Rose."

INTERLUDE: MONDAY, JUNE 4, 1951

There were elevators, and there was a long stairway tucked away behind side doors, but the main artery of Hellmouth Park's subbasements was an architectural feat: a long, very gradual corkscrew corridor winding between rooms on either side. The rooms were numbered 1A to 9Z, but the two young people had only reached 1D.

Rooms 1A to 3Z were a wax museum, every room open to view behind a door of reinforced plate glass. The exhibits looked almost more real than reality itself. True, these two young people had lived relatively safe and sheltered lives. Nevertheless...

"Oh, *yechh!*" exclaimed the girl, having moved on to 1E, an exhibit of a self-hanged man. "Look how *long* his neck! Oh, Solly, do you think they...exaggerated it?"

Tearing himself away from the morbid fascination of 1D—the arsenic exhibit—the boy joined her. "Well," he said after a sober moment, "they always said, 'Let's stretch his neck.'"

"And his *face!* Oh! No wonder they put hoods over their heads! Solly...I don't think I want to go any farther, after all. I...think maybe Clement was right."

Solly bravely went on to 1F, glanced in, and hurried back. "Yeah, April, you could be right. Next one's a guy who...I think they call it, 'ate his gun.' Makes this one look..."

"Solly," April said, swallowing hard, "this is probably educational. I mean, in a wholesome way. Really putting people off the idea of suicide. I mean, even the overdose of sleeping pills in 1A—with all those nightmare creatures and the woman screaming in her sleep..."

"Yeah... Unless they've got some farther along... Unless all this builds up to something that looks not too bad...in comparison. If all that's really true about Hellmouth Park renting subbasement rooms out where people can..."

"It seems to me they're getting *worse.*"

"Second level down's supposed to begin with the *really* bad stuff—deliberate torture... And the whole third level to show scenes from the Kali Camps and Eugenics Farms like they really were... And after that, the private party rooms and stuff beginning with 4A. For anybody who's still in the mood."

"Or smart enough to go straight down by elevator."

But from 4A down, all the rooms would probably have solid doors, shut tight. Solly and April exchanged a glance, and both of them, as though by unvoiced agreement, pointed up. Then they headed for the nearest stairwell door.

Which opened when they were halfway there, and a park employee came out, costumed in demon red tights, with pitchfork, horns, and a tail.

He took a good look at them and chuckled, fondling the tines of his pitchfork. "Well, well, well! What are you two infants doing down here alone and unattended?"

"Go on!" said Solly. "Dungeons are open to the Public."

"To the twenty-five and older crowd. You two are, what? Sixteen? Seventeen?"

"Think higher," Solly said like a challenge.

"Eighteen, at most. Think of that, only seven years shy."

"We're old enough to buy three percent beer and four percent wine," April put in boldly.

"And float your pudgy little selves silly?"

"I never saw where it said twenty-five and older," Solly lied.

"No, of course you didn't," the employee agreed amiably. "Nobody ever reads signs. No matter how big and prominently posted. We could wallop you in the face with our signs, and you still wouldn't read 'em."

"Of course not!" said April. "We'd be knocked out." She had in fact pointed the notice above the entrance out to Solly, and they had decided jointly that ignoring it would add to the zest of the adventure.

"Makes no difference," the demon told them, grinning.

"It sure doesn't," said Solly, "because we're just on our way out right now!" He took April's hand and stepped toward the door to the stairs.

The demon held his pitchfork across it like a crossbar.

"Look," said Solly, "I don't even *believe* in all this junk. So cut out the jokes."

"We don't care what you believe or don't believe about the Hereafter. We're Hellmouth, right here and right now, and we've got our own guiderules—"

"So what can you do about it? Kick us out? We're on our way out anyway, so what's this with stopping us?"

The demon looked from one of them to the other, back and forth. "True love between you two?"

Solly and April exchanged a long look. Turning back to the park demon, Solly asked, "Does it make any difference?"

"Maybe. Maybe not." The demon shrugged. "Depending."

Solly gave April another look, rather longing, and made his decision. "Well, we're just good friends. *Really* good friends."

"Not as in girlfriend and boyfriend?"

"My boyfriend didn't want to come in here." April spoke as firmly as Solly had. "My boyfriend is too smart."

"'Smart' meaning 'scared,' huh?" The demon tsked, shook his head, and looked at Solly again. "Son, it oughta be a cinch for you to pluck the lady away from a scaredy-cat wimp like that."

"Clement is no scaredy-cat wimp!" April flashed back. "He's a vampire and—"

"A vampire?" The demon's interest seemed to ratchet up even higher. "We should be right in his cup of blood."

"Yeah, a *good* vampire," said Solly. "And smart. We should've listened to him—"

"Okay, infants, tell you what I'm gonna do." The demon slid his pitchfork from crossbar to diagonal position across the door. "I'm gonna let you go on out now, if you promise you'll bring your vampire boyfriend back to us."

"He won't come," said Solly.

"Not even for a summer job? Kids your age and summer jobs go together like red and hot, and Hellmouth Park can always use a good vampire."

"We'll promise to take him your kind offer," said April, "and bring him back with us next time we come."

Solly looked at her, but the demon said, "Fair enough for Hellmouth. Okay, infants, *ciaou,* and looking to see you back real soon." He moved out of the doorway.

April and Solly lost no time in making their exit, but said nothing else to each other until they were safely out of the building into the night—it was only about 0300. At last, halfway across the black cinder ground, he congratulated her, "That was neat! Clem'll never go for it, but who cares? 'S long as that floater back there did."

"That's why I said it that way. And I don't intend on going back there at all. Ever."

"Me neither. Who needs it?"

As picketing Hellmouth Park became for some a life career, the pickets' earliest camp lean-tos had grown up into a neat white frame building that housed comfort station, shower stall, kitchen with serving window, and small dormitory. The Heavenmouth pickets had a similar one painted navy blue, and the two picket lines had been known to share supplies.

As they made their way across the cinder field, a tall marcher in gray detached himself from the picket line and sprinted toward them. "Hey!" said Solly. "There he is now!"

"What? Oh, yes, so it is! I forgot about his borrowing that old gray suit of his cousin's. He looks so different out of black, I almost didn't know him."

By now Clement had reached them. "You okay?"

"Hey, no problem, we're fine. Where's Cake-o?"

"Catching a nap in the resthouse over there." Clement jerked his arm at the white frame building. "We didn't expect you for a few hours yet."

"Yeah, well, you know." Solly gave a grand shrug. "It all gets to be pretty much the same old thing in there. Too much of a bad thing, you know?"

* * * *

Heavengate Amusement Park had been planned to present a wholesome contrast to Hellmouth. Yet, once, inside, the discerning visitor might glimpse a certain underlying similarity. Here were the same basic rides, with angelic white pegasi in place of black nightmares on the merry-go-rounds; the same restaurants, with angel's food in place of devil's food; the same theaters and peep-shows, with uplifting family-oriented fare in place of violence and naughtiness; the same waxworks, of Biblical and other inspirational scenes in place of horrors—although with here and there a grisly martyrdom in which the saints wore vacuously blissful smiles throughout their tortures; and the same subbasement private party rooms, wherein good, clean celebrations presumably took the place of orgies.

"I don't know…" Clement mused as the student foursome sat in the Sunrise Room waiting for their Crack of Dawn breakfast. "It's nice, but… I don't know."

The Sunrise Room was a small family restaurant pocketed into the eastern side of the rooftop gardens. Like the amusement rides, it was partly inside the domelike Crystal Cloud Palace and partly in open air, and it afforded splendid views of the daily phenomenon whose name it bore. It was also, unlike the Sunset Room on the western side of one of the lower floors, very budget-friendly.

"It's certainly a better place to visit than Hellmouth Park," said April, cocking her head in the general direction of the rival establishment across the cow pasture.

"I'd never even try to debate that point with you," Clement agreed. "All the same, this place… It makes me think of the story Professor Sharma tells, from her people's holy books. About the hero who refused to enter heaven when they wouldn't let him take his faithful dog in with him."

"Do you mean," April said with the hint of a twinkle, "that you'd stay out of heaven if you had a dog and they wouldn't let it in with you? What about a girlfriend?"

"I especially wouldn't go in if they tried to keep you out, April. But more likely it'll be the other way, and you'll have to beg them to let me in with you."

"Then what's the point of all the work you put into it?" Solly wanted to know. "Always being good and never drinking or—"

"The point is, functioning here and now." Clement spoke as though he was weary of repeating it. "If I didn't keep trying to be good, do you think I could be sitting here right now with you floaters, in a place filled with crosses and things, waiting to watch the sun come up?"

"But I see what Clement means," said Keiko. "And his Professor Sharma, with that story about the hero and his dog. It's like what some poet we just studied—Ralph Waldo Emerson?—wrote, 'Find me, and turn thy back on Heaven.'"

Just then the serving angel, in a costume modified for convenience while waiting tables, having high cherub wings and tucked sleeves, arrived with their orders: Crack of Dawn specials with eggs, ham, and pancakes for three young appetites, and for the fourth, a bowl of oatmeal.

"Never going to put any meat on your bones this way, young floater," the angel teased pleasantly, setting the oatmeal before Clement.

"I snacked earlier," he explained with a grin.

The angel refilled their coffee cups and moved on. "'Snacked'?" Solly repeated. "Isn't that sort of a fib? You *ate* earlier, if 'eat' means getting your main nourishment."

"Well, this isn't pinching." Clement touched his crucifix earring. "Either it was the mildest kind of white fib, or else anything liquid counts as a snack to people in general. This looks like real homogenized cream, anyway," he observed, pouring it over his cereal. "I guess she really hopes to put some meat on my bones. Too bad it won't work."

"You'll probably never have to worry about getting fat at all," Keiko remarked comfortably. "When the rest of us grow old and have to start watching our intake, you'll still be able to feed your face to anyone's heart's content."

"Besides," said April, "this simply isn't the kind of place where we'd want to ask for his regular."

"I'm not sure why not," said Keiko. "They advertise a ninety-nine and three-quarters percent success rate in getting every special dish anyone wants to advance-order, and that almost has to include things like black pudding and czarnina."

"That's a couple of the fancier restaurants here," said Clement. "Maybe even the Cloud Garden on the other side of the roof. The Sunrise Room has a set menu."

"But a pretty good one," said Solly, tucking into his ham. (He was liberal in his ideas about kosher.) "And they say the sunrise always looks good from here, no matter what the weather's like anywhere else."

"Besides," April went on to Keiko in a low enough voice not to carry beyond their table, "why do you think he's here in mufti?"

"Not for Heavengate," Clement answered for Keiko, although lowering his own voice. "Because of that other park across the way."

"Yeah," Keiko told April. "We were all through it yesterday. Don't you remember?"

April shot a glance at Solly. He said, in the most lowered voice yet, "Lady, I think maybe you'd better relay the message now."

Clement and Keiko heard, sat, and waited. After a moment, Keiko said, "Well, what message? Relay it, or I'm going to eat before my food gets ice cold."

"It's for you, Clement," April said in embarrassed tones. "The truth is, we came out earlier than we'd planned because we…er…may have gotten into a little bit of trouble back there."

"But you're all right?" Clement's hand tightened to white knuckles around his spoon. With painstaking effort, he released it to the plate beneath his bowl.

"Oh, sure, sure!" Solly said quickly, if softly. "The truth is, we snuck down to the twenty-five-and-older area for a look at their wax museum, and a guard or something caught us."

"When he let us go," April finished, looking and sounding more embarrassed than ever, "he said to tell you they always have jobs ready for…people like you."

Keiko whispered, "You told him Clement's a…?"

April nodded miserably. "It just slipped out! I'm not even sure how. Somehow, it just…slipped out."

Clement nodded, picked his spoon up again, and began eating his oatmeal. First Solly, then Keiko, and finally April followed his example. After several minutes, Clement broke the silence. "It probably wouldn't have made much difference, whatever I wore. I was in mufti that other time, too. Three years ago. I wasn't quite sixteen, and we were all dressed in jeans and sweat shirts—Ted and Omar and me—and the people over there saw it anyway, as soon as they looked at me. I never figured out how. I hope maybe they saw it too, over here at Heavengate, and feel okay with it. Anyway. I've got no interest at all in going to work for them over there. I've got a summer job waiting for me at the Sundae Palace in Maplehaven, with room and board at Uncle Don and Aunt Nettie's, and that's where I'm headed tomorrow."

Solly jerked his head in the direction of Hellmouth Park. "I've heard the pay is really good, over there."

Clement gave him a stare. "There isn't enough money in the whole world. If I wouldn't go in for love—" He glanced at April—"unless I heard you floaters were in danger, think I'd ever go in there for *money?*"

PART II
FALL, 1951

CHAPTER 8

FRIDAY, OCT. 5

"I was born," said Pater Fairchild, "the same year the University of Minnemagantic was founded, 1884. Pi Rho has been a presence here since the university's second term, and never, it seems, more attractive to pledges than in this first semester of the first year in the second half of this Twentieth Century."

"Yeah," Spud said happily. "I guess having us a resident vampire helped out."

"It probably did not hurt," said Mendoza, a senior this year and on the committee thanks to his being Prexy of the Purple Rose.

"Yeah, nineteen still on our pledge list," said Solly. "How many of us did you have at this point last year? How does it compare?"

"Ten," said Spud.

"And how many do you want left for the Midnight Haze?" Stale wanted to know, cracking his knuckles.

"The Pi Rho ideal," Pater Fairchild reminded them, "is ten initiates each year. The ideal is rarely achieved. That is one reason we have brothers living outside the house."

Yeah, that and maybe marriage. Spud remembered the big party they'd thrown last winter for Carl Avosso and his bride Milly Wanamaker, and then Carl moved out of the Rose house right away, into his wife's apartment near the hospital, and Jack Goodbody moved in.

"Nine's a lot to weed out during Hell Week," Stale said doubtfully. "Unless we make it a lot tougher on them than you floaters made it on us..."

"Eight, at maximum, during Hell Week," Fairchild told him. "In order to begin with an even number for the buddy system, we shall need to cull at least one tonight."

"Cull more of them, if you must," Mendoza suggested lazily. "An odd number, of course."

"Yeah," Spud agreed. "Don't leave it all on Hell Week hazing. I don't think I'm gonna do all that much bullying and stuff, myself. Upperclassman and all."

Mendoza smiled. "Nor, I think, can you rely on our vampire to do a lick of it, sophomore or not."

"Me," Stale said with a big grin, "I'm looking forward to being on the giving end this year. And I bet we can count on Fletcher, too, upperclassman or not."

Pater Fairchild gaveled for order. "Nineteen being an unusually large number for us since before the War, I have gone back to a practice they employed in those happy, long-ago times, and had copies of the list made for each of us. I propose we spend ten minutes going through these names, each on his one, each of us lightly lining out nine names. At the end of the ten minutes, we will compare. Any pledge whose name we have all lined out, shall be eliminated. Next, anyone on whose name four of us agree, then three, and so on. With luck, this method may whittle our list down to manageable length with little need for further debate."

He passed out the copies of the list, along with sharpened pencils. Spud's copy—probably everyone's except the house father's—was a carbon, but pretty clear. They got to work.

Ten minutes later—actually more like fifteen—they found that everyone had agreed on four names and four guys had agreed on three more, so that brought it down to an even dozen, and they decided to stop with that, and keep Hell Week activities no worse than last year, because Pi Rho could live with twelve Sunday initiates.

"But what about the Midnight Haze?" asked Stale, cracking his knuckles again. "I've gotta say, from what Fletcher and some of the other brothers've told me, I'm kind of sorry I missed out on the way it used to be."

"Some floaters," Spud told him, "don't even know when they've got it good."

"Well," Stale argued, "I don't know about that, but I do know I'm the only Class of '54'er in the I. C., and if we don't attract a few more frosh this year—"

"The Inner Circle lies in danger of quietly snuffing out?" Mendoza replied, with so slight an accent on the "quietly" that Spud wondered if he'd just imagined it.

"Can't see that happening," Solly remarked, confident like only a brother could be who'd never poked his nose even as near as Spud had to the I. C. "Long as the hunt is on, we'll have somebody to direct it."

"I wonder," Mendoza murmured, "whether the hunt might not be redirected at targets closer to home."

"Its present targets might be closer home than you seem to suppose, Mendoza," Pater Fairchild told him a little sternly. "But this is business for the Inner Circle, not the Pledge Committee."

Mendoza smiled and opened one hand in acknowledgment. Spud admired his senior poise. But then, Mendoza had always been poised, ever since Spud first saw him, back when he was only a soph but still looked mature and worldly-wise to the frosh pledgling Spud had been at the time.

Stale spoke up again. "But it comes pretty close to Hell Week business, I guess. Didn't the old, traditional way you had of doing the Midnight Haze net you more…"

His voice trailed off. Spud glanced over in time for a good glimpse of the looks both Mendoza and Pater Fairchild were giving the speaker.

"More bullies among the brothers, you were about to say?" Mendoza asked softly.

"Yeah, yeah, that was what I was gonna say," Stale mumbled.

Spud guessed it wasn't. There were enough rumors, enough speculation, that Spud guessed Stale'd been close to bending I. C. secrecy. What the whole purpose was of I. C. secrecy, Spud wasn't sure. Probably some lodge-like kind of mystique. Everybody knew the I. C. mainly talked about hunting down deathguards. Maybe they figured putting on a big secrecy front helped inspire the rest of the Rose into keeping not too far behind them in righteous zeal. Anyway, Mendoza had Stale pegged pretty well. Stale *was* kind of a bully, even with his own classmates, Lord help the frosh! Maybe came of being one of the oldest in the Class of '54, thanks to his birthday falling just a day the wrong side of the cut-off for the Class of '53. At least he was open about it, not kind of sneaky, like Fred. Yeah, they were buddies, the three musketeers of them, but sometimes Spud wondered… If anybody was going to make Hell Week live up to its name for the Class of '55, it was floaters like Stale Drinkwater and Fred Fletcher.

"Hey!" Spud said suddenly. "Long's we've got a house vampire, and long's he's probably not going to be giving any of our pledglings any grief at all the rest of the week, why don't we give him the same part in the Midnight Haze Saturday that I had last year—make him the Lord High Pooh-Bah or whatever we'll call it at this year's campfire?"

"I call that," said Mendoza, "a true inspiration."

Spud grinned, feeling honored and happy.

And there was no more talk about going back to the way they used to do the Midnight Haze, up until last year. Just give it another couple of years, Spud thought proudly, and the national protocol will be our U. of M. tradition and nobody but alums and Prof Fairchild will remember it ever was any different.

CHAPTER 9

ABOUT A WEEK LATER: SATURDAY, OCT. 13

Clement sat where Spud had sat last year. Maybe not the exact spot. (Battlefields that had been turned into memorial parks—how did they *know* that where they had a little marker was the exact spot where such-and-such a hero had fallen? Had they had somebody there at the time, watching to put in a golf marker?) But the same spot relative to the campfire, on an old wooden folding chair turned into a throne by plumping a pillow on the seat and throwing a plush blanket over the whole arrangement. Set up on a portable platform about a third of a meter high.

They had talked him into playing tonight's Lord High—in his case, Vampire. Solly and Spud and Ramon and some of the others had talked about how well that role fit with his having kept in the background all through Hell Week proper and given this year's pledglings no grief. "It'll make your presence all the more effective at the Midnight Haze," Ramon had said. "All the more authoritative."

"And don't let 'em *all* sing all the way through," Solly had said.

"Only the best singers?" Spud had suggested.

"Huh?" Clement had protested.

"Or the worst." Ramon had given them one of his elegant shrugs. "I think we may trust the rising star of the School of Music to judge the best and the worst."

"Either they *all* get to finish their songs," Clement had said firmly, "or *none* of them."

"Then you better make it none," Spud had declared.

Ramon had nodded. "The protocol is still rather fluid, but I imagine that 'none' would be best."

So now here they were, sitting around roasting things and waiting for the pledges to get loose and make it to the campfire. The wieners smelled good, but the Lord High Vampire had promised himself not to eat a bite until all this year's pledglings were safely folded in. Not even a s'more. It wasn't that he was hungry, exactly. He couldn't be, not really. He had drunk his nourishment and eaten a fair amount of bulk at dinner. And sworn himself to fast until the last new little brother had made it.

Sort of by way of penance for the role he was going to have to play in this evening's "gag rule." It *was* just a role. He kept reminding himself. As much a role as Papageno last fall, or Major-General Stanley in the spring operetta. He kept reminding himself. To keep his jewelry from giving him any pain.

Things looked different from up here on the throne. A makeshift throne on a makeshift platform. Still, things looked different. Just a year ago tonight…not quite to the date, that's why they used to talk about "a year and a day"…when he'd been one of the pledglings (gadfly! how young the frosh looked this year!)…bumping along those back roads in the trunk of an old jalopy, gagged and blindfolded and trussed like a Thanksgiving turkey…then bound to that tree…

But by the way the older brothers talked, those who still talked about it, last year's Midnight Haze had started a new and milder tradition here. Things used to be a lot worse. For floaters like Fred Fletcher and…yes, Spud admitted it, too, even if he never volunteered reminiscences about it.

But Pi Rho was a national fraternity, and tonight's ceremony, like last year's, followed the protocol approved for houses all across the R.S.A. So…Clement should study up on all this a little more. It was his own fraternity, after all. Hadn't things used to be…wilder everywhere, during the Intermission between Acts I and II of the Last Great War? Maybe the University of Minnemagantic Pi Rho house had just been a little slower than others in changing gears.

What about Inner Circles? Did the chapters at other universities have them, too? And how uniform were *they* across the country? Equally secretive everywhere? Too much secrecy, Clement thought. Everyone knew the Inner Circle kept charge of directing and coordinating the watch for deathguards—as if any of those would ever come up here to Hodag Crossing (well, maybe *en route* to Canada). But they must've served some other purpose, those Inner Circles, back before the War and during its Intermission. How much secrecy did it require, to direct and coordinate the affairs of a Greek house? All the members would find out the important stuff anyway, as it filtered down in guiderules and new, revised traditions and such, like this Midnight Haze. So all that secrecy did, was inspire whispers and rumors. Some fairly outrageous whispers and rumors. Some of the brothers speculated that the Inner Circle was a purgatorio.

Clement knew a little about those. They had been big in the Twenties, when things got wild because of international inflation and counterfeiting. They faded a little during the Thirties, but had been revived to an almost public level as a home front effort during the War's Second

Act. They claimed forerunners in things like the flagellant movements of the Middle Ages. People devoutly hurting themselves and each other with various mild (that is, not causing permanent damage beyond a little scarring) tortures, as penance for sin—their own and the world's. In fact, right after his accident, when he came out of the hospital a vampire, Clement had thought semi-seriously about scouting around for one and joining it himself. He remembered the long talk he'd had about it with Father Mike at Saint Basil's in Galop de Vache, where he spent his high school years September to May with Uncle Jan and Aunt Cele. Father Mike had explained that purgatorios were a perverse—that had been his exact word, "perverse"—blot on the Christian tradition, that no monastery worth joining ever indulged such practices nowadays, that as a Church we'd grown beyond all that kind of nonsense, thank the Lord! And as far as Father Mike knew, mainstream Protestants had never even started down that particular perversion of piety. All of which meant that it was highly unlikely the Purple Rose's Inner Circle included a purgatorio, and the speculation that it did was just the same kind of shivery storytelling it tickled people to whisper about. The same kind of shivery storytelling rumors Clement learned now and then that people were repeating about himself.

"You'll have a hard enough time of it," Father Mike had told him, "if you really decide to go around costumed like Bela Lugosi. Trust me, son, very few people would ever notice the length of your dogteeth."

"But they'd notice me drinking blood, padre. What'd I do, have to sneak all my real meals alone somewhere after dark? How bad would that look if anybody ever found out?"

There were rumors about Hellmouth Amusement Park, too. The difference was, a lot of those rumors were probably true. Or even milder than the reality. Unless it had all been some kind of nightmare, the time he sneaked over there with Ted and Omar, and Hellmouth Park threatened to drown him in their underground lake of blood unless he went to work for them as a vampire. Thank God he'd still been a week and a half shy of turning sixteen and legal age for signing contracts. Looking back, it really seemed a lot more plausible as a nightmare, and some of the rumors had Hellmouth Park sneaking hallucinogenic drugs into some of the refreshments they sold, even air squirting out through their ventilation jets... Why had he even been visiting Uncle Buck and the guys in Udder Delight at the wraparound end of April that year, anyway? Oh, yes, that was one of the years he spent the summer with Cousin Donna's family in Maplehaven, so spring break had seemed like a good time to get in a visit with Uncle Buck's family.

Heavengate had already been built that April, but not yet open for business. And already at the beginning of this last summer, after only a few years in business, he'd noticed Heavengate showing a little wear and tear around the edges. If it was true that both those parks were owned by the same...corporation or conglomerate or tribillionaire or whatever... Clement could believe it. Heavengate Amusement Park looked like a plot to cheapen people's ideas of Heaven. Well, April had really, really wanted to see both parks in one outing, and make her own comparison.

That was April. She had a mind that had to look for its own answers, examine the evidence for herself and sift it empirically. That was one of the many things he loved about her. And it didn't even seem to make any difference to her, either way, his being a vampire. She loved him just for himself, Clement. She'd have gone for plain old Clement Black as soon as for Clement Czarny, the dracula. She'd shown that from the first.

Funny. Away back before he hit his teen years, he remembered planning sometimes to be a priest or monk when he grew up, when he wasn't planning to be something else, like a polly or robber or fireman or cowpoke or doctor or circus clown. Like every other kid, he supposed. In a way, wasn't he turning out to be something a little like a circus clown as it was? "Lord High Vampire" and all. Thinking about the priesthood or religious brotherhood had pretty well stopped when he woke up in the hospital and found himself a vampire, and at almost the same time—so nearly that he had never been able to make it clear in his own mind which came first—realized there was a basic reason for the difference between boys and girls, and it promised some pretty good things, after all! He didn't think he'd ever given another thought to maybe becoming a priest, until after he got seriously involved with April. Funny. Paradoxical, wouldn't that be a good word for it?

It might be like finding himself a shield in case things didn't work out with her. But could anyone be a good priest if it'd only been the fall-back career choice? He'd have to be a secular padre, of course. Or, if the priesthood wouldn't take a vampire, one of the missionary-type friars. Thinking about a lifetime cloistered away from the complementary gender might have sounded good to a prepubescent kid, but he was old enough now to understand that social life would turn out to be pretty much a desert if shut away from friends like Keiko. For one. And Cousin Donna—

There! North side of the campfire clearing—the first pledge to make it to the fire. Tony. Still—or again—obediently gagged. Tony Tallpines. Made sense he was first, with his Cinnamon heritage.

Tony didn't hesitate a minute, but came right around the fire as if he'd already spotted the Lord High before actually poking his face into the firelight, knelt to him, bowed his head, and waited. *Deja vu!* Just a year ago...

"Well, well, well," Clement delivered his scripted line. "Our first little one. Rise, turn around, and present thine infant face to our circle of brethren."

Tony obeyed.

"Does anyone here among us claim this infant?"

"That'd be me." Stallion stepped forward.

"Thou know'st what to do, O brave one."

Stallion undid Tony's gag, handed him the sheet of paper—they'd streamlined things a little from last year's procedure, given every sponsor his own fledgling's lyrics—and stood back. Tony looked over the lyric, nodded, and started singing.

> *"Follow the Rose and drink some more,*
> *Drink some more, drink some more.*
> *Tip up the bottle and we'll booze some more!*
> *Follow, follow the Rose."*

And...Gad—fly! he was good. Clement had had some advance warning, Tony having come out for Glee Club first thing after matriculation, but...

> *"Come on and take another swallow!"*

Clement knew he should have given the thumb's-down after about half a line, but already by then his earring had been pinching. Badly. By now his fraternity ring had joined it, searing a line around his finger, and even through shirt and undershirt, he was starting to feel his cross heat up.

Why? Just at the thought of playing this trick on the pledges? But it was all only part of the script! They'd understand...the way he'd understood...almost at once...

> *"Follow the Rose and drink some more,*
> *Drink some more, drink some more.*
> *Trot out your poker deck and play some more.*
> *Follow, follow the Rose."*

No! The problem was—*envy!* After a frosh year of being the Hodags' top new baritone...with daydreams of a Met career (along with his lovely soprano wife), Clement Czarny was hearing his position challenged...a greater baritone voice than our vampire's is here...

"To the grand house where we gather,
Where the sparks fly, and beer flows.
How much fun it is in beer to wallow."

The other brothers were starting to look a little twitchy. Was it that obvious to everyone? Or chiefly to him—because his own musical studies had trained his ear to judge quality like that—and were the other floaters just wondering why he hadn't given them the thumb's-down yet? Or maybe both: they could hear it, and it made them wonder all the harder why their Lord High Vampire wasn't cutting it off.

Follow the Rose and drink some more,
Drink some more, drink some more.
Don't want to be a pipsqueak any more?
Follow, fol—"

Just in time, Clement gave the thumb's-down, Stallion slapped the gag back over Tony's mouth, and all the rest of the group sang the limerick about the rotten radio crooner, while Clement settled back, shaking inside, but relieved to feel his jewelry relaxing to normal. Maybe... just maybe...he'd managed to slay the green-eyed monster. At least for tonight. He might find it rising from the tomb again all semester...all school year...maybe his entire college career...and even longer...but having Tony as a frat brother, getting to know him better as a person and not just as a rival voice...that could help. Clement hoped.

Back to the immediate future. Having let the first pledgling almost finish his song pretty well obligated the Lord High Vampire to let all the others sing their lyrics all the way through until the last couple of words.

In fact, three of them—the worst three—Brant Epswich with a croaky voice, Al Koby who was completely untunable, and Joe Doe who confessed right off that he didn't recognize the tune and had to make up his own—Clement let get all the way through, and then led a round of applause in place of the bad crooner limerick.

CHAPTER 10

ABOUT HALF A WEEK LATER:
WEDNESDAY, OCT. 17

Carl Avosso paced the Expectant Fathers' Waiting Room alone, popping cough drop after cough drop in his state of nerves. Helpless. Absolutely helpless for anything but waiting and praying.

Not too helpless to have gotten Milly into this in the first place. Not too helpless to marry her as soon as she knew—and her sister and Dr. Shammari knew—and then Carl knew because they told him. But before the world at large knew.

Milly had told him he didn't have to do anything about it. Even if the Procreational Permit system had been started up again yet after the War, being a healthy nurse she'd have been as good as assured of an almost automatic Propermit for one, any healthy father. She had her full and equal rights under the Law, and their baby had full and equal rights, and only the oldest generation still alive could remember out of personal experience that it had ever been any other way, back before the Great Reform and the administration of President Susan B. If they were still living in the Bad Old Days, she might not even have told him. But today, his daughter—if it was a girl—would wear her daddy's family name in any case, so Milly thought it was only fair that daddy should know—

That was when he'd kissed her into silence, and eventually told her he would have been proposing in any case, come June. They'd just hurry things up a little.

They could still have waited till after graduation. Maternity bridal gowns were still around, after the big fashion they had been in the Twenties, even for brides who were still virginal. His own mother had worn one. But what reason had Milly and he had to wait? Valentine's Day falling in midweek that year, they were married the Saturday before, February 10, and the Pies opened both houses, Rose and Sighs, for a gala reception. Then he passed the house presidency on to Alfie Taylor and moved right into Milly's neat little three-room apartment near the hospital where she worked, while Jack Goodbody went from the top of the waiting list to Carl's bed at the Rose house. All working out to a happily ever after for everyone. Until now. This was the first hitch…

The door opened. Dr. Shammari. In one step, Carl was face to face. "Doctor?"

"M. Avosso. Will you please have a seat?" Medically serious. Professionally serious. Not good.

Heart thudding, Carl sat. Words choked up at his lips, but he knew his questions would probably get answered quickest if he just let the doctor take the lead.

"M. Avosso, your dear wife tells us you were aware this is not her first pregnancy?"

What was this, wasting time asking *him* questions? "Ancient history, Doc. She was seventeen, being kind to a serviceman about to be shipped to the front. What—"

"Who was the father? Can you tell us?"

"Hank somebody. She never told me his family name, just that he was killed in action, and then she lost the baby on Victory in Eurasia Day, some kind of accident when the celebrating got out of hand. What—"

"It was unfortunate, that accident…"

Carl wanted to give the physician a good shake. "Dr. Shammari. *How is my wife?*"

"Forgive me. She is doing well. As well, perhaps, as it can be expected. I feel very sanguine that we will save her. It is the child, the boy…"

"What? What's wrong? God, Doctor—"

The East Indian headed him off with two raised fingers. "We deal here, M. Avosso, with something that medicine is being too slow to understand. It has, apparently, to do with the blood. That first child. There are cases in the literature that suggest…the first one she might have had without complications. It is unfortunate if we have no way to consult the record, even to learn what was the father's blood type. A sample would have been best, but even to know the record—"

"Dr. Shammari. Is the baby dead or not?"

"Oh. Forgive me. The boy still lives, but by…I think we would say, a spiderweb. You must prepare for the worst. Nevertheless, there is something we can perhaps… I must warn you, it will be almost to experiment, an experiment of desperation. But it is the only hope we see—"

"Anything! Just do it!"

"We ask first the permission of the father."

"You've got it!" What the hell had the Indian been beating around the bushes for all this time?

Still the doctor seemed to hesitate. "It would be an exchange trans-fusion. This would mean draining your son of blood completely and replacing it."

Carl's own face probably went white.

"M. Avosso? Have we still your permission?"

"That's *it? That's* our only hope?"

"It is the only hope that we can see here at this hospital, Dr. Sharma and I. And it must be done soon, if it is to be done. There is not the time to convey your son to a larger place or to consult with other physicians elsewhere."

"What about Milly? Have you explained all this to the *mother,* for God's sake?" Or was Milly even conscious? "What condition is she in?"

"We have explained it to her, as much as her condition allows. She has trusted her baby and herself both into our hands."

"Then do it! Do whatever it takes! Anything! To save them *both*, but just please make sure you save *her.*"

"You will sign—"

"Anything you like! Just get me the forms and I'll sign them. Just… Doctor, if it *should* have to come down to a choice—"

The doctor cut him off. "The baby is delivered. That was not the chief trouble. We can do our best for both, freely. There will be no ques-tion of choosing mother or child."

"And Milly—you think she'll be—"

"Yes. We believe your wife will live, will recover fully. Only, you must be tender, you must understand…"

Carl felt his muscles relaxing a little. "Poor Milly. If she loses this one, too—"

"M. Avosso. Whether this beautiful boy dies or, we hope and pray, lives, in either case, we think you would be very unwise to 'try again.' We do not yet know enough about these cases, cases like yours, but from the too little we know, it seems that the first child sets up a…reaction in the blood of the mother, which attacks its brothers and sisters in the womb, during the pregnancy. Also, it can be, finally, to the very serious risk of the mother. No. You will be wise not to try again."

Stunned, Carl could only whisper, "Then do whatever you can. Only… You weren't lying? You think *she'll* pull through, at least? How soon can I— Is her sister with her? How soon can I see them?"

"She is in the charge of her sister. I do not need to tell you what a fine nurse your sister-in-law is, like your dear wife when she is not herself the patient. I leave it to your sister-in-law to say when you can go to them. Now, M. Avosso, I go to send someone with the forms for your signature, and, if we can, to save your son."

They had reached the small hours of Thursday morning. The new-born was resting in its oxygen tent in the Intensive Care ward, the new mother in a tranquilized sleep in her room, the new father nodding off in a chair beside her—the other side of the room being at present unoccupied, he might well be stretched out on its empty bed by morning, but let his sister-in-law, that excellent Nurse Dolores Wanamaker, remind him of the hospital guiderules, if she so chose. The doctors were too tired, sitting side by side in the hospital's Coffee Room, gathering energy for the decision whether to go home at once or first snatch a few hours of sleep on hospital cots.

"It is perhaps early to be sure," the Muslim doctor congratulated the Hindu, "but it seems that we may well have saved the infant, my friend, with your inspiration."

Slowly, carefully, sleepily, Dr. Sharma lifted a cup of coffee to his lips and sipped. "I think it was thanks in large part to you, my good friend and colleague. Somehow... Somehow it brought into my mind your case these five? six? years ago of our young student for whose diet you must prescribe raw blood."

"How is that?"

Dr. Sharma thought...seemed to doze off...caught himself and thought again. "No. I cannot say. Maybe it was only a... Who can tell how our minds work? Who, even of those who study the...psychomystique...of us poor humans? Only that young Charny's case, also, had to do with the blood, and strong symptoms of hemolytic shock."

"Which were gone when I saw him."

"But you trust the word of our good nurse."

"She was one of the few who kept her head sober that day, even in this hospital where all should have been sober."

"It was the day of Victory in the Pacific, was it not? All had cause to celebrate that day."

"Within reason. For some of us to celebrate too much, was to risk making still more casualties, after the hostilities were ended." Dr. al Shammari sighed, shook his head wearily, then smiled. "But tonight, my dear friend and colleague, tonight I think and hope that we have won a victory which may last and spread and help many. We must publish this."

"Yes..." the other said reflectively. "We must publish, must we not? For the benefit of the world...."

CHAPTER 11

A FEW DAYS LATER: FRIDAY, OCT. 19

Professor Sharma had chosen *The Barber of Seville* for this fall's opera, and almost every baritone in the School of Music, plus Professor Ives who taught Advanced Music Theory 201 and The Masterworks of Bach 301, plus a graduate teaching assistant from the School of Science who sang in the Lutheran Church Choir, plus the owner of the Hodag Crossing Barbershop, had shown up to audition for Figaro. Half a dozen of them, including the barber, had survived the Wednesday auditions and sat here in the auditorium waiting for tonight's finals, but Clement wasn't really worried. Except about Tony Tallpines, and maybe M. Carlson, the barber, who had his own almost stereotypical Italian mustache. His casting in the role would be great for town-gown relations.

But wasn't Professor Sharma above politics? After seeing what politics running amok had done in her native India... No, Professor Sharma would cast it as she judged best for the show in and of itself. And hadn't she cast Clement as last year's Papageno? When he was only a frosh. Now, with all last year's training and development having gone into his voice...

His earring pinched. Too much self-confidence—it was shading over into vainglory. Before the metal started heating up, he turned his thoughts to April, waiting eagerly in the chair beside him, scanning her audition aria.

Too bad Figaro wasn't Rosina's love interest, or anyone else's, not in Rossini's opera. If they did Mozart's in the next few years, she could go out for Susanna.

"The transposition is okay," April murmured in his ear, "but sometimes I wish I were a mezzo or even an alto, and could do it the way Gioachino first wrote it."

"You'll do fine," he whispered back. "And you'll look wonderful. Audiences really expect beautiful young romantic heroines to be sopranos, anyway." Bolstering up someone else's confidence cooled his jewelry right down. Unlike bolstering up his own too high. Maybe he should go over and give Tony a good-luck clap on the back? Fraternity brother to brother? Maybe M. Carlson, too. Town-gown relations and all…

He went over and did it. Well, M. Carlson he didn't clap on the back, but he shook his hand and when the older man, looking friendly and sincere, comic mustache and all, congratulated him on last year's Papageno, he found it painless to smile back and say, "Thank you, M., it's nice to be remembered so long." Tony, he clapped on the back with his left hand while exchanging the Pi Rho handshake with his right and saying, "Go to it, brother, just sing as off-key as you like." Which same words Tony repeated back to him, with a self-conscious little frosh grin. It all tamed Clement's jewelry down so much that he went on wishing well to his rival baritones and everybody else until Professor Sharma called for order and got the Friday finals underway.

M. Carlson sounded like he'd practiced Figaro's famous aria and practiced it hard. He sounded exactly like a good Barbershop Quartet baritone who had practiced Figaro's famous aria to death. But Tony… Tony's voice was like Grade A-plus cream going into the perfect cup of coffee, yet also, somehow, spot on for comic effect. If Tony's voice and M. Carlson's appearance had been combined in one man, Professor Sharma could have planned the whole production around him, and Clement thought he wouldn't even have minded losing out, not too much. The other three floaters were makeweights. But when Clement's turn came… it was going great, right up until the next to the last note! He *flubbed* the next to the last note!

He lingered long enough to go up to Professor Sharma as the last few people were leaving. He knew he shouldn't—shouldn't say anything about it—but none of his jewelry was hurting, so whatever trying to explain was, it wasn't sinful. Probably a mistake, but not a sinful one. "Professor Sharma…I just wanted to tell you—I *know* I flubbed that one note."

She gave him an understanding look. The red bindi on her forehead made him think of that third eye that was supposed to give adepts who had learned how to use it a special, spiritual insight. "Clement. We all know of what you are capable. Believe me, if you do not get this role, it will not be because of the one unfortunate wrong note you sang tonight in your nervousness."

She smiled and clapped his upper arm in a gentle, encouraging way that somehow told him he wouldn't be getting the part this year.

* * * *

Joe Doe didn't really like Stale Drinkwater that much, fratty bro or not. Stale'd been one of the worst all Hell Week—"Come'n, just play like you're a man and take it!" And he hadn't toned it down all that much in the week after formal initiation, even if he seemed to act happy that now the new brothers had the ground beneath their feet to stand up and push back.

But Joe Doe's real name was Josef Dostoevsky. Like the famous Russian author, so he and his mom and grandfather had worn it proudly, right up till the end of the War. Then, when it all came out about Stalin's Eugenics Farms...that was when they Americanized it and he became Joseph Doe. Maybe a good thing more ways than one. He couldn't help suspect the Purple Rose had rushed him just for the sound of the name "Joe Doe."

Like so many other Russian-Americans—people of Russian descent all over the world, Joe guessed—he felt so guilty about what the Russians had done back in the Old World, that when Stale whispered him an invite to the Inner Circle, it just seemed like the least he could do to try and make up a little bit for all that guilt by association.

He couldn't help wondering why Czarny wasn't part of the I. C. You'd think a vampire with a Russian-sounding name and so all-fired... clean...a style of living... But Fred had warned Joe that Clem was one of the bros—including most of the Purple Rose, actually—they wanted to especially keep in the dark about it. Was being some kind of wonderkid in the School of Music—operas and all that—really more important for a Friday night?

Getting whipped hadn't felt good, but at least Joe felt...a little cleaner, somehow, now it was over. For the evening. He wasn't sure he wanted to take four years of it every other week or so. Or even one year of it. Maybe they'd let him go honorary, just come in later for the business meeting. Along with Hartwick. Of course, it helped Gale Hartwick to have a big brother who was not only a Pi Rho alum, but a FIDO-WC man.

Anyway, it had seemed like longer than the Last Great War itself, Intermission and all. But now they were finally settling down to the business meeting. Pater Fairchild—he didn't take any active part in the suffering stuff—too old and venerable—just oversaw and monitored. Carl Avosso, who was in grad school now and maybe phasing it out, but had let himself get whipped tonight in gratitude or purgation or sympathy or whatever for his wife's trouble—and danger, if Joe had it right—having their baby two days ago. Mendoza, the dark quiet senior, house prexy this year. John Rogers, Fred Fletcher, Al Koby whose name had been Americanized from Kobayashi, and himself—Joe Doe, the other frosh in the I. C. And Gale Hartwick, who had come in while all the others were finally rubbing down, and put on some coffee for them.

Joe would rather have had a beer, but Pater Fairchild had guiderules for I. C. meetings, and one of them was, If you're going to drink anything else but coffee, make it tea. Or just plain water.

Gale brought the tray out and poured and served the pater's coffee. For everyone else, the whippers served their whippees and then themselves. Even before everybody had his cup—John and Al were taking the tea route, Al dunking his bag up and down, up and down, up and down—Joe wished he'd just let it sit quiet and steep, like John was doing—Pater Fairchild was asking, "Well, Hartwick, what do you have for us this evening from your brother at FIDO?"

Fred had explained to his frosh recruits that the house father never asked Hartwick that question unless he already knew the answer was yes, and had seen what it was first for himself. This was his way of alerting the I. C. and making sure they saw it next, before the newsrags and Post Offices got it.

"Dmitri Garbanokov," Gale answered proudly, producing a black sheet of paper. "The notorious Bear of Yemtsa. Just a small photo, but it's a good, sharp profile, and very well documented and authenticated. It should enlarge nicely for the papers."

Mendoza, who was sitting nearest to Gale, took it first, lifted the cellophane a moment to get a better look at it, and remarked lazily, "Does it seem to anyone else that our redoubtable FIDO man is paying more attention to Russian than Indian deathguards?"

"Speaking of that," Carl said, and hesitated when everybody looked at him. Then he coughed and went on, "Pater, you've talked some about the Sharmas. Well, just night before last, Dr. Sharma saved my son's life."

"That is certainly a point in his favor," Pater Fairchild nodded.

"So you can see why I'd as soon drop him and his wife from our list of suspected deathguards."

The pater shook his kindly silver head. "Avosso, Avosso! Need I remind you that no one small good—however large it may appear to you or to any of us as individual beneficiaries—can ever balance out such guilt as that of the Kali Camps and Eugenics Farms? Nevertheless," he added, smiling, "I have yet to see any reason to suspect either Dr. or Professor Sharma beyond that svastika in her scarf, which, as has been pointed out to me, may have an innocent and coincidental explanation. As of the moment, I believe we can concentrate our attentions elsewhere with reasonably easy minds."

Carl grinned like he was relaxing.

"How did Dr. Sharma save your newborn?" Mendoza asked. "If I may inquire."

"Well…in lay terms, it involved a complete change of blood. Somehow draining out all the blood he had from Milly—that was killing him somehow, some kind of reaction—and filling him up again with a more compatible blood type. I guess it was sort of almost experimental. I didn't even ask to watch how it was done."

Mendoza nodded like he was storing textbook facts for a test that wouldn't count for that much of his grade.

Pater Fairchild had a studying kind of look on his face, too. "And this technique was Dr. Sharma's inspiration, Avosso?"

"Well, I thought so, somehow, but…" The grad student frowned in concentration. "Now I'm not quite sure whether Shammari ever actually said which one of them first suggested it, just that it was the only hope 'they' could see."

"Tricky," Joe ventured to put in, "with the names so much alike—Sharma, Shammari."

"Both are recent immigrants from India," Pater Fairchild said. "And this procedure…fortunate though it proved this week for your own family, Avosso… How shall I put this? It has the sound of something that might almost be grounded in the 'medical experimentation' of the Kali Camps."

A shivery moment of silence fell on most of the bros, but Mendoza said, "Shall we now regard all unusual lifesaving techniques as pointers to deathguards?"

"I think you take my meaning and intention better than you pretend, Mendoza," Pater Fairchild said with a very slight frown. Then, to Gale, "Hartwick, suppose you were to send your brother what we know of these two physicians, and see whether he cannot definitively clear them."

"Also Professor Sharma," added Fred, who liked to complain about not getting into the Minnesingers himself when his fratty bro was such a pet of the vocal music director from India.

"Both Sharmas," Pater Fairchild agreed, "the doctor of medicine and the professor of music."

"Dr. al Shammari," said Mendoza, "was, I believe, already well established at Hodag Crossing General Hospital in 1945."

Avosso said, "He escaped from India in '42, I think it was. He and his wife, but she was killed in the escape. Milly told me. I think her sister Dolores told her. Dr. Shammari himself doesn't talk about it much, I guess it was pretty bad."

"Having escaped India as early as that," said Mendoza, "would seem to place him above our suspicion."

Pater Fairchild thought about it and shook his head. "Not necessarily. Although if he and his late wife—assuming that rather sketchy piece of information to be reliable—were escaping from work they had come to find personally distasteful, it might certainly go far to influence the Court of World Justice to leniency in his case."

"Dr. Rabar al Shammari is Muslim." said Mendoza.

The Kali Camps mostly killed Muslims. At least for starters.

"I've never seen him bowing to Mecca or anything," said Avosso.

"It is far from unknown," said the pater, "for fugitives to hide their true allegiances under more acceptable masks. Many Spanish Inquisitors were secret Judaizers, and today many supposed Muslims may secretly be Hindus in hiding."

"Gandhi's a Hindu," said John Rogers.

Pater Fairchild nodded. "And may eventually help remove the guilt of the Kali Camps and Great Persecution from his co-religionists as a people. But in the meantime, a fugitive Hindu deathguard hiding in our R.S.A. might consider it well to pay lip service to Mohammed's creed."

"Except that it seems he does not," said Mendoza.

"And Dr. Sharma makes no bones about being Hindu," said Avosso. "Him and his wife both."

"A Muslim in name only…" Pater Fairchild let his voice trail off.

Mendoza said, "People fall away from other faiths and practices. Why not from Islam as well? Especially after a shock like losing a beloved spouse in that manner. If al Shammari were trying to hide being Hindu by pretending to be Muslim, wouldn't he want to make himself appear especially devout?"

John Rogers said, "Maybe Dr. Shammari just slips out of sight or something when it's time to bow to Mecca. Look at our own vampire. Probably the most devout floater the Purple Rose has had this century, but you'd never know it just to meet him at a party or in a class or something."

"I do not call Czarny's sincerity into question," Pater Fairchild said dryly, "but how much of your impression may be due to the contrast between his actual daily life and the popular stereotype he so carefully cultivates in his wearing apparel? In any event, I think that this is not the time to discuss our house vampire."

Mendoza seemed to give the pater a kind of a funny look before saying, "Is it a time to wonder whether the murder of Irina Kiripovna near the end of the War could point in any way to the activities of Russian deathguards in greater metropolitan Hodag Crossing?"

The idea of "greater metropolitan" Hodag Crossing made them laugh all around before Pater Fairchild said, "M. Kiripovna herself could hardly have been a deathguard, having immigrated here about 1922, if my memory serves, when she was younger in years than the century.

Though already experienced in…let us call it, the oldest profession. Nor can I see why a Russian deathguard who had seen the handwriting on the wall as early as 1944 and fled to America should have courted attention by murdering a Russian…woman of the night. For myself, I have never seen any compelling reason to question the sheriff's official theory that her death resulted from some bizarre and unfortunately unwitnessed accident."

Mendoza raised one eyebrow and said, "A bizarre accident indeed, involving a fatal fall from a position of standing on the ground, onto a picket fence, with impaling force. No wonder, at least, if the poor prostitute's death remains a favorite local folktale for Hallowe'en."

Joe shivered pleasantly, thinking about Hallowe'en just a week and a half away. On a Wednesday this year. Pi Rho's Hallowe'en Party, with a friendly vampire in the house!

Should be a lot more real fun than these doggone I. C. meetings.

THE NEXT DAY: SATURDAY, OCT. 20

Oh nine fifteen hours, and Keiko sat trying to study in spite of her worries about Clement. Last year he had come to her straight from the final auditions, that same night, certain he'd gotten the part he wanted, and glowing about it. This year…the fact that he hadn't given her the news already last night suggested it was still in doubt, and he had to wait for it to be posted on Prof Sharma's office door this morning…

Tap, tap-tap-tap, tap, tap. Clement's knock at Keiko's door.

Appear casual, Ko-Ko girl! She leaned back in her desk chair, reached around, and turned the door knob. "'S open. Come on in."

She clunked her chair's front legs down onto the floor as Clement came in, squeezed by her, and sat heavily on the bed. "Ko-Ko. Thanks."

"Uh-oh. Bad news?"

"They posted the cast list. Babs Thorvald came out and tacked it up at oh nine hundred on the chime. Exactly when Professor Sharma promised to have it up."

Looking at him, listening to him, Keiko guessed right away, "And you didn't get the part."

He shook his head.

"Oh. Too bad." Weak response, Ko-Ko girl, very weak. "Pretty stupid of Professor Sharma, I'd say."

"No! Professor Sharma always casts for the good of the show. How she sees it. Going over on the stage. For our audiences."

"Well… Who got it, then? Who did she cast as Figaro?"

"M. Carlson. With Tony Tallpines for understudy."

"I thought she didn't go with understudies or double casting."

"She is this once. I guess M. Carlson himself requested it. Anyway, there's a little note to that effect on the posted sheet. April got Rosina," Clement added, sounding as if he was trying to force himself to be a little more upbeat.

"Mmm. M. Carlson—isn't he the town barber?"

"And owner of the shop. I go there for my own haircuts." Clement gave a forced-looking grin. "So I've got to keep on good terms with him. When you don't reflect in the mirror, you've got to be able to trust your barber."

"You always try to keep on good terms with everybody. Someday it's going to break you up, whenever you come across some bad-minded floater you can't keep on good terms with."

"Maybe," he agreed heavily, without arguing.

They'd been over it often enough, about his reflection, which everybody else saw—or anyway thought they saw. It was all bound up in Clement's ideas about the laws of mysticism and physics. Keiko asked, "What part *did* you get?"

"Officer of the Watch who comes on in one scene to try to arrest the tenor. I guess Professor Sharma wanted somebody tall in the uniform."

"And I guess she cast M. Carlson because of how they're trying to encourage townspeople getting involved. How come she didn't at least make *you* his understudy?"

"Professor Sharma casts for the good of the show," Clement repeated. "She doesn't play local politics. Tony's about the same height as M. Carlson. With a little padding, he can wear the same costume. And his voice is better than mine."

"In *your* ears, maybe," Keiko said at once. "We none of us sound exactly the same to ourselves as we do to other people. But I'll buy the costume argument."

"Ko-Ko. Thanks." He reached out for her hand. She seized it eagerly.

They sat a few minutes in silence. He lifted his other hand and swiped its heel across his cheeks, each in turn. The gesture looked somewhere between impatient and self-accusing.

"Rosina. Figaro's love interest?" Keiko asked at last.

The vampire shook his head. "Figaro's the cupid in this one. Count Almaviva's Rosina's love interest."

"Oh. Who got Count Almawhosis?"

"Dick Walters."

"Don't think I know him."

"With the Minnesingers. You'll be seeing more of him. Good tenor. Pretty handsome too, to go with the voice."

You're handsome, Clement Czarny, she thought. Probably much too handsome for me. I guess we wouldn't make a very good matched team. People would think, What'd he ever see in her? With April, now…people would all see a good matched team *there,* right at first glance! Aloud, she said, "Well, if Figaro isn't anybody's love interest, and the tenor is, maybe Professor Sharma didn't want to dilute the romance angle by having too good-looking a cupid."

"Don't try to swell my head again."

No, Keiko had meant it. That jerk of a tenor last year, who made a pass at every floater of the complementary gender and whose name she couldn't even remember this year—*he'd* been too handsome for his own good. Prof Sharma could go ahead and put Clement on the same stage with *him*—especially with Clement made up for the comic role, especially with Papageno's own Papagena—and not worry about diluting what's-his-name's?—Palomino's romantic beauty. But with whozit—Walter Dicks?—yeah, even sight unseen, Keiko guessed there could be a problem. People wouldn't know which one was supposed to be the romantic lead. A middle-aged town barber with his own funny trademark mustache had to be a lot safer choice. Not that she explained any of that aloud to Clement, not after his plea not to swell his head. (Fat chance of that!) Instead, she went on, "Ooh-kay. Here's a consolation prize, maybe. The Thespians are talking about doing *Dracula* this fall, as long as we've got a real, authentic vampire for the lead. If you weren't going to be too busy with the opera and stuff."

"When did this come up? Did I miss a meeting?"

"Hasn't come up yet at a general meeting, I don't think. They just started talking about it last week in Backstage 101." Keiko didn't join anything, not even school clubs of an extracurricular nature, but she was taking Backstage 101 in hopes of increasing her exposure to Clement by working behind the scenes for shows he was in, and everybody enrolled in any theater course counted as an ipso facto member of the Hodag Thespians.

"I'm not sure," Clement said slowly, "that I really count as an 'authentic' vampire in quite that sense."

But she could tell the idea was grabbing him already. "Authentic enough for us, old bloodsipper," she said with an extra squeeze to his hand. "I don't guess that Officer who comes in to arrest whozis is going to make excessive demands on your time and energy."

"No, I guess I can squeeze it—can come and try out, anyway. Speaking of time," he went on, "I guess I should be going. April's meeting me at B & Z this morning when it opens at ten hundred."

"Oh?"

"We decided to get pinned."

Keiko swallowed. "Hey, that's great!" she said as sincerely as she could, hoping she didn't sound too much like she was forcing it. "Congratulations! Yeah, I guess that oughta help take the sting out, too."

"Ko-Ko… Thanks. Well…see you later. Joining us at the House tomorrow afternoon?"

"As per usual." She gave him a grin. He didn't act like he noticed how shaky it felt.

It was a very mixed relief when he left to meet April. Well, Keiko told herself firmly, pinning doesn't really take it any farther than it's been up to now, just makes it a little more formal. Pinning isn't so much, not really, just an engagement to think about getting engaged…somewhere down the road…sometime after graduation, and that's still almost three years away for all three of us.

And maybe he's getting pinned with her, but it's *me* he came to right away this morning, to kiss his big disappointment and try to make it a little better.

CHAPTER 12

STILL SATURDAY, OCT. 20

Not quite ten hundred hours on a Saturday morning, but they never minded opening the B & Z for business a few minutes early. "Well," October remarked to his wife as she returned to her counter after unlocking the door, "we seem to be holding our own here. Might've been a good move, after all. Looks like we might be able to roast a duck *a l'orange* for Christmas this year."

"Careful about gourmandizing, dear."

"The food goes right in and out again. Pretty much like your stock of jewelry that way." Aurea didn't even have a jewelry box of her own these days, only one ring stand beside the sink and another one on the dresser, for both their wedding bands at night. Sometimes when people never took their wedding rings off at all, it got so they *couldn't,* and in case of emergency the doctors had to cut the metal off the finger. Neither Aurea nor October especially wanted that to happen to them. Years ago, the night they'd met, she'd had enough trouble with one of the many extraneous rings she used to possess and wear in those days.

"Well, I know," she went on this morning. "But it isn't the actual eating of the food, it's the daydreaming about it too far in advance."

He could have observed how long she daydreamed about her jewelry creations before crafting them, but instead he only agreed, "You're absolutely right, Aurie. Thanksgiving first. One holiday dinner at a time."

It was good that, a decade later, they were able to joke about the failings that had given them so much grief that terrible night—gluttony for him, avarice for her.

He opened the small new shipment from Classic Twists that had been delivered late yesterday afternoon. A book titled *Chess As War Is Really Played* caught his eye. He fished it out, started examining it, and grunted.

"What is it?" Aurie asked from rearranging her display cases.

"Somebody wants to make chess more like real war by introducing an element of chance. Rolling dice every time one piece attacks another. Instead of instantly being captured, the attacked piece gets a chance to turn the tables. In the case of a queen and a pawn, a very, very small chance for the pawn. Likewise, a pawn had better think several times before trying to capture a queen."

"It sounds complicated."

"Most of the book seems to be tables showing what rolls of the dice give the capture to which piece. I think Classic Twists has a real loser here."

"Well, we might give it a test run some evening. Though it sounds like we'll spend most of our time checking those tables. And do people really want their games of chess to be more like real war? so soon after the real war we just fought?"

"I doubt it. I think what chess players really like about their game is its mathematical geometry and certainty—beauty, in its way. Although..." He took another look at the book's opening paragraph..."the authors may have some point when they argue that this business of identifying chess with actual war can give rulers and generals false ideas about such-and-such a maneuver will always and invariably prove successful."

"Oh, I don't think anyone can really believe the chess-war comparison any longer, not after what the world's been through this century with the Last Great War."

"And yet it's true," October said slowly, "strip away the fantasy elements, the gnomes and elves and unicorns and such, and some of these new rolegame scenarios are about war, and more popular among the college kids than I thought they'd be."

"Speaking of college kids," Aurie said, looking toward the door, "here are some— Why, look who it is!"

It was Clement Czarny, the college vampire, and a young lady who belonged to the same "club" as October himself—people named for calendar months. Czarny had not been in B & Z since picking up his doctored fraternity ring about a year ago, but October had naturally followed what anybody in town could see of his collegiate career, attending a few of the swim meets held here at the U. of M., most of the Minnesingers and Music School choral concerts, two performances of last fall's opera and three of the spring operetta. Besides singing opposite Czarny in *The Magic Flute,* M. April Greenhill had window-shopped B & Z rather often and come in several times for a closer look at the jewelry, three or four times even to buy a piece. Aurie had remarked that the young woman was building a nice, tasteful collection, to which Octie had replied that all the jewelry Z sold was tasteful. To which Aurie had replied in turn that none of the games B sold were exactly in bad taste, and so on...

"M.'s Bradley and Zimmerman," the young vampire began this morning. "Again, the jewelry side of your shop."

October nodded, and Aurea stood ready.

"We'd like to look at pins," M. Greenhill said with that bold-shy smile teenage ladies so often used in such situations. October often wondered if they practiced it in a mirror.

"A matched set?" Aurie said as if she needed to ask. October knew that, students being students and most of them on some kind of budget, she would show them the least expensive first.

They were half an hour choosing, during which time October made two small sales to other customers: one who bought a bag of jacks and one who bought a set of plastic gameruler's dice for rolegaming. And a silver-haired pair of late-season tourists came in and browsed around for a few minutes, with smiling glances at the young pair looking at courtship pins.

When the choice seemed to have settled down to one of two sets, and there were no other customers in the shop at the moment, Czarny left the final decision to his girlfriend while he came over to the game side for a look at the collectors' chess sets.

October seized the opportunity to tap *Chess As War Is Really Played* and inquire, "Could I maybe interest you in a bold new concept? Using dice to introduce an element of chance into the game of chess?"

"Thanks, but I don't think so." Czarny shook his head. "Not today. I just barely know how all the pieces move. But these fancy sets fascinate me. Especially the ones that look as though they might make good playing pieces on a rolegame board. Someday, when our train comes in, maybe April and I can buy a few."

"Interested in rolegaming?" October began, turning toward that section of books and boxes.

"When would he have the time?" M. Greenhill asked from the jewelry side of the small shop. "Clem, I think I've made my choice."

Nodding to October, and stealing one last glance into the case of collectors' sets, Czarny returned to his girlfriend. Together they made their purchase, bade the shopkeepers a pleasant good-by, and departed talking about where they would perform their private little ceremony of exchanging the "His" and "Her" pins—maybe in the park by the Hodag Fountain, drained now for the winter but still framed by lovely old fir trees.

"Nice-looking young pair," October observed, joining his wife at the window to watch the students stroll away.

"Well...I don't know. I'm not quite sure..." Aurie let her voice trail off, then gave her head a quick shake. "But it's *their* lives, after all. Someday, 'when their train comes in' and he has the time, if he's still living in these parts, we might invite him to join our game club."

"Two minds thinking along the same tracks," October agreed. Their game club met, usually, twice a week. The Tuesday evening session was dedicated to giving new games a test run. Maybe one of these Tuesdays would be a good time to test run Classic Twist's new chess with dice thing.

CHAPTER 13

ALMOST THREE WEEKS LATER: FRIDAY, NOV. 9

Matthew Fairchild felt less satisfied than he might have. True, to-night's active meeting had had six participants: Mendoza, Rogers, Fletcher, Drinkwater, Koby, and Doe. Also true, this year they had gained two—Koby and Doe—from the frosh class, thanks largely to Drinkwa-ter's enthusiasm. But Nathaniel Shin had indeed dropped completely out of active participation, out of even the hunt; and Fairchild could hardly help fearing that Drinkwater's motivations and, for the matter of that, his close friend Fletcher's, were somewhat…shall we say…less than purely idealistic? That to them, the search for justice might be a mere excuse for the pain, and the business of the hunt meetings afterward of second-ary rather than primary importance. As for the two frosh lads, true, their motivations seemed purer, but also less…motivated. Koby's surname had been Americanized from Japanese, Doe's from Russian, so that both might well be less intent on bringing the truly guilty to justice than on re-paying the cosmic balance for some fancied association guilt of their own innocent selves. Nor did Doe's determination strike his house father's as of the steadiest. Fairchild would be pleasantly surprised if young Joe Doe lasted out the year as a regular attendee of the Inner Circle.

Were all this not sufficiently disquieting, at the last meeting they had overridden their pater and voted to postpone the meeting that ought to have been held last Friday to this Friday instead, pleading that last week's Thursday had been the ancient Christian feast of All Saints and the following day the traditional Catholic commemoration of All Souls. This postponement moved all subsequent meetings to one week later, which would likely result in the one that by this new schedule should fall on December 21 being canceled altogether on grounds of proximity to the Yuletide holidays.

Since Fairchild had never thought that any but the truly greatest and happiest religious feasts of the calendar should be grounds for postpon-ing meetings of the Inner Circle, and since for himself he should have thought All Souls' a particularly appropriate day for such a meeting, he wanted to suspect that the vampire brother's observance was having some out-of-measure effect on the fraternity house as a whole. And so far as Fairchild knew, Czarny was barely aware of the Inner Circle at all, unless as a shadowy background entity that kept charge of the all too rarely consulted dossier of deathguards-at-large which resided in Fairchild's office back at the Pi Rho house.

The calm and impartial part of his mind feared, however, that he himself was merely finding in Czarny's supposed influence an excuse, that the true problem was a general flagging of interest in the hunt. After six years only! Even had the statute of limitations applied, it would not yet have run out.

The oldest of these young men had been no older than their middle teens when the War ended and the truth of the Kali Camps and Eugenics Farms was discovered. At that age, it should have sunk very deeply indeed into their impressionable young minds. Yet the process of aging had the effect of making it seem farther in the past for them than for a man of Fairchild's age, to whom the years went past like blinks. As for the frosh, how much younger yet had *they* been at the War's end!

What was needed, was something to reawaken the scent in their nostrils, something to make them remember that even this speck on the map that was the University of Minnemagantic and its miniature surrounding hamlet of Hodag Crossing might see the coming of a fugitive deathguard. Professor Fairchild was in strong hopes that young Hartwick might supply such a reawakening alarm whenever he arrived at the hunting cabin for this evening's business meeting.

Pending Hartwick's arrival, Mendoza broke the silence. "Easier, this semester, to call Czarny Kittridge's pet than Sharma's." Referring to the senior professor of the Dramatics Department and director of the play that had just entered its rehearsals.

Rogers said, "Unless Sharma refused him Figaro because she knew Kittridge wanted to take advantage of him for Dracula."

"Naw," opined Fletcher. "That'd be more reason for Sharma to've cast him. These things work by rivalries."

"Not always," Fairchild balanced the junior's generalization. "Although for myself, I have some reservations about the Hodag Thespians using Czarny in this way."

"Oh?" said Mendoza. "Because his casting seems to have been a foregone conclusion, or because you object to the play itself?"

"More nearly the latter," Fairchild replied. "These things should not be made light of."

"I guess they're doing it pretty seriously," said Drinkwater. "As seriously as— Hey, here comes Gale blowing in."

Yes, here was Hartwick the younger, arriving with a puff of white flakes, which he cut off by shutting the door and shaking himself out of his coat and muffler.

"Hartwick," Fairchild greeted him. "I see the snows of November are upon us. How does it bode for the roads?"

"Oh, no problem for us tonight, Pater. Just a few off-and-on snow showers. Nothing serious."

"No serious weather, you mean?" said Rogers. "There's usually something more or less serious on the deathguard front when you grace us with your belated presence."

"Possible sighting of Petrovka in the Minneapolis-St. Paul area." Hartwick smirked, gave his head a "Shucks, folks, ain't much" shake implying the opposite, and added, "Coffee made? Yes, I see it is."

"'Possible sighting,'" Fairchild repeated carefully, for the sake of the gathering. "How nearly verified, and how recent?"

"Yesterday evening," Hartwick answered the second part of the question first, pouring himself a cup of the black brew and adding two spoonfuls of sugar. "Made by a floorwalker at Minas-Field-Scott's. Being only a store employee, he figured he had no authority to do anything else but step outside for the nearest polly, and by the time they got back, the suspect had disappeared."

"The glimpse of a floorwalker," said Mendoza.

"In your own father's employ, Mendoza," said Fairchild.

"My father is as good as retired, and living comfortably with my mother on their Florida estate. Leaving his chain of stores to his partners and their local managers. It is precisely because I have glimpsed the inner workings of these stores myself, in my process of deciding whether ultimately to claim inheritance in the Minas merchandising empire or sell out to the heirs of Field and Scott, that I feel less than impressed by the sightings of a floorwalker. Some employees, of course, are more competent than others."

"The one who thought he sighted Petrovka is M. Frederic Davenport," Hartwick supplied.

Mendoza shook his head. "Unfamiliar to me."

"But Minneapolis isn't that far away," Doe said eagerly. "Maybe tomorrow—"

"It is far enough," Fairchild cut the frosh off sternly, though privately delighted at this spark of enthusiasm. He hated to risk quelling any part of it, yet he stood *in loco parentis* to these lads, and frosh were very young. "It is distant enough that any extracurricular wraparound foray should be left strictly to upperclassmen. Fortunately, we have two alum brothers stationed in the Twin Cities."

"I've already phoned Shepkowski and Hollinger," Hartwick informed the meeting. "Hollinger had already read about it in the *Press*."

Fearing he saw interest slacken in more young face than one, Fairchild added, "But let us bear in mind that distances we can cover in six hours, they can cover equally quickly. Faces that have appeared in the Twin Cities area may reappear in Hodag Crossing, *en route*, perhaps, to Canada."

"And where one of the Demon Doktors of Novgorod is," Drinkwater pointed out, "the other one probably is, too."

"Assuming that it was indeed Kosya Petrovka," Mendoza observed almost absently. "I suppose M. Davenport failed to make timely use of the surveillance cameras, or you would have mentioned it."

"They got one surveillance-camera photo that Davenport thinks shows her, and turned it over to the police. Hollinger promises to send a copy of what they ran in this morning's *Press,* but he warned me it's just one face in a crowd of shoppers, too small and blurry to say anything except that it doesn't rule her out. But they had the police artist do a sketch from Davenport's description, that I guess makes it pretty obvious. They'll be getting that to FIDO, and Lance'll make sure we get a copy here."

"A recreation by a police artist who expected to hear Kosya Petrovka described," Mendoza murmured, "and drew accordingly, to order for a witness already confident enough whom he had seen to alert the pollies."

"Mendoza," said Fairchild, "a little skepticism can be healthy, too much can stifle action."

Mendoza smiled and spread his hands. "Consider my observation unvoiced. Hartwick, your brother has made the Russian deathguards his special study, I think?"

"Ever since the War was being fought," the younger Hartwick answered proudly. "Even before we knew about the Eugenics Farms. Back when we thought Russian spies were all we needed to worry about."

Mendoza nodded. "In contradistinction to the deathguards of India?"

"FIDO partnered him with a floater who specializes in the people who ran the Kali Camps. Floater named Maklowski."

Mendoza said, "Interesting."

CHAPTER 14

ALMOST THREE WEEKS LATER:
THURSDAY, NOV. 29

Keiko was working backstage lightboard and sound effects—mostly barking dogs—and almost wishing she could watch the play from out front. Like the Pies, who were here in strength to cheer their fraternity brother on. In Keiko's admittedly biased opinion, he was magnificent.

Things were moving at a pretty good pace for Opening Night. They had already reached the scene in Act II where Dracula slips in and confronts Van Helsing. Van Helsing at the mirror giving his face a medical once-over for symptoms of stress and overwork, when the Count slips in through the window and comes up behind him.

Whether the faulty psychomystique about Clement and mirrors was the vampire's own or everybody else's, at least he could see for himself that whatever he was wearing reflected. If the play was logical about it, Van Helsing should have seen Count Dracula's empty clothes coming up behind him. According to Clement, seeing his facial make-up reflected with no face beneath it was maddening enough in itself that he didn't have to act all that hard when he threw the flower vase against the mirror. Both vase and mirror were the cheapest dollarstore specials you could buy, new ones being needed every time.

"I dislike mirrors," Clement was saying as Count Dracula. "They are a playground for human vanity." In fact, offstage, he sometimes complained how hard it was to keep himself shaved, combed, and otherwise groomed by feel alone. Oh, Clement, thought Keiko, you need a good life partner to help you with all that. And I'm not sure about April. You need *me!*

She snapped her mind out of daydreaming and back to the action onstage. Van Helsing was accidentally on purpose cutting his finger, just to make sure he had the right vampire. Making a greedy snap at it—that *was* acting. Clement said he was always tempted to ask if he could lick anybody's fresh little cuts, but it was all he could do not to gag at the capsule of stage blood Winsor Grant popped as Van Helsing.

Now…the *piece de resistance,* the ultimate in Van Helsing's arsenal. What it really was, of course, was a circle of thin white cardboard. But Clement's *"Sacrilege!"* sounded as genuinely outraged as if the prop *had* been an actual Consecrated Host.

Prof Kittridge had rehearsed that and rehearsed it. "No, no, Dracula! You're outraged because he's using it against *you!* Because it's giving you unbearable pain even at that distance, and it may keep you from getting your victim. Not because he's mishandling something 'holy.' Dracula doesn't care about mere 'holy' unless and until it gets in his way."

"I'm very sorry, Professor Kittridge, but the line *is* 'Sacrilege!' As I see it, there's still just a little trace of old-world piety in the character, just enough to make it not too ridiculous for them to talk about this famous 'look of peace' on his face right before his corpse crumbles away. If he wasn't outraged at the way he sees Van Helsing mishandling the Host, he wouldn't cry 'Sacrilege!' He'd say, 'Oh, damnation!' or 'Curses, foiled again!' or something like that."

By the first dress rehearsal, Prof Kittridge had given in, called it in keeping with Clement's overall interpretation, and let him do it the way he wanted. They said movies were the directors' canvas, legitimate theater the actors'.

But it was time for Keiko to get ready. There…Clement jumps out the window, spreads his cape, gives his laugh and ducks down—just as Willie in the light booth flips the bat stencil over the spot on the window—and Keiko raps her boards together for the gunshot sound.

They'd talked about how to do the bat, decided, Why mess with some wired model almost guaranteed to look slow and hokey, when a stencil across the lights should be just as effective, and a lot cheaper. Keiko thought the stencil was probably much more effective. She peeped out at the audience and saw Theda, this year sitting with the other Pies, her new Greek sisters and brothers, making that little shooing movement above her own head.

* * * *

Maybe I should take Acting 101, Keiko thought during the Intermission. Try out for the same plays he does. Be able to spend some of the time between acts in the Green Room with him and the other actors, instead of here behind the curtain, sweeping up broken mirror and helping change sets. It really isn't all that much, after all, just brushing against each other now and then backstage, where we've both got to concentrate on cues and things.

Yes, and how would it feel if I got a part and he didn't? Look at what happened to April this semester. She sang the lead and Clement was onstage for about two minutes, never even near her.

Well, Sharma's loss, Kittridge's gain.

* * * *

The big scene change in Act III could have been tricky, seeing they didn't have a revolving stage. Good thing the vault was scripted to be as bare and dark as possible. So they just rolled the big, pale gray coffin downstage center, opened the curtains only about halfway, and used weak spots to help out the flashlights in the actors' hands.

Keiko hated this final scene of the play. Clement's actual part was pretty well over and done with at the end of the scene just before this one. The only thing in the coffin was a small, tight bag of stage blood to squirt up when Van Helsing and Harker pounded the stake into it. Clement was crouching behind the coffin to give his one little groan, and then be ready to clamber up into it during the blackout before final curtain calls. But even when Keiko knew exactly how they were doing it, and how safely for everyone involved, it still seemed so graphic, so…nightmarish…

Doggone it, all he had was some kind of really rare, really puzzling medical condition. It wasn't as if he really *was* any kind of "horrible, undead 'thing.'" He was probably the pick of all the male students at this person's university! She was glad the role had helped him get over his disappointment about Figaro and all that, and his interpretation of the big, famous bloodsucker was probably the best one she'd ever seen or could imagine…all the same, something about his doing it made her just a little bit uneasy.

* * * *

In the reception line, Clement stood next to Winsor to emphasize that they were really friends offstage. Not too long after the Rose brothers and Sigh sisters, M.'s Zimmerman and Bradley of B & Z came through to congratulate them.

"I saw what you were doing with the character," the game seller told Clement, shaking his hand. "Giving him a human side."

"Even a rather vulnerable side," added his wife the jeweler.

"I liked it a lot," M. Bradley finished. "But—just a friendly warning—the critics may not."

FROM THE NEXT DAY'S REVIEWS,

FRIDAY, NOV. 30:

Hodag Crossing Currents:

The Local Arts:

"What might otherwise have been a reasonably competent rendering, for a school production, of the famous vampire play is masticated to a mushy pulp by the most inept portrayal of the title character it has ever been this reviewer's bored displeasure to see…

"What audience member did not vicariously pound the stake in with Winsor Grant's quite adequate Van Helsing at the end? Alas, that Dracula will once again rise from the grave for three more woefully mismatched encounters with his adversary."

(For Frank Bashaw, this translates into another reviewer's mild annoyance.)

* * * *

John Carpenter's Quick Picks:

"Go if you want to see good sets, good costumes, and a fine supporting cast. Not if you want to be scared."

* * * *

The Hodag's Yawp:

"The Hodag Thespians' *Dracula* was promising very well, right up until the title character's initial appearance left many of us in the audience wondering if something Really Major was going to be changed and this time the bad guy would turn out to be somebody else, possibly Renfield, so ably carried off by Ted Appledore through his many lightning shifts between sane and insane, or even Van Helsing himself, Winsor Grant giving his righteousness a strength and stage presence rarely seen except in the major villains. If Dracula had been a truly worthy opponent for this Van Helsing, maneuvering about on Holly Sendak's strikingly macabre sets, it would have been a show to send delightful shivers of many kinds and every level up and down our spines…"

("Pundita" makes no reference to last year's Magic Flute, *suggesting the byline may have changed hands.)*

* * * *

Gregory Sierramentez's "At a Gulp":

"2 stars. For the sets, costumes, effects, and most of the cast, it would have been 4 stars. Too bad the lead crashed it. Czarny, go back to singing amiable buffoons."

* * * *

The Galop de Vache Times:

"With fair weather predicted for the wraparound, you might enjoy a drive to Hodag Crossing for the university's new production of *Dracula,* featuring an actual, practicing vampire in the lead role....

"Young Clement Czarny (Class of '54) has suffered since age thirteen from a rare condition which has the medical profession completely stumped. All that the doctors seem able to say for sure is that to avoid malnutrition and possible starvation, the young man must have raw blood in his diet, and plenty of it. Fortunately, animal blood will do, if spiked with two or three drops of human per glass. Figuring it best to be open about it, Czarny told this reporter in an exclusive interview that he has adopted the Dracula 'uniform' for his everyday wear...

"Unfortunately, he seems to depend too much on his daily diet and not enough on his acting, letting his natural amiability show through until this time the play comes off as more tragedy than parable of the triumph of good over evil. Nevertheless, this reporter—while not the paper's drama critic—found the show as a whole worth the drive."

(John Wordwright, who signed this feature article, stretched a point in talking about his "exclusive interview," which in fact comprised a couple of quick questions and answers while shaking hands in the reception line after the show.)

INTERLUDE: SUNDAY, JUNE 1, 1952

This year they didn't even attempt what everyone had come to call the "Dante Tour" of both parks, usually beginning with Hellmouth. This year the four of them just went straight to Heavengate for the afternoon.

April had a summer job lined up for herself singing in the Heavengate Choir. She had tried to talk Clement into applying for a place in it, too. Good practice and very good pay. But he wanted no summer job that would bring him within sight of Hellmouth Park every time he showed up for work. Uncle Buck and his wife had bought the little drugstore in Udder Delight, so Clement planned to put his Sundae Palace experience to use by helping them make the kind of showpiece out of the soda fountain that a village with that name really needed. Uncle Buck's adopted older son Omar having left home for a job in Chicago, they had cleaned out his old bedroom for guests, which this summer would mean April, while Clement bunked with his younger cousin Ted. That arrangement pleased April almost as well, and Clement much better than if they'd both been singing at Heavengate.

"I wish I could be so happy about it," Keiko confided to Solly. "For their sakes."

He nodded. "I know what you mean."

They were having a cup of coffee together in Angelo's while giving Clement and April time to stroll hand in hand through the newly planted Elysian Fields surrounding the park building.

"We're a funny foursome," Solly went on.

Keiko nodded. "Yes. By rights, I think you and I are supposed to be sabotaging and undermining and I don't know what to pry them apart so we can get them for ourselves."

"I guess I wouldn't really know how. If she doesn't want me for myself…"

"Me neither. No more than Clement would know how to bite someone's jugular." Keiko added a little cream to her coffee and stirred it. Around and around and around. "All the same… I don't know if it's just jealousy talking here…but I don't feel she's really…right for him."

"I know exactly what Clem sees in April. She'd be right for just about any male floater, I guess."

"I'm not knocking her. Don't think that! It's just that…for *him*… Well, remember last winter when he got those terrible reviews for his Count Dracula?"

"I thought she did her best to buck him up."

Keiko shook her head. "She tried to make him get angry with the reviewers."

"Well? We were all pretty sore about it. All the Pies—both houses— we were talking about making some kind of big public protest—"

"I'm glad you didn't. Don't you see, Solly? Not even you, his best same-gender friend? That was the wrong approach completely for someone like Clement. He *can't* let himself get mad about something like that. His Jiminy Crickets won't let him. Not when it's only himself who's the victim. If they'd panned *everybody*—but they just panned Clement, while they praised—well, in Bashaw's case, as good as praised—everybody else. He couldn't let himself get angry at the reviewers without risking looking like he thought they were wrong about everybody else as well."

"Yeah…looking at it that way… So that's why April couldn't seem to cheer him up. How'd *you* do it?"

"I didn't, not really. The company did, when they took Van Helsing's little curtain call speech, you know, the one about 'Go home and sleep well and remember that there really *are* such things,' and gave it to Clement instead. Some of us sort of thought that maybe Mendoza put that idea in Winsor's head when he came visiting backstage right before the second performance. Anyway, that was what Clement needed, to get him through the rest of the shows. The vote of confidence from the rest of the cast and crew. If anything like that ever happens again…"

"Yeah? What'll we do?"

"Well," Keiko said slowly, "I've thought what we should have done right away, and the best thing might be to try and persuade him that reviewers can be honest and still dead wrong. About one thing and not necessarily about anything else. Maybe his Papageno and Major-General were *too* good, too much to their taste, and they couldn't get past that and accept him playing a serious character. And then, his Count Dracula was too different from their preconceptions—from what *they* thought the character ought to be. They were so hung up in their own preconceived ideas, based on every other actor's interpretation over the years, that they didn't even try to see what Clement was doing with the part. He was too avant-garde for the local critics. But the word of mouth must've been great—we sold every show out to standing room only."

"He was saying that night, after the first performance, that that old floater from the games and jewelry shop gave him a really nice compliment, so he knew at least part of the audience saw what he was trying to do."

"Yes. M. Bradley. I've been making it a point to check B & Z first from now on, whenever I think they even might have something I'm in the market for."

So Keiko and Solly sipped their coffee and waited for their so far (darn it!) just good friends. While Heavengate and Hellmouth stood and brooded at each other across the cow pasture, and visitors wondered how many of the rumors were true: Were both amusement parks really under the same ownership—even management? And did Hellmouth Park really facilitate suicides in some of its subbasement "dungeons"?

PART III
FALL, 1952

CHAPTER 15

FRIDAY, OCT. 3

"I was born," said Pater Fairchild, "the same year that our school here was founded, 1884. Pi Rho has been a proud presence at the University of Minnemagantic since its second term."

The pater had started out every year's Pledge Committee meeting with this same speech. Well, maybe not quite word for word. Spud couldn't remember it exactly word for word. But the same substance, year by year. Since this was the third and last year Spud was going to hear it, it had a rather nice, homey sound. The sound of tradition.

And it was interesting how Spud came to be sitting here to listen to these basically-the-same words one more year. He'd never expected to get elected house president. It had come as a big surprise to him, almost behind his back. So here he sat, in the same place Carl Avosso had when Spud was a soph and Ramon Mendoza when Spud was a junior. They were both graduated now, but not actually all that safe in the wide, wide world. Carl was still right here in town, working on the hospital administration staff, living with Milly and their son—almost a year old now, the Pies should throw a surprise party or something; was one year old too young for a surprise party?—in their neat new little bungalow near the hospital. And Mendoza hadn't flown even that far. He was still right here in the Purple Rose house, taking advantage of his option to keep his old room as a grad student while he worked on his advanced degree. Like Spud was hoping to do—get an advanced degree, that was. At some other school—Michiana, maybe, or Astoria State. Not that he didn't like it here; he just wanted to see someplace new, broaden his horizons a little. His grades weren't exactly *cum laude,* but they weren't that bad for basically a football major. Good enough to get him into a fair to middling university for some postgraduate work in Philosophy and Lit.

So here they were, four Committee members and the house father, *deja vu* all over again with its changing cast. This year Spud as the token senior by dint of his office as prexy, Solly Goldfein as token junior— Spud kind of wished Prof Fairchild had named Clemmie to that post, but the pater never seemed to've quite gotten over his adverse feelings toward the vampire, no matter how well he kept them from showing. Clemmie's best chum and roommate was coming pretty close, though, and next year, if Clemmie found himself elected house president, like Spud had this year, he'd be sitting here on the Pledge Committee at last. Meanwhile, Joe Doe and Tony Tallpines for the sophs, and thirteen possible pledglings on the list, so all they had to do this evening was weed one out. Just one, to get an even number. Ten might be the ideal, but two extra, they could live with again this year.

But they argued a long time about which one to weed out. The choice finally narrowed down to Doug Middleton or Gary Wilson. Not knowing anything to complain about in either one, Spud more or less just sat back and let the argument roll on by. Right up until Solly said, "Mendoza told me during rush, that he thought one time he saw Wilson looking a little fishy-eyed or something at Clem—at my roommate Czarny." Even as a junior, Solly still had trouble sometimes remembering the pater's preference for last-naming everybody.

"I call that," said Pater Fairchild, "a weak and tenuous argument. Wilson strikes me as a fine lad, and Mendoza…"

"You've always shown a lot of respect for Mendoza, Pater," Spud remarked.

"A respect I continue to feel. But Mendoza can…occasionally…be just a tad imaginative when it comes to our vampire. Let us put Wilson to a vote."

It split. Solly and Spud—swayed by Solly's argument in the absence of anything else—for striking Wilson off the list, the two sophs for keeping him on. And Pater Fairchild broke the tie in favor of Wilson.

Then they voted on Doug Middleton, and came out Spud and Joe for, Solly and Tony against, and once again, after a very long hesitation, Pater Fairchild decided that he could not in fairness rule against Middleton where he had ruled for Wilson.

Seeing the debate about to start all over again, Spud felt an inspiration. "Hey, fellows, fourteen wouldn't be *too* many to start Hell Week with, would it? We had a dozen last year, and it came out okay."

"I am of two minds here," said the pater. "Whom would you propose reinstating?"

"How about Val Saladin?" Solly asked like he'd been hoping for the chance.

"Okay by me," Spud agreed. "Anybody remember why we crossed him off in the first place?"

"Clem—Czarny liked him a lot," Solly added. "During Rushtide."

Pater Fairchild cleared his throat, and for a minute Spud thought he was going to object. But all he did was call for a vote, and this time all four brothers carried it unanimously, and Val Saladin was their four-teenth pledgling.

CHAPTER 16

NOT QUITE A WEEK LATER: WEDNESDAY, OCT. 9

Clement tried to get as much of his sleep as he could during the day, freeing the small hours of the night and pre-dawn for study. It wasn't always easy, what with classes and swimming; fortunately, the practice rooms were available clockround to School of Music students entrusted with keys to Foster Hall, and most stage-show rehearsals were held in the evening. This semester he had a couple of hours most weekdays between his last afternoon class and dinner. Almost his only command to the pledglings this Hell Week was to leave his naptime uninterrupted.

This afternoon he was dreaming about being onstage in front of a full audience, and not having the faintest idea what play he was starring in or what the plot was, when a raucous commotion of shouts and grunts and yipping and thudding feet roused him out of it. Sitting up and blinking, he found his and Solly's bedroom crowded with frat brothers—more at the door trying to crowd in—the little pup he had sent pledge Wilson to the pet store Monday to buy, because the house had decided to have a mascot, yipping her tiny yips madly on the bed, and…Spud and Solly wrestling above him with Gary Wilson himself?

"What's going on?" Clement asked groggily, sitting up and hearing something clatter heavily to the floor.

"This———" Spud use a word Clement hadn't heard very often in his life and always tried his darndest to forget—"tried to stake you while you were sleeping!"

"What?" Clement sat up a little higher, came a little more awake.

Val Saladin, the other pledgling in the room, stood up and nodded soberly, handing Clement one of the things it must've been that clattered to the floor.

A sharpened hardwood stake.

Someone had tabbed the ceiling light on to help the last daylight filtering through the curtains. Blinking again, Clement spotted the mallet, probably iron, lying on the floor.

"Thank our Lucky Chances," said Solly, "that Val wondered why he needed to haul that damn rucksack of his upstairs."

"He…tried…to…*kill*…me?" said Clement.

It almost seemed to him that Gary Wilson snarled. He could have been mistaken. In the emotion of the moment.

"Somebody go call the sheriff!" Spud shouted to the mob at the door.

"He tried to murder me?" Clement repeated.

Then too many voices were coming at him at once, anger and rage and thanks that he was all right, they'd gotten here in time… Clement's silver cross and fraternity ring were on the dresser, but he rarely took his crucifix earring out just for before-dinner naps, and it was starting to throb and burn in his earlobe. He picked up the yipping puppy, who fell quiet in his hands, licking his fingers for all she was worth, and started petting her quickly and gently. "Please, everyone," he said aloud. "Please. Just leave me alone for a little bit. I just need to be alone for a little while."

"Clem?" said his best chum.

"You, too, Solly. I'm sorry. I've just got to work this through by myself. For a few minutes. Alone. Noble can stay," he added as Val reached out, offering to take the puppy. "No one else. Please. Just…alone."

Solly nodded. "We'll be right outside the door."

"Shut it behind you, please," said Clement.

Solly and Val were the last to leave, shutting the door behind them with a soft click.

* * * *

It seemed like a longer time for them, waiting there outside the door, than it probably was. Once Solly thought he heard Clem stifling sobs.

"O lord and master," Val whispered, still trying to keep up the pledglings' Hell Week ritual, "what happens now?"

"Shhh, Val. We've just got to wait and see."

At last they heard them letting the sheriff in at the front door. The door noises and voices came right up the stairs, and even if most of the actual words were muffled, it was easy to guess more or less what was being said. And here came Spud's solid footsteps up the stairs.

Solly tapped on the door. "Clem? I think the sheriff's here."

Spud reached them just about the same time the bedroom door opened. Noble jumped out, tail wagging her whole back end, and started licking Val's shoes.

"Angels, Clem!" Solly exclaimed softly, "Look at your ear!"

"You know I can't." A shaky grin. "Feels like it must look pretty bad, huh?"

The lobe was all red and swollen until the tiny little platinum earring was just a dimple lost in the swelling.

"I can't get it out," the vampire almost apologized. "No—don't you try. It's still too tender. Don't worry, it should be going down soon. The thing is…" He looked at them all in turn, each one in the eye… Solly, Val, and Spud. "Brothers, this was just a Hell Week prank that got a little out of hand. Nothing else. He wasn't really going to try to stake me. It was all a misunderstanding."

"Jesus, Clemmie," said Spud, "we all know that ain't the truth. That motherlicker tried—"

"It was just a prank, Spud," Clem repeated, looking back at the prexy. The football star was stockier, but the vampire had maybe a quarter-head on him in height. "Just a Hell Week stunt that got a little bit out of hand."

"Clem," said Solly, "you know you can't lie."

Clem opened his hands and held them up before his friends. The shape of a cross was branded livid and blistering in each palm. "I was holding my silver cross between them," he explained very softly. "I know it's even worse to send a poor little floater to prison for maybe the rest of his life, out of plain revenge, than to stretch the truth a little."

Val tried, "But he's dangerous—"

"To who? Just to me. Nobody else. He thought he was protecting everybody else. If there are any other vampires around, I've never recognized them, not even the one who must've bitten me. Not even being one myself. And there's too much literature, too many stories about us being evil 'things'—Saints, I even acted in one myself, last year! Too much of society telling him he was doing the good and…and righteous thing. No…brothers…please, just follow my lead."

One by one, they all nodded. The puppy sat, looked up at them, and whined a little. Clement picked her up and cradled her in his hands, gingerly patting her head, and they all headed downstairs to face the sheriff.

* * * *

Sheriff Ole Nurmi had rarely seen a kid whose looks he liked less than he liked this Gary Wilson's. Pleasant enough features, but sneery. At least he wasn't acting rough or violent. Not saying or doing much of anything. Nurmi probably wouldn't have needed to bring Pat O'Donoghue along on this one. Or could've just sent her out alone. Looked like she could've cuffed Wilson and hauled him in all by herself, even without a houseful of frat brothers ready to lend the sheriff's deputy a hand. But the call had sounded almost hysterical, if you could use that word for a houseful of young men.

"Now, let's make sure I've got this straight." Nurmi spoke as the voice of mature authority—the most mature man here present, if you didn't count Professor Emeritus Fairchild. "All of you agree that one of your new pledges tried to pound a wooden stake through your frat brother, the vampire? That's your story?"

Nods and vocal assents all around the living room.

"Any idea *why?* Hazing get a little out of hand?"

"On the contrary," said Fairchild. "Czarny was sleeping at the time. And of all the brothers, even among the upperclassmen, I must acknowledge that Czarny is the one least likely to give any pledgling grief."

One of the other frat fellows said, "As well as I can put things together, the whole reason Wilson rushed us and pledged and went along with everything up to now, was to get his chance at our vampire. Lugging that stupid rucksack around every time he came to the house..."

For almost the first time, Wilson opened his mouth. "I just wish—"

"Careful there, son," the sheriff said, a little reluctantly, glancing at Pat with her notebook in hand. "Anything you say could be taken down for evidence against you and all that."

"What is this?" New voice from the stairs. Nice, rich baritone voice. "What's going on here?"

So it was true. Czarny really did dress like that all the time, not just when going around in public. "Enjoyed you in the play last year, son," Nurmi greeted him. "And the G. and S., of course. That opera, too, even if I'm not usually all that much for grand opera."

"I made him go," Pat boasted. "What's in the works for this year, M. Czarny?"

"Thank you. Thank you very much. It's still early days for this semester, but Professor Sharma has mentioned Marschner's *Vampyr* as a possibility. But what's going on?" Czarny repeated, looking all around the room. "*Handcuffs?* Oh, come on, brothers, isn't this taking a haze just a little bit too far? Even getting our good sheriff and company in on it? Isn't that like a 'false alarm' or something?" Czarny turned back to the sheriff and deputy. "Or did they somehow enlist your help ahead of time, M.'s?"

"What is this?" Nurmi asked in turn, looking around again. A lot of puzzled young faces, some outright incredulous, a few nodding like they agreed. The sheriff looked at the ceiling and gathered his thoughts. "We were told this young fella—'pledgling,' you call 'em?—just tried to pound a stake through your heart, M. Czarny."

Czarny cleared his throat and said, "Then please let me apologize, Sheriff Nurmi. This is all a giant misunderstanding, a real waste of your good time. It was all a gag—a prank, a Hell Week joke. Sometimes when we get a little too rough on the pledglings, they strike back. We don't mind. In fact, we like it. We encourage the spirit it shows. Wilson was only planning to put a little scare into some of his hazers."

Deputy Pat took advantage of Czarny's pause to say, "All the same, think we could have a look at that stake and mallet?"

"Hey," said one of the three boys who had come down with the vampire. "Think Clem here can't tell stage props when he sees 'em?"

"But now, please, M.'s," Czarny went on to the officers of the local law, "isn't it time to call it off? Get him out of those handcuffs and get back to your real business?"

Nurmi took one last look around the living room. About half the frat boys were nodding now, making little noises like they were agreeing, even looking a little shame-faced about the whole thing. Most of the ones who weren't nodding agreement, were still looking puzzled. And none of them was raising any protest. Fairchild looked bemused. Feeling relieved, because this Gary Wilson seemed like such a nice kid, Sheriff Nurmi nodded to his deputy and said, "Okay, Pat, take the bracelets off him and let's get back to our business of waiting for a real call. Greeks!"

* * * *

On the porch they almost bumped into a tall, dark young man on his way to the door. "Sheriff Nurmi?" he asked at once. Gratifying to get face recognition from a potential voter. "Has the Purple Rose done anything to earn an official visit?"

"Apparently not," said Nurmi, still feeling just slightly off kilter. "You one of 'em, too?"

"You look a little old for a college man," Pat appraised him. "Counselor of some kind?"

"Graduate student, and the dim light could have an aging effect on my appearance. Again I ask, why this visit?"

"Some kind of hazing stunt that got out of hand, I guess. No, don't worry, nobody hurt," Nurmi anticipated the next question.

"Is it true," his deputy clarified, "that your pledges may try to get back at the older members during this 'Hell Week' of yours? That the older members sometimes encourage it?"

"It was true in my salad years," the grad student affirmed warily. "By all that I have seen, it remains true today."

"So that's okay, then." The sheriff relaxed a little. "Seems one of your pledges got up a little skit with your vampire—re-enacting that play, I guess—and some of your fraternity brothers took it a little too seriously, thought he really intended to pound a stake through his heart."

"I see," said the grad student. "A planned skit, you say?"

"That's how it looks from here. Well," the sheriff tried to sign off with his well-practiced slogan, "next time we meet, here's hoping it's nothing professional."

"As you say. Sheriff Nurmi, I think that this is not the first time that something with the strange appearance of vampirism has called you out to Greek Town?"

"Not recently," Pat answered at once for her boss.

"Some years ago. Six, I believe, or seven. A Russian-born 'woman of ill repute' discovered staked through the heart? You held your office already at that time, Sheriff Nurmi, did you not?"

"Oh!" Nurmi remembered. "Oh, yes. The 'Hallowe'en Hooker,' they're calling her now, aren't they? Actually, not a 'stake' as such, a broken point from a picket fence. Pretty messy, but had to've been some kind of freak accident."

"Seven years ago?" Pat asked. "Was the War still going on?"

"Yep. Wartime." The sheriff shrugged and looked around. Couldn't see much in this neighborhood of irregularly shaped lots. But... "Yeah, I think they took the fence down right after we got done investigating, but I'm pretty sure it used to be right about...somewhere over there. Yeah, funny coincidence all right, so close to your 'Purple Rose' house. Stake-like board through that poor working lady's heart, and now you Pi Rhos have your own resident vampire." Nurmi gave his head a shake. "Funny coincidence, all right. Just plain coincidence, of course. They happen. Well, next time we meet, here's hoping it's nothing professional," he repeated, and this time the sheriff and deputy got successfully away.

MEANWHILE

As soon as the sheriff and his deputy had left and closed the door behind them, Gary Wilson said, "There! Doesn't *that* convince you? What was *that* but the vampire's hypnotic power?"

"What?" cried Clement, stunned and astonished. "It was no such—"

"Okay, 'power of suggestion.' Same thing."

"It was simple cooperation," Clement insisted. "Nothing else. All of us cooperating in a bluff, and thank Heaven it worked! Everybody, thanks. Thanks for helping us out, there. Thanks a lot."

"Any time, Czarny." Spud gave him a clap on the back.

Wilson threw up his hands.

Pater Fairchild coughed and said, "I should think, Wilson, that you might act a trifle more gracious about whatever it was that just transpired here, seeing that you yourself are the chief benefactor, having been saved from a very unpleasant experience at best and, at worst, a lifetime behind bars."

"Hey!" said Stallion. "We *can* still throw him out, can't we? Will you let us do that much, old bloodsucker?"

"That's up to all you floaters," said Clement. "I'd just like to go back up and try to finish my nap." Yeah, he told himself wryly, good luck with that!

"You can't kick me out," said Wilson. "I depledge. Right now. And I'm transferring to Madison or Minnesota or somewhere just as soon as—"

"Good," said Ramon Mendoza, opening the door and coming in. "If you, as I take it, Wilson, are the idiot who just tried to stake our man Czarny."

Fearing whether their bluff had been a complete success, after all, Clement stared at Ramon and began, "How did—"

"Fear not," Ramon replied. "Our good Sheriff Nurmi took pains to explain that it was some Hell Week skit that took a number of you in too completely. I read between the lines, although not telling him anything of what I guessed. I only regret, little brother, that I was not here at the time," he added, gazing back at Clement. "It would honor me to offer you the use of my bed, while I sit watch at my desk until the Van Helsing we unknowingly harbored is safely away from the house."

"We'll appropriate his mallet and stake," said Spud.

"Yeah!" said Solly. "I don't see how taking away a murderer's weapons could count as stealing. How's your ear, Clem?"

"Feels much better, Solly. Thanks."

"Looks a lot better. I think I could get that stud out for you pretty easily now."

"No, thanks, leave it. It'll be okay."

Val Saladin suggested, "We could mount them for a trophy—the stake and mallet, I mean."

"No!" Clement exclaimed, alarmed at what he saw in Val's expression. It looked far too much like hero-worship—fine in a puppy's face, not in a fraternity brother's. Thank goodness that at least Val had said "trophy," not "relic."

"I'm leaving right now," said Gary Wilson.

Nobody stopped him. Fred Fletcher even said, "Don't forget your coat, Van *Hel*sing. *We* sure don't want it lying around here."

* * * *

Half an hour later, lying in Ramon's bed, with one mellow lamp across the room shedding light on Ramon over his books, while the smells of dinner drifted upstairs from the kitchen stove…feeling safe and comfortable and still keyed up anyway, Clement thought the thing that kept worrying him most was how, when he sent everyone away so he could cope with it alone, he had found himself thinking he wished he had Keiko there, he might have been able to talk it over right away with her.

Why Keiko? Shouldn't April have been the one to jump into his head at that point? And he didn't think April had ever come into his mind at all until now. But Keiko had at once. Why?

When he woke, with no awareness of having fallen asleep, it was almost midnight. He sensed it at once, even though Ramon was still, or again, reading at his desk. But a dirty plate sat on his dresser.

Somehow, as Clement had sensed the time, Ramon apparently sensed that the sleeper had awaken, because he turned, smiled, and said, "We decided to let you sleep through. Guessing this has proved more of a Hell Week for you this year than when you were a mere pledgling yourself."

"Thank you."

"You can have a sandwich, potato chips, and your glass of blood right now, or young Saladin waits ready to warm up a plate of tonight's Mulligan stew for you."

"Tell Val to get his own sleep. The blood and sandwich will be fine. He shouldn't have stayed up."

"He likely would have anyway, thanks to the tensions of this evening and his own ongoing need to keep his grades up. He fetched his books over here for the night." Ramon hesitated before adding, "I believe he is rather proud and eager in his hopes of warming a meal for you. He insisted on supplying five drops from his own finger to your thermos of Cora Cluck." Chicken's blood.

"If he wants to do it that much, tell him I'd be honored."

Ramon stepped over and opened his door. Val was sitting just outside, nodding over a book by one of the hall lights. At Ramon's nod, the pledge was out of his chair and heading downstairs.

"Tomorrow evening—in a few moments, today in the evening—is the choosing of 'big brothers,'" Ramon remarked. "After this afternoon—in a few moments, yesterday afternoon—all our remaining thirteen will no doubt want you. But I should judge that young Saladin has the strongest claim. It was he who wondered why Wilson should be hauling that rucksack upstairs for a presumed comfort break, he who alerted Bartlett rather than take it on his own pledgling authority to follow Wilson and the puppy up to your room alone."

Clement sighed. "I'm afraid he hero-worships me."

Ramon smiled. "Disabuse him gently."

"Well...I only hope I can be as good a big brother to him as you've been to me."

"I was not here tonight," Ramon said on a note of calm self-accusation, "when my absence could have been fatal to you. Thank God for Saladin and Bartlett and the others."

"You can't be everywhere at once," Clement answered almost absently, still worried about Val's hero-worship and how little he himself deserved it.

NEXT MORNING: THURSDAY, OCT. 10

When Keiko came down at 0630 for breakfast, there was Clement waiting for her in the dining room of Thelwell Hall. "Ko-Ko," he said, "can you get a roll or something and come over to Rayburn where we can find a private room? I don't want anyone overhearing us."

Her heart thudding hard and fast, she went through the line, where she got an orange juice, an apple, two hard-cooked eggs, two doughnuts, and a coffee, all boxed to go. As much as looked plausible for one student. She didn't want to look like one of these floaters who tried to sneak meals for half a dozen friends out of their single ticket. Regular food was just bulk and roughage to him, but she made sure to choose things she knew he liked the taste and texture of.

Had he—oh, God, please!—broken up with April or something? And come back to his good ol' study buddy? But he hadn't looked or sounded romantic.

Being so early in the morning made it simple to find an unoccupied privacy alcove in Rayburn Student Center. They settled in. She handed him the apple, an egg, and a doughnut, and waited.

He didn't start eating until he finished telling her what had happened yesterday at the Pi Rho house. Neither, after her first sip of orange juice, did she.

"My *Lord*, Clement! He tried to *kill* you!"

A shaky grin. "That's more or less how *I* reacted."

"But you're *sure*? It wasn't—I don't know—just some kind of a put-up job or something? Your whole doggone fratty house trying to put one over on you?"

He shook his head. "They wouldn't all do that to me. They wouldn't have done anything like *that* even when I was a frosh going through Hell Week myself. Not Spud and Solly and Val and the others. They'll convince you."

"But you let on to the sheriff it was all a joke. Was that very smart, if the—jerk—really meant it?"

"It was the rest of his life, Ko-Ko."

"I care a whole lot more about the rest of *your* life. There's a time and a place for forgiving, and that wasn't it."

Again Clement shook his head. "It's *always* right to forgive. At least—for someone like me. The crosses and sunlight and things… Anyway, I'm afraid I haven't forgiven him yet. Not really."

"Sure sounds to me like you have."

"Not here. Not in my heart. That I almost don't have any more. I think there's still a lot of anger in here."

"Well, I should think so! I should *hope* so!… But the crosses and stuff aren't bothering you about it?" she pressed him, looking at his earring, which today seemed to be resting quiet in a healthy-looking earlobe.

"The trick seems to be, acting as if you've forgiven, and letting your heart catch up."

"Well!" Keiko took a swallow of her cold coffee and asked, "What does April have to say about it?"

"I haven't told her."

"Huh?" In her thoughts, Keiko added, You came to me first?

"And I don't think we should tell her. It'd only worry her. It shouldn't go any farther than the Purple Rose brothers. And you."

Good luck with that! she thought. Aloud: "Clement… I really think, if you're really serious about April, she should know."

"Not yet, anyway! Think I haven't thought hard about this myself, Ko-Ko? If Professor Sharma does decide to do *Der Vampyr*, and casts—"

"Clement! Now, that really *wouldn't* be smart! If *Dracula* brought out a crazy kamikaze like Gary Wilson—"

"It's just the chance actors have had to take all through the centuries. As long as plays and operas have villains, somebody's got to play them. It's a great part—one aria that really explains what Lord Ruthven is going through himself, makes him almost sympathetic—something they never gave Count Dracula. And after those reviews last year…it'd probably be good for me to try it again, after being thrown like that. And this time, no stakes involved at all—he gets struck down by lightning from…Heaven or Hell, that part isn't quite clear to me, but no mere human agency, anyway. And if I do it, I plan to play it as if he really loves all his victims—"

"April would be singing his main beloved victim, I suppose?"

"So you see how important it is to keep what really happened yesterday a secret? Most importantly from the legal authorities, but also from April and Professor Sharma and the School of Music. From April, at least until after the opera is either behind us, or Professor Sharma decides to go with *Don Giovanni* or *Madame Butterfly* this year, or maybe *Falstaff*."

Keiko considered getting the talk back to this staking attempt, and decided to keep it where Clement seemed more comfortable. "I hope not *Falstaff*. I mean, I'm sure you'd be great in that part, too. I just wouldn't much like seeing you padded up like Santa Claus on his own 'naughty' list."

CHAPTER 17

ABOUT TEN DAYS LATER: SATURDAY, OCT. 18

Formal initiation had been just a week ago tomorrow, and tonight Spud, Fred, and Stale had brought Val Saladin and three more of the new frosh brothers, along with dates for everybody except Fred and Stale, out to Hellmouth Park. "Okay, newbros," Stale had said, "you think 'Hell Week' was Hell? Come on and see what it's *really* like."

Except that Hellmouth Amusement Park was just a lot of fun and games. Strictly for laughs.

Well, maybe not for everybody. First off, they all spent about an hour in a little movie theater on the third floor, that was posted "Off Limits To Anyone Under 25," but Fred had talked to the demon at the box office—all the park employees Val had seen were dressed up like demons with horns and tails and usually pitchforks, or else like damned souls not wearing much of anything but costume chains and fake blood—and Val guessed a bribe changed hands, but that seemed to be standard operating procedure here, where 16-to-25-year-olds had to pay a higher entrance fee anyway than the 25-and-up crowd. Anyway, once inside, they'd watched a stag movie that made Val very glad his date, Debbie, was quite willing to neck and pet in their double seat—all the seats in this little screening room were doubles.

That must be why his own special "big Pi Rho brother" wouldn't ever come along to Hellmouth Park. Poor Clement! Having to go through life keeping his conscience as clean as a nun's! But what a floater he was! What a heroic floater! Val guessed he wouldn't tell Big Brother Clement everything he and Debbie were up to here together.

After the stag movie, they all went straight down to a long table for twelve in the Blue Blazes Room.

All the restaurants of Hellmouth Park specialized in hot foods. The mildest you could get was in the Devil's Little Acre Room, where they claimed to serve an "Arctic Chili" that would have been only three-star hot anywhere north of the state of Texacali, where it'd be called "mild." And, of course, they served Devil's Food Cake everywhere in the park—that was plain old Devil's Food Cake, with or without plain old vanilla ice cream—melted and warmed up. Otherwise, for anything solid that didn't take a couple of layers right off your tongue, you had to go up to the kiddieland on the top floor.

At least they kept you well supplied with cold beverages. Enough of his big brother had rubbed off on Val that his "I Bet You Can't" glass held nothing but plain iced tea. He thought. He hoped they hadn't slipped a little vodka or rotgut or whatever into it, seeing he was eighteen and a college man.

"Okay," Augie was challenging Fred at the head of the table and Stallion at the foot (the only two who hadn't brought dates of their own, saying they planned on sampling the park's riper employees). "So far, we haven't seen a damn thing worse than Hell Week at the Purple Rose."

"Yeah," Pete put in. "A helluva lot better, in fact."

"So where's this bad stuff you primed us for?" Nebbie wanted to know.

One of the Sigh sisters—Rosie, Pete's date—giggled and said, "It's so *juvenile* of you brothers still to be doing your silly Hell Weeks! The Sigh sisters outgrew all that kind of thing *years* ago." Rosie had two or three shots of something in her tea, for sure.

"Patience, chicklets, patience," Fred assured them all. "After dinner, the dungeons!"

Stale smacked his lips. And then wiped his eyes. They were all wiping their eyes every mouthful, the food was so spicy. And gulping from their glasses after every bite.

Val coughed and found himself half whispering because there was so much pepper and stuff in his hamburger, "I thought you couldn't go down there till you were twenty-five."

Fred, who acted pretty used to hot food, waved his hand. "That rule's just for the masses. Not for college fraternity men."

"And sorority women," Spud's date Theda added.

Debbie either winked at Val across the table or blinked because of her stuffed chili peppers.

"I don't know," Val insisted. "Solly said last summer he and Clement's girl friend got in trouble down there…"

"Solly just didn't know when to wave the tridols," Stale said confidently. "You've gotta do it ahead of time. Well in advance."

"Yeah," Fred agreed. "Don't worry, chicklets, no sweat. We've already got it all cleared and arranged for you frosh floaters."

For a minute the table fell silent. Then Augie's date Mattie said, "So tell us, bros, 's 't really true that that Wilson floater tried to stake your pet vampire during Hell Week, and that's the story behind why you kicked 'm out and he left school?"

"We didn't 'kick Wilson out,'" Fred answered, making it sound like he meant they did. "He 'depledged,' and transferred to greener pastures—for his type."

Spud, the big senior who wasn't saying too much this evening, spoke now. "Seems Gary read about Clement in that article they ran in the Galop de Vache paper last year, about how our Hodag Thespians had a real vampire playing the part here. I guess Gary Wilson's from one of those families that thumps the Bible till it squeals, and he decided here was his chance to make the world a little bit safer for his kind of good people. That was why he enrolled at the U. of M. and pledged Pi Rho and went through all the rest of it, just watching for his chance at poor Clemmie."

Nebbie's date Candy said, "Yeah, well, m' own folks can thump the Good Book pretty hard, too, and from what I've seen, come Judgment Day, I'd rather take my chances alongside our vampire than with anybody like Gary Wilson." She took a long swallow of whatever she was drinking and added, "Or with any of the present company, either, for the matter of that."

"Then isn't it a little daring of Clement to play another stage vampire this year?" asked Theda.

Val said proudly, "Clement says if every actor who ever got threats because of playing a villain let it spook 'em off, who'd they ever get to play the villains? Besides, Lord Ruthven gets killed in the end by a bolt of lightning, not a stake through the heart, so that shouldn't inspire any copycats. And it's a good baritone role, and Prof Sharma really wanted—"

At the table next to theirs, a woman jumped up and started shouting. Everybody looked around. The other person at that table, a stocky gray-haired old guy, was doubled over into his dinner plate. His glass was upset and dripping all over everything.

"He's choking!" Spud exclaimed, jumping up. He was closest and got there first, but all the other Pies from that side of the table were there almost as fast, crowding around. So were people from other tables. By the time Val—who'd been on the far side of the Pi table—got around, there were too many bodies in between. He could make out Spud thumping the gray-haired man, hauling him up and down by the armpits, but...

"It is too late!" the woman said, with a funny kind of sob. "He is dead."

"Outta the way!" some park demons were shouting, pushing through. "Outta the way!"

"He is gone," the woman repeated.

Being toward the back to begin with, Val was one of the first to get pushed aside. He got back to his chair and sat down again, shaking.

Pretty soon the rest of the Pies were back in their chairs, too. Except Spud, Fred, and Stale. The big football player was still trying to revive the old floater. The park demons and a couple of the chains-and-fake blood damned souls were having to pry him away so they could get in with a stretcher. Fred was staring at the choking victim kind of open-mouthed, and Stale... Val wasn't sure what Stale was looking around for...then finally he noticed that the woman who had been at the same table with the man who choked didn't seem to be anywhere around any longer.

When the three upperclassmen finally got back to the Pi table, Val said, "Bros...I don't think I want to go down to the dungeons any more."

Everybody made noises of agreement. Nobody tried to argue. Only Fred said, "Look. Anybody else have any idea who that was?"

"Yeah," said Stale. "Looked a lot like the Demon Doktors of Novgorod."

"What?" Spud asked. "How the heck could you tell? How can any-body recognize anybody, choking like that?"

"I thought the woman looked like Kosya Petrovka," Stale said. "Made me take another look at the man. Build matches, probably about the right age. The face, yeah, I'll give you that. Pretty damn hard to tell by the face alone, under conditions like that. But with the build right, the age right, that Slavic type of face, and then the woman—pure coincidence?" He shook his head. "Pretty hard to believe in that much coincidence. And she hurried herself out of sight pretty damn quick, didn't she? Why'd she take off like that, if she was concerned about her dear *tovarich?* Why don't we head right on down to that subbasement level where they have the Eugenics Farms waxworks and take a look at the Demon Doktors? Their waxworks here are supposed to be better than most photographs."

But everybody else except Fred wanted to head back to Hodag Crossing right away. Finally Fred and Stale talked Spud and Theda into taking advantage of the advance arrangements and bribes after all, go down with them and check out the wax dummies of Feodor Blazhenov and Kosya Petrovka, while all the younger Pies went over to Heavengate and waited for the older foursome there.

CHAPTER 18

AFTER THE WRAPAROUND: MONDAY, OCT. 20

Jason Maklowski, son of Chicago steelworker Joe Ponchewski and his sturdy wife Barbara Maklowska, had been a two-year-old "jechanko" (to use the family's own half-Americanized pronunciation) when the 20th century came in, which had made him a hair too young for Act I of the Last Great War, and a hair too old for Act II. Never mind. When the Army bumped him on account of his age and premature potbelly, the Federal Investigative Departmental Office had been happy enough to find a use for him and his grasp of Slavic languages, going back to a childhood spent tumbling up in the ethnically diverse neighborhood around St. Hedwig's: Poles, Belorusskies, Bohemians, Slovenians—all your standard Bohunks in general—and one Swedish family.

Anyone might think, when the War's final curtain uncovered those damn Eugenics Farms and Kali Camps, and FIDO organized its War Crimes Division, Jason Maklowski would have wanted to specialize in the fugitive Russian deathguards. Hadn't a good half of their victims been his own ethnic group? Maybe that was the trouble. Too much chance of finding some aunt or uncle or cousin twice removed in the lists of Eugenics victims. Oh, yeah, they tried to slot him there. They tried hard. By giving him a gung-ho young partner fresh out of college, who apparently hadn't thought about much all through his university days except Russian spies and how to spot them. Tricked themselves. Made it quite easy for Jason Maklowski to slide over to the Kali Camp deathguards and free Hartsie to concentrate all he liked on the Russian ones.

Now here they were at the top of the Upper Midwest because Feodor Blazhenov had choked to death on some piece of overspiced meat at one of the Hellmouth Park eateries, and his partner Kosya Petrovka had been sighted in the same place. Mere sightings weren't all that uncommon, and most of them worth less than your average newssheet horoscope. But the dead man turning out to be the real McCoysky made it a good chance that this time the sighting of his fellow deathguard had been genuine. And Hartsie being an alum not only of the University of Minnemagantic, but of the same frat house half a dozen of whose current members had reported the sighting, made him and his senior partner the logical team to send out. In somebody's opinion. Not necessarily Jason Maklowski's, but what the hell, with retirement waiting to welcome him a decade down the line, why complain? He didn't mind airplane meals (though complaining about them was obligatory for air travelers), and he always enjoyed university towns. Especially whenever he got a few hours clear to wander around the campus.

If he'd been directing this operation, he and Hartsie would have rented a car and driven straight out to Hellmouth Park—about an hour away—for a look-see on the spot. But car rental wasn't exactly deluxe at the tiny Hodag Crossing airport, and this Pi Rho frat house had its own semi-trained team of deathguard hunters who kept in close contact with FIDO-WC, mainly through their alum Hartsie. Both FIDO men would be getting together with the Purple Rose so-called "Inner Circle" later on tonight. Meantime, Hartsie'd walked over to Greek Town, and Maklowski had his couple of hours free and clear.

He usually gravitated to the music part of the school, because it wasn't only gangsters who liked opera. It was also a few of the people on the right side of the law, like Jason Maklowski. And these days some of the best opera in the country was going on in the university schools of music. He was a regular subscriber to *The School Opera Scene*, as well as *Met News* and a couple of lesser magazines on the subject. With luck, he might be able to sit in on a student recital or two.

The School of Music was in an old redstone building, Foster Hall, cornerstone reading 1898. Old as Jason Maklowski himself. He went in and wandered. Always gave him a pleasant sense of freedom, being a harmless sightseer unconnected with the university. Like he had permission to wander the halls at will during school hours. Did anybody ever outgrow their school days? These corridors even had pretty much the same look and feel as those of St. Hedwig's, grown a little older and shabbier since the teens of this century...

Music was coming from one of the basement rooms. Baritone and soprano...sounded like an operatic love duet, with piano accompanying. Then a third voice came in with them, a tenor. Singing in English, baritone asking soprano for a kiss, tenor protesting.

Maklowski opened the door.

Not a recital. A rehearsal. He'd lucked in on more than one of those, too, in his time. Looked like an early rehearsal, almost a preliminary one, just half a dozen people in the room: three young men, two young women, and someone behind the piano.

The three who weren't singing at the moment he opened the door all looked at him. After a few more bars, the tall-and-dark young baritone and his strawberry blond soprano let their voices die and also looked at him. The piano stopped as the player behind it stood up and looked at him, too. Older woman, looked East Indian. Refugee from the War? Lot of them around these days.

"Don't mind me, folks," the FIDO man told them with a grin. "Just wandering in search of beautiful music for my ears. Mind if I sit back there and listen in?"

"Be our guest, M.," said the piano woman. "I am Professor Sharma. These are M.'s Czarny, Greenhill, Kemper, Walters, and Thorvald. We are in very early rehearsals for our opera next month."

"Yeah, I figured it was something like that, soon as I saw it was a rehearsal, not a recital. What opera? I'm something of an opera buff, myself."

"It is *Der Vampyr—The Vampire—by* Marschner."

"With a real vampire in the title role," the strawberry blond said, beaming up all over her face at the baritone. "But a dear, friendly one."

"That so?" Something rang a bell, something Maklowski had read in *The School Opera Scene* a year or two ago. "You the same one who sang Papageno, I think this is the same university? a few years back?"

The tall baritone bowed and grinned. "I could be. It was my first role here, the fall of 1950."

"Would like to've caught that. Well, let me just sit back here and listen while you rehearse away."

Maklowski chose a chair near the back of the room, sat, rested one elbow on the fold-up writing paddle, and listened. With open eyes. Something about Professor Sharma…

"Clement, I know it is early yet to think of these fine points, but cannot you be a little more…the one who deceives, who lies to the young woman? You want only to bite her neck, after all."

"I'm sorry, Professor, but doesn't he really love them all? Isn't he going to explain to his friend in a few minutes how terrible it is to long to spare someone you love, and have to drain them anyway, in spite of yourself?"

One of the tenors—Kemper—said, "Remember those rotten reviews you got last year when you tried to make a sympathetic floater out of Dracula."

"I wasn't really trying to make him 'sympathetic,' just to make his motivations a little more…human. And we sold out every night anyway. But in that play I was sort of going counter to the actual script. In this one, there's already a lot of commentary to the effect that Lord Ruthven is supposed to be a hero-villain, with a definite sympathetic side. And I'm a year older, hope I've learned something in the meantime."

"And I like the romantic effect," said the strawberry blond. "After all, Emmy's not really a fool. Didn't she herself just sing the vampire legend? I think she'd tune right in on any insincerity in Lord Ruthven, and how could he take her out from under her fiance's nose *then?*"

"Very well," said Professor Sharma. "We will try it as you wish, and see. But if it does not seem to be working as we put this piece more fully together, you must be prepared to change and to follow my direction."

Jason Maklowski cleared his throat and said, "I'm just a visitor here, M., and like I say, I don't really know this particular opera. But it sounded great to me just the way they were doing it."

The kids already seemed to have carried their point about Czarny's interpretation. What the FIDO man really wanted was a closer look at Professor Sharma, her reaction to his buttinski comment.

Turning, she gave him a pleasant smile and said, "But you know much of opera, it seems, and the opinion of the listener who knows is always welcome. The English words—can you understand them well?"

"Oh, very well. They're coming through fine and clear. Excellent enunciation, people."

"That is good. And may we hope that you will attend a performance?"

"If I'm here in town, I'd surely love to do just that." And unfortunately, Jason Maklowski thought, maybe a lot more than just that. Unfortunately for himself and everybody else concerned. They seemed like a bunch of nice, happy, hard-working college kids with a sympathique music professor.

And it'd be a pretty darn thick serving of coincidence.

All the same, he was very glad that some sixth sense had kept him from identifying himself as a FIDO agent.

A FEW HOURS LATER

Of course, tonight wasn't the first time Theda Jones had been out to the Pies' hunting cabin in the woods. Especially since becoming a Sigh sister. Pi Psi used it too. Their all-girl slumber parties on fall and spring wraparounds were legends of poetic beauty, all the more so when some of the brothers came out and gave them a surprise serenade. When the vampire was among the serenaders, it never went any farther, and all the men's pleas to be let in were only a big joke…until after Clement and his closest buddies had left for the night. And when weather permitted, the brothers and sisters held their big joint party out here, just before the holiday break. But this was the first time Theda had ever been the only sister among so many brothers, and she was loving every minute of it.

There was Pater Fairchild. And two FIDO-WC men, guests, one of them quite old, at least in his fifties, looking respectable and professional as the Secretary of State. And the other one was Gale Hartwick's big brother, family ties as well as fraternity, who'd kept the direct communication line open ever since the end of the War. Then there were three more alum brothers: Jack Hollinger, who worked in the Twin Cities now; John Rogers, who had taken a good job in Galop de Vache after graduating last spring; and Carl Avosso, who was in the Hodag Crossing Hospital administration, and married to one of the nurses.

Rich and handsome Ramon Mendoza, still decorating the Purple Rose house as a grad student. And Fred Fletcher, Stallion Drinkwater, Joe Doe, Al Koby, Pete something and Augie something—she hadn't quite learned all the new frosh brothers by family name, even though Pete and Augie had been in the party at Hellmouth Park the day before yesterday, and seen the deathguard die.

This year's whole Purple Rose Inner Circle—the Purple Sigh didn't have one—and some members back from the past. And an extra FIDO man as guest! Yes, this was a pretty big thing tonight. She felt both glad and proud that she had pestered Fred and Stale and little sophomore Joe Doe until they let her in on the secret, at least far enough to wangle Pater Fairchild's permission for Theda Jones to represent the sister house at this very special meeting. If you could call it "represent" when they'd sworn her to secrecy in case anything transpired here tonight that they decided to keep from public consumption.

Secret from the rest of their own house, as well. From floaters like Spud Bartlett (Theda was a little sorry about that, having the ideas she had about making him her special beau) and—this had really surprised her—the vampire himself. In fact, Fred and Stale and the two soph brothers had warned her specifically not to let anything out of the bag in front of any of Clement's special buddies, particularly Val Saladin, who idolized his big brother.

Why this secrecy even from the rest of their own house, Theda wasn't sure. But she suspected that the Inner Circle must be involved in other Deep Mysteries, things they hadn't told her about yet, and it added to her delightful, shivery feeling. Other things besides the hunt for deathguards? What? Ongoing espionage? Against whom, with the world finally at peace? Undercover work for…who? Hugging herself inside, she sipped her hot tea and watched all the males settle themselves respectfully around her, each in his own place before the fire.

When everyone was settled and attentive, the meeting got under way. Pater Fairchild called the roll, thanked the alum members for being here, and finished with a hearty welcome to the two guests. Then, at last, they got down to serious discussion. Lance Hartwick began: "We've known since late Saturday night that the man who died in the Blue Blazes Room of Hellmouth Park that evening was indeed Feodor Blazhenov, one of the so-called Demon Doktors of Novgorod. What we couldn't be absolutely sure of until today, when it was verified by our associate forensic examiner in St. Paul who actually did the autopsy, is that it was not a simple accidental asphyxiation on a bite of hot food. It was cyanide."

There was half a second's silence before everybody—almost everybody—started talking at once. Theda didn't. What use would it be? The floaters who knew anything would be able to share it sooner without superfluous questions cluttering up the air. She glanced at Lance's partner, her fellow special guest, the old guy M. Maklowski, another one who wasn't saying anything, yet.

He did shortly, making it obvious that his partner had already shared the data with him. Naturally. He coughed for silence. When he had it, he said, "Cyanide deaths are deliberate. The question is, deliberate by whom. Was it suicide or murder?"

"And does it matter?" said the frosh Augie.

"It may," Pater Fairchild informed him. "Although less, perhaps, than this question: In either case, suicide or murder, why in so public a venue?"

"To give Hellmouth Park a bad name?" asked the other frosh, and everybody laughed for a second or two before Pater Fairchild went on,

"It is well known, albeit in that form of word-of-mouth which can be mistaken for mere rumor, that, for a fee, Hellmouth Amusement Park facilitates suicides, arranging to so dispose of the bodies as to make it appear either accident or inexplicable disappearance. In the case of Blazhenov, one must wonder, why not simple disappearance? Unless even Hellmouth relucted to soil itself with a deathguard any longer than absolutely necessary."

"So it could have been murder," said Lance Hartwick.

"Objection still stands," said Jack Hollinger. "Why in a public place?"

"How better to get the body disposed of?" Lance replied easily. "Let the stretcher-bearers carry it away off your hands into those of the proper authorities, while you, the murderer, melt away in the crowd and disappear yourself. Chances are she didn't expect him to be autopsied for cyanide. Expected it to pass off as the choking accident it looked like."

"You sound like you know whodunit," said Joe Doe.

"I think it should be fairly obvious," Lance replied. "Who else but his dinner companion? To whom the world would owe a debt of gratitude, if she were not another deathguard herself. Kosya Petrovka."

"That isn't yet absolutely verified," said the older FIDO man. "It could've been another woman who resembled her."

"But why'd she kill her friend and partner?" asked Augie. "Probably her only friend in the whole world."

"Maybe a suicide pact," suggested Carl Avosso, "and she got cold feet at the last minute. Or went out to do it someplace else so it wouldn't look too conspicuous. We might still find her body somewhere. Maybe in one of those subbasement rooms below Hellmouth Park."

"Let us hope," said Pater Fairchild, "that we find her alive. Her notorious consort has already cheated the Court of World Justice. Let us hope it can still try at least one of the Demon Doktors of Novgorod in public."

"What great difference?" murmured Ramon Mendoza. "Death by cyanide in a crowded restaurant, or by the rope before a crowd, remains death."

"The difference, Mendoza, lies in the moral lesson to the world, that these things must never happen again."

Mendoza yawned. "How long will the world at large truly remember? Or care?"

"Here's another thought," said Gale Hartwick. "The Russkies themselves are trying to get their deathguards quietly out of the way. They secretly hired Petrovka to cyanide her *tovarich,* and now they plan to doublecross her and do her in somewhere else."

Lance nodded. "That isn't bad, younger brother. Means we'd better find her in a hurry."

The older FIDO man grunted. "If Hellmouth Park had charge of the doublecross, she's dead already. Otherwise, she's in Canada by now."

"So?" said Lance. "No country in the world offers legal sanctuary for a deathguard."

"So our course of action is to alert our Canadian colleagues and step in only if and when they ask us," the older agent replied. "Jiminy Ketchup! you'd think these northwoods had a couple of Russian spies behind every pine tree."

"You might be surprised," Lance told his partner. "During the War, there was one right here in Hodag Crossing, operating out of our little local brothel. Excuse me, M.," he added, looking at Theda.

She chuckled. "How pre-Reform of you, M. Hartwick!" Did they think no Sigh sister or other college woman ever snuck over to that side of town to window-shop the male prostitutes? Why, once she had even spotted Ramon Mendoza lurking around that services-both-genders shop. Who'd ever have thought? Not that one Pi had any business tattling on another one.

"You cannot mean," Ramon Mendoza was saying slowly, "the 'Hallowe'en Hooker.'"

"Oh, is that what they're calling her, now? What else do you think got her killed?"

"The common opinion," said Pater Fairchild, "would seem to be that Irina Kiripovna was a vampire."

"Because of that picket fence post?" Lance grinned and shook his head. "Well, I guess she could've been that, too, Pater. But the picket fence had to've been a coincidence. A lucky coincidence, maybe. She wasn't here in Greek Town that night on a service call—well, maybe that, too, if she was trying to bake two or three cakes in one oven—she was here thinking she was going to get secret info about troop movements from someone she thought was a sell-out, who, instead of selling her secrets, put her out of all action permanently."

"Interesting," Pater Fairchild said with a nod.

Mendoza added, gazing at Lance Hartwick, "And you would know all this because…"

"Well, that was my own last year at the U. of M., and I knew that informal double agent personally. Classmate of mine. Who told me about it over beers down at the Old Muskie. You'll keep it all hushed from the local law, of course? Our secret patriot did the nation a big service, even if it can't be recognized officially. The Old Muskie still here?"

"It is Hogebloom's Party Shop now," said Pater Fairchild. "A change—very marginally—for the better."

The older FIDO man coughed and said, "Let's get back to current concerns, shall we? M. Avosso, by our best sources, your Dr. Rabar al Shammari checks out. The story as you have it here matches everything we know, with just enough allowable variance for individual memories to, as they say, enhance plausibility. Down to the tragic death of his wife Fariza during their escape from India in '42."

Carl seemed to relax a little. "I'm glad about that, M. Maklowski— may I call you Jason?"

"Why not? We're all friends and hunting buddies here. Or oughta be."

"Dr. Shammari has been a good friend to us here. Even if…" Carl grinned apologetically… "Even if I felt like he'd rubbed me a little wrong last year, that time we almost lost young Carl, maybe even Milly. I guess I must've been pretty tense myself, pretty easy to get rubbed wrong. But looking back, yes, he was good. Even if the other medic should probably get most of the credit for saving the baby—Dr. Sharma."

"Sharma." Jason (Theda figured, since he'd given Carl permission, she could first-name him too, at least in her thoughts) raised one eyebrow. That looked a little funny for an old guy with a potbelly, but she politely kept her chuckle deep inside, as he went on, "I just met a Professor Sharma at the School of Music this afternoon. Any connection?"

"A spousal one," Pater Fairchild replied. "They, too, are refugees from war-torn India, although later ones. They arrived here shortly after the War's end, and in these few years have earned for themselves places of respect, she at the university, he at the hospital. Our young Czarny swears by her as a professor of music and director of the school's opera productions."

"Hmmm," said Jason. "Maybe I should've said, everything on Dr. al Shammari checks out, assuming it's the same man. Maybe we can find some excuse to drop by the hospital tomorrow morning on the way to the airport and have a look."

After half a heartbeat, Pater Fairchild suggested, "Dr. al Shammari was the attending physician at the time young Czarny believes himself to have become a vampire, and continues to renew his prescription for blood. Not that it is so greatly needed at present, but should fresh blood ever become hard to obtain from butchers, as I have heard it already is in many cities…"

"Well, thanks. FIDO isn't interested in vampires as such, but being something of a follower of the university opera scene, I won't have to put on much of an act to sound interested in its rising young vampire baritone. Maybe even get a chance to chat a bit with the husband of his music professor, too."

CHAPTER 19

ABOUT A MONTH LATER: WEDNESDAY, NOV. 19

"As long as it's been this long," Jason Maklowski grumbled, "we could've waited half a week longer. Let the kids finish doing their opera."

Hartsie shook his head vigorously. "Too long already. Whole blame process took too blame long."

The two FIDO agents were on their way back to Hodag Crossing in FIDO's own small plane, with FIDO's own pilot, Alec Pfeiffer.

"For getting the doctor's prints to us on a hospital cafeteria glass—"

"Avosso took long enough doing that!"

"—finally getting sharp enough photos of their reasonably reliable prints from Vayalpad, giving Sanders and Estergard the time they needed to compare 'em—I'd say we acted with lightning speed on this one."

"Canada beat us to Petrovka last month," the younger man complained.

"Relax. Petrovka knew she was on the run. Indradatt and Asan don't know anyone's on their scent. They're not going anywhere. We'll be turning 'em over to stand trial right alongside Petrovka and Karpovsky in Geneva."

"Yeah. Do you believe that story Petrovka told, about why she got cold feet when it came to swallowing her own Hellmouth cyanide capsule?"

"About seeing devils from Hell actually swarming up and yanking her partner's screaming soul out through the top of his head?" Maklowski shrugged. "Yeah, I can believe her seeing it. Not saying that what she saw really happened, but these—'psychomystical' things—can be funny."

"They say we've all got one." Hartsie shook his head again. His huge gray eyes had an almost haunted look to them. "A 'psychomystique,' I mean."

Pfeiffer, the pilot, proved he was hearing at least some of their conversation by saying, "Polite way for atheists and agnostics to talk about the soul."

Touching off one of Jason Maklowski's pet peeves. "Hey! How often do I gotta tell you, quit lumping agnostics in with atheists. Us plain and simple aggies can't subscribe to atheism any more than we can to any other hard doctrine."

Hartsie said, "At least you'll get a chance to see your opera, Mak."

"'F they go through with it." Maybe they would, at that. The show must go on, and all that kind of thing. Especially with such a big boost of publicity.

Assuming everyone in the cast, chorus, orchestra, and stage crew didn't just walk out on it.

* * * *

The final dress rehearsal had started at 1400 sharp. Well, 1407 by the Wedderburn Auditorium clock, which was probably 1400 sharp by somebody's watch somewhere on or near campus. Wonderful how these fractional little time zones moved irregularly through small areas.

Several people had to cut afternoon classes, but School of Music productions counted as team sports—they *were* team efforts, even if the game was that everybody should win—so the rest of the university made accommodations for final rehearsals. And Prof Sharma believed in everybody on her team getting plenty of sleep before curtain time on Opening Night.

The spring operetta, being officially an extra-curricular production sponsored by the G&S Society, usually in collusion with the Hodag Thespians, had to do *all* their rehearsing evenings. Being a non-joiner of anything, Keiko wasn't officially a member of the G&S Society, either; but she sat in on most of their meetings, chiefly because—although he wasn't an official member, either, his schedule already being so tight—Clement made time to audition for their spring show. And this year they were already talking about taking advantage of *Der Vampyr* and doing *Ruddigore* as a spoof, maybe even re-using some of the same costumes and sets, casting Clement as the other Ruthven.

Meanwhile, Keiko was back at her old familiar place: backstage lightboard and sound effects.

For a final dress rehearsal, things were almost clipping along. They might, just possibly, be out of here by 2000 hours, right on Prof Sharma's schedule. By which time, Cast, Chorus, Crew, and Orchestra would have gotten themselves around their suppers on a catch-as-catch-can basis, inhaling sandwiches and stuff from refreshments tables backstage, in the Green Room, and in the musicians' warm-up room.

They reached Emmy's "Vampire Romance" aria. April was doing Emmy, arguably as important a role as the actual heroine, Malvina, and one that gave April another chance at love duetting with Clement. Darn it. Keiko wished April was doing Malvina, who from the word go wanted no part of vampyre Lord Ruthven, only Sir Edgar Aubry the tenor.

"Hush! That pale man is a vampire! May God protect us…"

Emmy had good songs, but she was really slow on the uptake. Has this folk-tale type of an aria about a legendary vampire, and then can't see that this handsome Lord Ruthven who comes supposedly to dance at her wedding and actually to romance her out from under her bridegroom's nose is a pale vampire himself, and she's just told the audience her own story. Where it fell down this time, was in how different Clement was from those wicked types he seemed to like playing on the stage… Keiko really, really wished he'd stick with amiable buffoons like Papageno. Maybe she would have been happier this term to see him as Falstaff, after all.

Here came Lord Ruthven now, stepping out from the crowd. Even the spot from the light booth overhead pretended not to notice him for half a second. Well rehearsed to heighten the effect of him just materializing there…

And…lights up at the backstage board, for the dialogue. That was Keiko's department. Now she softened the glow bit by bit, a crimson sunset on the flats, while the light booth had a soft white spot on Emmy, a stronger red one on Lord Ruthven, a subtly green one on John Kemper as George when he came on at stage back…

Clement made his exit, his part over for a little bit. A quick touch to his hand, and lights up a little for the George and Emmy dialogue…just a little, not too much. Didn't want to wipe out the sunset effect, leave most of the stronger lighting to the spots from the booth…

"Going okay?" Clement whispered at Keiko's ear.

"Looking great from back here!" She handed him his thermos and straw.

With only moments before he had to get back onstage, he unscrewed the thermos cap with one twist and inserted his straw while he murmured, "Maybe Professor Sharma can make her dinner at Dr. al Shammari's at 2000 hours."

"Maybe."

Clement took two long sips, handed the thermos back to Keiko, and watched for his next cue.

"I will break my terrible oath," Dick Walters declaimed as Sir Edgar Aubry. "I will reveal his dread secret, come what may!"

Clement's cue. He stepped back onstage to confront Aubry, and Keiko brought the sunset down one deliberately abrupt jerk, while Willie back in the light booth fiddled some more with the spots…darn!

He'd gotten something fouled up. Two- or three-minute pause while he worked it out, Prof Sharma standing there down front biting her tongue, glancing back around at the light booth, scribbling furiously on her note-board... Half a minute longer, and she'd almost certainly have stopped the rehearsal long enough to ask what was going on...but Willie got the spots right just in time, they'd get only the single scorching with the footlight review at rehearsal's end...

For now, this was Clement's big aria, about the legendary horrors of a vampire's existence. Hearing Clement sing this struck Keiko as a little akin to hearing Bishop Sheen seriously reading anti-Catholic propaganda aloud—as if that'd ever happen—but Clement put so much feeling into this song... He'd told Keiko once, while she was helping him learn his lines, that when he woke up in the hospital bed and found himself vampirized, if there was such a verb, at thirteen years old, for a while he had been in terror that maybe this really *was* the kind of existence in store for him, and how was he going to find maidens to feed on, if he never got any older? Fortunately, he grew up all right, still seemed to be a living human being, and figured out for himself that most of it was scare propaganda. That vampires had probably originally been shamans, super-sensitized to anything holy, and the first new religion that started the fashion for persecuting all earlier religions began by demonizing the earlier one's holiest people first and hardest. And from then on, once vampires were demoted from shamans to supernatural monsters, it just kept going downhill for them.

Keiko wasn't sure how he thought he could help the situation by humanizing vampire villains, but as long as *someone* was going to play them anyway, it might as well be someone who at least tried to make them a little bit sympathetic. And he was almost as eager to play non-vampire villains. More than once he'd said with a wink that he'd love to get his teeth into Scarpia.

Offstage again, briefly, leaving Dick Walters alone for Aubry's next aria. While the tenor was singing it, Keiko whispered, "Dinner at 2000 hours? They're really going New York, aren't they? Or even Continental European."

"Both doctors have tonight off, and Professor Sharma thinks Dr. al Shammari and M. Wanamaker want to announce their engagement."

"Oh. No wonder she's letting little things slide by. I hope this means she plans to keep her directorial notes short at the end."

April squeezed up and snuggled against Clement, taking full advantage of the fact that that was the way they had to make their next entrance. Keiko bent and made sure she had everything ready for the two shots later in the act, right after the comic relief scene coming up soon.

Babs Thorvald wanted to play Mrs. Susie Blunt, the comic village wife in this opera, who ran no risk at all of being bitten, the way Clement wanted to play Scarpia. She had even tried to talk Prof Sharma into transcribing the role for her. But with three sopranos in the opera already, Prof Sharma didn't want to lose the one alto role of any length, so the public librarian of Hodag Crossing, M. Wendy Geller, got Mrs. Blunt, and when Tony Tallpines had enough aging make-up on, he didn't look that much too young to be playing her husband, who had the comic drinking song. Poor Babs had to settle for Janthe, the smallest soprano part, bitten to death in Act I, scene 1.

* * * *

They got done with the actual rehearsing about a quarter till, but full dress rehearsal meant as much time changing out of costumes and make-up as a real performance. So it was almost 2030 on a chilly night just about two thirds of the way through November when they started their walk back to Greek Town. Just the two of them, the only Pies in this production. But they were the cream of the cream. Tallpines and Czarny.

Just a few old, dry leaves on the hardwood trees, rustling as if they enjoyed the secrets of the spooky opera, too. Just enough zephyrs of early winter in the night air to set the Cinnamon tingling in Tony Tallpines' blood. Just enough stars showing through the clouds...

"Sing it like that tomorrow night," said Clement, "and you'll be the hit of the whole show. You almost make me wish I was doing Tom Blunt instead. 'In the winter, let us drink!'" he sang from Tony's big song.

"Still late fall just now."

"'In the autumn, let us drink!'" Clement kept singing the song, one line here, one line there.

"Yeah, that's the whole point of the drinking song, isn't it? A stanza for every season, meaning 'Let us drink all year long.'"

They walked a while without speaking, just humming or whistling snatches of music, the vampire's long cape swishing to the beat of his steps. At last Tony broke the silence by asking, "Clement. What do you think of Linda Beauchamp?"

"Linda Beauchamp." A moment, as if Clement was sorting through his mind to be sure which one she was. "I think she's one of the best oboe players in the school." That had to be his honest opinion, too. The vampire couldn't lie. He could keep quiet about things, but if he said something, it had to be true.

"I think I'm in love with her."

"Make sure." Coming from another floater, that could have meant, Make sure by taking her to bed as soon as you can. Coming from

Clement, it meant, Whatever you do, make sure neither one of you will ever be sorry later…especially if it really is love.

"Clement, how about you and April?"

"How about us?"

"You two really in love?"

The vampire said slowly, "I think so. I've thought so since we were frosh. But, you see, Tony, I don't really have any…any personal standard of comparison."

"I thought I loved one girl all the way from eighth grade to halfway through my sophomore year in high school. And then I thought I loved a completely different one when I was a high-school junior, and by the time I graduated I thought I was in love with another one yet."

"It sounds as if you should have accumulated a fairly good personal standard of comparison."

"Thanks. And what I feel for Linda Beauchamp—beautiful name, isn't it?"

"A very beautiful name. Fits the lady."

"Anyway, it feels different from anything I ever felt for the other three. Hey! Is that a light on in our basement?"

They had come in sight of the Pi Rho house.

"It certainly looks like one," said Clement. "They must be having a meeting of some kind."

"The I. C.?"

"Or some new committee. Probably private." The vampire never showed much interest in anything he knew he wasn't supposed to know.

"Well," Tony went on after another couple steps, "maybe we can get together sometime, compare notes about how a floater can know for sure when he's really in love."

"Tony, I'd appreciate combing your experience."

* * * *

"What's going on in the basement?" Tony asked when they got to the living room.

Spud looked up from his favorite wing chair before the fire. "Some kind of special I. C. meeting, I guess. Very hush-hush. All I know's, Gale's big brother Lance and his partner are down there with 'em. Got in this afternoon."

Whoever was sitting on the other side of the fire—Steve Wu by the sound of his voice—asked, "Why are FIDO men like nuns?"

"Because they travel in pairs," sang Randy Lundquist from the couch, where he lounged riffling the pages of a book. "Anybody have a clue why *Moby Dick's* supposed to be a good story?"

"I liked it," said Spud.

"The football hero likes it!" cried Steve. "Good enough recommendation for anybody, I guess."

"Can I cite you in my paper, Prexy?" Randy teased Spud.

"'F you like," the big senior answered absently, eying the bundle of animated fur that was scratching at his chair leg. "I think Noble's asking for somebody to take her outside again."

"Let me," said Clement. "I still need to wind down after that final dress rehearsal."

"So do I, a little," said Tony.

"You've already got your jacket off. Just sit down by the fire and relax." Stooping, Clement caught the growing puppy up in his arms and went to find her leash.

It should hang either from a hook beside one of the doors, or from a doorknob. This time it was on the kitchen doorknob, so that was where Clement took her out and where, eventually, her little deposit made to the soil bank, he brought her back in. The phone was chiming as he closed the kitchen door, and somehow as he jumped to answer it, the leash slipped through his fingers and the lively little dog was bounding over to investigate the basement door.

The basement door should probably have been shut, with a private meeting going on down there; but someone had left it partly open, and Clement saw Noble take advantage of that space, even as he reached the telephone.

He picked up the receiver. "'Lo, the Purple Rose."

"Joe there?"

"Joe who?"

"Joe...king!" Laughter. Could be the new frosh bros at Chi Rho Epsilon again.

"Ace, queen, jack, and the game," Clement replied. "Sorry, wrong number." Grinning to himself, he cradled the receiver and went after Noble. They pretty well gave her the run of the house, but right now she still had her leash on, and there were all kinds of things it could get caught on, especially in the basement. So he'd better find her and get it off, private meeting down there or not. At least the Meeting Room door ought to be shut.

It was, but Noble was sniffing and scratching around it and, as Clement stooped and unclipped the leash from her collar, words came through.

He shouldn't have listened. But he couldn't...*not* listen. He scooped Noble up and kept petting her to keep her quiet, and afterward he never remembered whether or not his earring had pinched him for eavesdropping.

"And you're sure Indradatt's at home tonight?"

"Unless he got an emergency call. Both of those doctors—Sharma and Shammari—are scheduled off duty tonight." That voice was Carl Avosso's.

"We aren't interested in Rabar al Shammari. He's exactly who he says he is. It's Dharmik Indradatt we're after, *alias* Pundarik Sharma."

"And his wife, Ganesa Asan, *alias* Kastha Sharma."

Professor Sharma—a *deathguard*? Oh, no, no, no!

Pater Fairchild was saying, "The opera rehearsal ought to be over shortly, if it is not already. It was to have begun at 1400, and I have rarely heard of a final dress rehearsal at this School of Music requiring more than six hours. Seven at the utmost."

And Dr. Sharma? Who had saved Carl's baby son? No, oh, no, this *couldn't* be right!

"You'll want a woman with you to help bring a woman in. Aren't you floaters happy you let me in on this?"

"Maybe that was *why* we let you in on the secret, Theda." So it *was* Keiko's old friend from Thelwell Hall days, who'd joined the Sigh sisters last year.

"Okay, men and lady, let's go. Me, Hartwick, M. Jones, and…let's see… Okay, how about we make it both Hartwicks in the first car. The rest of you divide yourselves into groups and we'll meet you at 1410 Anthony Drive."

"I believe you can rely on us for the remaining group divisions," said Pater Fairchild.

"Never doubted it. Let's see here…ten of you, better make it in three cars. One car somewhere as near as possible to the back door. Two cars, if possible, and you men inside be ready to move. Otherwise, park down the street. Let's go!" the stranger's voice repeated. Clement thought he had heard it before, somewhere, somewhen, but right now he was more concerned with getting out of sight behind the door when it opened.

In the light that showed through the crack between the open door and the door frame, he could see just enough of their faces…Theda, the brothers Hartwick, an older man whose face seemed to strike a chime somewhere, but Clement couldn't quite place it. He kept his hand gently cupped around Noble's jaws, hoping she didn't whine…

So far, she didn't. None of the four turned around for any reason. They passed by and headed for the stairs. Holding his breath, the vampire concentrated hard on their footfalls going up. Even if the fellows still in the Meeting Room didn't shut the door again while they were dividing up into their groups, maybe as soon as all of the first four were safely up and away, he could slip over to the stairs—

Noble whined. As Clement tried to readjust his hand, she shook her head free and yipped.

Several voices cried things like, "What was that?"

Clement broke for the stairs.

They stopped him right away. So much for vampire super-speed.

At least none of the first four had come back down. Maybe if he hadn't waited quite so long…

"Czarny!" said Pater Fairchild.

Maybe if he hadn't been holding the puppy as he tried to run, instinctively not dropping her on the concrete floor, consciously not squeezing… "Here," he said lamely, turning to Ramon—*Ramon!* Yes, Ramon was one of them. "Take her. Please."

Ramon took the puppy. Pater Fairchild said, "Bring him inside and close the door."

They did.

There should be ten of them, according to what the older man had said. Clement looked around. Pater Fairchild. Ramon. Carl Avosso. John Rogers. Joe Doe and Al Koby, Pete Temple and Augie Rasmussen. And Fred Fletcher and Stallion Drinkwater were the ones holding him. (No wonder their grips felt so tight.) Yes, ten.

"What have you heard?" asked Pater Fairchild.

Clement made the best attempt he could under pressure. Instead of answering the question, he tried explaining, "Noble slipped down here with her leash still on after her little walk. I had to get it off before—"

"That was not what I asked you, Czarny. What did you overhear?"

"A…I'm afraid, Pater, sir, some things I shouldn't have. That weren't meant for my ears. I'm sorry, sir, but you can hear more down here—even with the Meeting Room door closed—than you can ever hear upstairs."

"Czarny. With no more evasions. What, *exactly,* do you know?"

Fred twisted Clement's arm. Unnecessary. Questioned like this, vampires could either tell the exact truth, or say nothing at all, or lie and open themselves up to any kind of pain the interrogators wanted to apply from crosses and holy things, which Clement suspected could be worse for somebody like him than anything in your standard knotty-pine torture chamber. No other choice.

Clement decided on silence. Even though silence answered Pater Fairchild's question as well as they needed.

The house father nodded. "Rogers, Temple, Rasmussen, with me. You others, bind our vampire brother, gag him, and lock him in this room. Then, follow us. Use your own discretion in choosing your parties."

Ramon spoke. "Why not simply lock him in? Sir." The "Sir" was almost insolent.

"Oh, that's right, Mendoza. You were not a witness to what transpired the night of the attack on Czarny's life. How he persuaded sheriff, deputy, and most of his own fraternity brothers who were there present in the living room that it had been a mere bagatelle and no matter for legal action of any kind. Allow him means to summon assistance, and we may find most of our own house pitted against us."

"How do we know," Ramon drawled, "that Czarny is pitting himself against us?"

"I should think that much must be perfectly obvious from the fact that, having learned what he has clearly learned, he has voiced no spontaneous plea to join us. Gag him first," the Pater directed them, "and avoid looking him in the eye. But bear always in mind that he is your fraternity brother. Let him suffer no more discomfort than absolutely necessary. Remember that you are responsible for producing him whole and unharmed when tonight's work is over."

Then the house father left the Meeting Room with John, Pete, and Augie in his wake.

It was one thing for him to say, "Gag him and bind him." Another thing for them to do it, now that it wasn't a question of voluntary submission to fraternity hazing. Even with six of them—five, actually, since Ramon stood back the whole time keeping the wiggling, yapping puppy out of the way. But...so much for vampire super-strength. When Fred, Stallion, Joe, and Al were all four sitting on top of Clement—Stallion clamping his mouth shut with one hand—Carl and Ramon, still carrying the puppy, left to get the ropes and gag from the chest where they were stored between Midnight Hazes.

Ramon came back alone. "Carl has taken charge of returning Noble to the brothers upstairs," he explained, tossing down a choice of gags and supply of ropes. "Doe and Koby, do the work."

"Aww," said Fred. "How often do we get—"

"*You*, Fletcher, would be entirely capable of tying him up with so many tourniquets, and so would Drinkwater. As Pater Fairchild emphasized, our fraternity brother is to suffer no lasting damage, regardless of his convictions on any one particular subject, Tonight's work being over and done with, we will be responsible for producing him again safe and unharmed."

Clement still made it as hard as he could for them but, forbidden to do any actual tying, Fred and Stallion held him down, and they were the strongest of the four. In about ten minutes he lay bound, gagged, and panting.

Ramon had spread a sleeping bag out on the floor. "Move him onto this." When they had, he bent over and asked, "At need, can you breathe through that gag?"

Tempted to get a little something back by not responding at all, Clement felt his earring pinch, and nodded.

Ramon put an old but reasonably clean pillow under his head, dropped a blanket over him, murmured, "We will be back as soon as possible, little brother," and squeezed his right shoulder.

Then they all left, tabbing off the light and locking the door behind them. He heard the tumblers fall into place, then Joe asking, "Maybe we'd better bolt it, too?"

Ramon answered with a counter-question. "And whet the curiosity of anyone who may by some chance descend to the basement?"

Then there was silence. They had all left.

* * * *

Left him alone, gagged, bound hand and foot, helpless in the dark, in a locked room.

This time, a blindfold would have been superfluous. Even though the room really wasn't all that dark, to vampire eyes. Maybe not to anybody's eyes, with all that nightglow coming through the curtain across the window, high up there.

The binding and gagging were almost equally superfluous. Assuming that, "free of his limbs," he could have made enough noise to bring somebody downstairs, who would it be? Solly? Was probably all the way up in their room, combing the books. Spud? Was a close chum of Fred and Stallion, even if he didn't go along with them in everything and hadn't seemed to know anything about what was happening at tonight's meeting down here. Tony? Steve or Randy? Anyone else in the house? On the whole campus? In the whole town of Hodag Crossing?

Keiko. In the whole world, Clement thought, there was only one person who might understand him tonight. Maybe even forgive him. Keiko Kato. And…possibly, just possibly…the Pope. Who else? Nobody else. Nobody else in the world.

Wouldn't his attitude look as…outrageous, as unjust, as unrighteous to all the right-minded people in the world as it obviously did to all those who had been down here tonight? Val Saladin…Clement might have grinned, if not for the gag. I guess *this* would show Val what clay feet his idol has. It would surely end *that* problem, anyway.

Helpless, humiliated, and uncomfortable. Not that uncomfortable right now, except for the arm he was lying on…he should be able to roll around a little from time to time… Still, it'd probably get worse.

And there was no way he could wipe his nose. Helpless, humiliated, and uncomfortable.

Wait a minute! Why should *I* be the one to feel humiliated? Shouldn't all the humiliation go to those floaters who did this to me? Left me like this?

Wish-for-vengeance alert! Earring check. No, no pinching, no burning. Ring finger? Also feeling okay. At least two parts of his body felt comfortable. So that hadn't actually been a vengeful desire, just... Well, I'm not sure what. Maybe figuring out that I shouldn't feel like the humiliated one helped me forgive them all...at least as well as I can, right now...Ramon, too! Even Ramon!

No problems with my jewelry during the fight, either. Fight? Hard scuffle, at least. Yes, if we've established that vampire super-strength is as tall a tale as vampire hypnotic powers, at least I think I gave a fair accounting of myself on a purely human level. Five against one, after all. I really do *not* have any reason to feel humiliated about this.

Unless it's because of my attitude.

Why *didn't* I jump right in and volunteer to side with Pater Fairchild and those FIDO people and the rest of the brothers? The side of truth, justice, and the right-thinking way? Everyone knows that the death-guards—

Wait! Maybe it was all a gigantic mistake! How could they *know?*

That older man...the one Clement could...almost...place—Gale's brother's FIDO partner... Wait! That stranger who had come in on one of their earliest rehearsals in Foster Hall...yes! That was him!

And, somehow, it carried conviction. The FIDO man must have seen, back then...taken a month to make sure...

Clement choked back a sob, thought a second, decided what difference could it make, here and now, and he could always breathe through the gag if his nose clogged up, Ramon had made sure of that. So he sobbed. Professor Sharma! Professor Sharma—a deathguard! Professor Kastha Sharma had been Ganesa Asan, Kali Camp *deathguard!*

Wait...wait...wait. *Had been.* Wasn't the tense important? Weren't religion and our whole modern system of court justice based on the idea of *reforming* criminals? Hadn't the Sharmas shown that they *were* reformed? Hadn't they lived good lives here in Hodag Crossing, done good work, benefited the whole community? What was the good of going after people when they were *already* reformed? Didn't it make hypocrisy out of the whole doggone legal and religious system?

"Vengeance is Mine, I will repay..." A lot of people seem to take that as a commandment for *us* to exact justice, here in this life. Doesn't it really mean the opposite? If there's any vengeance that has to be taken, isn't God commanding us to leave it to Divine justice?

But "an eye for an eye, a tooth for a tooth..." And that really means, no more punishment than in fair and exact proportion to the injury. And how could any one deathguard—how could all the deathguards put together—ever possibly be punished enough for all those millions of deaths, all that incredible suffering in the Kali Camps and Eugenics Farms?

And now his earring was starting to feel like a red-hot bolt through his earlobe, his fraternity ring throbbing on his finger, his cross starting to burn even through his shirt and undershirt.

"Father, forgive them, they know not what they do." He couldn't actually whisper it, because of the gag, so he thought it, over and over, until the pains in his ear and finger subsided and the cross stopped feeling as though it might set his shirt on fire (which it never actually had).

And that establishes that, whatever is really right and just here in this plane of existence, it can't be for a vampire like me to judge. A vampire *has* to forgive, no matter what. No matter, even, who it is who suffered the wrong.

And that was maybe why vampires weren't fit to live with normal, healthy, right-minded people.

One advantage he had. If he could only have used it. If he could have gotten back upstairs in time. Professor Fairchild and the FIDO men and the others thought Professor and Dr. Sharma were at their own home at 1410 Anthony Drive, near the hospital. They didn't know about Dr. al Shammari's engagement dinner party at 278 Traut Road, on the other side of town. So it might take them a little while to find the Sharmas...

Which meant Clement would lie here that much longer, bound and gagged and getting more uncomfortable by the heartbeat.

All right. *He* wasn't in ultimate danger. Not like the poor Sharmas. He wasn't in danger of anything except being bound and gagged alone in the dark...

You'd think Carl would have known about the engagement party. Being married to Nurse Wanamaker's sister, and Dr. al Shammari intending to become Carl's own brother-in-law. But Carl hadn't said anything about it. Had he forgotten in the excitement? Or had he deliberately not said anything? He'd never come back in here, either, after leaving the room with Ramon to get the ropes. Could it be...?

Better not even think that way. If Carl had suddenly gone AWOL, surely they would have made enough fuss about it, that Clement should have heard something, even down here. Unless they didn't want to alert anyone else… No! Better not even think that way. If the Sharmas are going to get any warning at all, it's up to me…

Only, *how?*

As long as he wasn't about to risk shouting and banging for help, and be shunned for his pains by every right-thinking brother in the house, he might as well try to make himself a little less uncomfortable. He started chewing at his gag.

Let's see…what was that plan I thought out two years ago, riding bound and gagged in the car trunk? Blindfolded, too, that time, superfluous as it was… Use my fangs to chew through the gag, wiggle my legs through the circle of my arms to get my wrists in front…

Why not just lie here and relax…as well as I *can* relax…and let things take their course? I'm helpless, nobody expects me to do anything. In fact, the forces of righteousness expect me *not* to do anything. Don't *want* me to do anything. They'll have me loose by morning, in plenty of time to rest up comfortably for the Opening Night performance…

The Opening Night performance! The opera! The show Professor Sharma had directed him in all this last month!

Even as he found himself sobbing again, he discovered that, hardly aware of having done it, he had wiggled the blanket off his body, wriggled his legs almost through the circle of his arms…

Being in good condition, with swimmer's muscles, had to help. Maybe a lot.

Having sharp fangs helped, too. For once.

His legs were through! His hands were in front. There! The gag was chewed through! He fumbled it out of his mouth, found an almost-dry spot to blow his nose in, clumsily but adequately…then got to work chewing the rope around his wrists.

He nicked his skin and flesh quite a lot. Fortunately, he managed to avoid the veins. But there was a fair bit of surface bleeding. His own blood, when he swallowed it, gave him nothing but empty calories. But that was as good right now as sugar cubes for a normal person—quick energy—so he licked greedily the whole time he chewed at the rope…

And was free!

Free of his limbs, anyway. As soon as he had the rope off his wrists, it took only a little extra fumbling to get it off his ankles as well.

He massaged his wrists and ankles as thoroughly as he could. It took time, and did nothing to stop the minor bleeding at his wrists; but by all he understood, it was probably essential, after being tied up like that. Pulling his shirt cuffs down as far as they would go over his wrists, he stood and worked feeling back into his legs by walking to the light button and tabbing it on. Not that he needed the illumination, but it made the room seem slightly more cheerful, and he needed cheerful. He knew it would be useless to try the door, but some need in the human psycho-mystique made him try it anyway. It was useless.

He turned and considered the window.

In their confidence that he was tied up until they untied him, they had left the long meeting table and its dozen chairs in the room. Why hadn't they tied him up to one of those chairs? Seemed almost as if... Well, if he stood on a chair—better, if he dragged the table over and stood on that—being as tall as he was, he could not only open the glass pane but probably hoist himself high enough to crawl out.

He dragged the table over—a good, solid old pine one. He jumped up on it, drew the curtain back from the window, and found himself staring into a face.

The face of October Bradley.

CHAPTER 20

IMMEDIATELY FOLLOWING

"M. Czarny?" said the co-owner of B & Z, Good Games & Fine Jewelry. His voice came through muffled by the window pane.

Clement flipped the catch and swung the window open. "M. Bradley? What—?"

"Call me October." The shop man's eyes seemed to look beyond Clement into the rest of the room. "Are you wanting to get out?"

"There's a storm window. I didn't remember that."

"Just two minutes." Already October was twisting the fasteners. It couldn't have been much longer than the promised two minutes before he had the storm window out and lying on the dead grass. "Here," he went on, reaching through the open space for Clement's hands. "Lord, what happened to your wrists?"

"My own fangs. Useful for chewing ropes off, if you don't mind a few nicks."

"It must be a long story," said the older man. "But first things first."

Even for a floater as thin as Clement, the basement window was a tight squeeze...but worth the effort. He was glad of October's help, and told him so as soon as he was safely outside.

"Any time," said the shop man. "My car's over there." He pointed to the curb.

"Is that M. Zimmerman in it?"

"Yes. She insisted on coming. Call her Aurea."

"Call me Clement." As they trotted over the lawn to the dark Rockne, Clement went on, "But how? Why?"

"You called. I came."

In his astonishment, the vampire halted. "I *called*? When? How?"

"About...half an hour? ago. I can't explain it. The sense just came over me, 'Young Czarny's—Clement's—in trouble. He needs help, right now.' So we hopped in the car, and I followed the...I guess you might say, vibrations in the air." October shrugged and repeated, "I can't explain it. I just *knew.*"

Would that have been about the time Clement had wondered who in all Hodag Crossing would even be willing to come to his assistance, if they knew? "It must be a long story," he said as they started running again.

"We'll have to take turns," October replied, "when we have the time."

They reached the car, where Aurea sat waiting behind the wheel. October eased Clement into the front rider's seat and took the back seat himself. "Where to?" said Aurea.

"278 Traut Road," Clement answered at once, then hesitated. "But if you knew why, you might not want—"

"First things first!" said October. "In this case, getting there."

"278 Traut Road," Aurea repeated, putting the Rockne in gear and pulling smoothly away from the curb. "That's in the W.I.N. east of campus, isn't it?"

"Not far from here," October agreed from the back.

The W.I.N. was the "War Intermission Neighborhood": moderately large single-family homes built in the 1930's, still looking pretty new and well kept up, though the saplings planted to line the streets had grown into sizable shade trees.

"May I ask what's at 278 Traut Road?" Aurea added.

Clement sighed and shuddered. He *had* to tell these good people. He couldn't risk letting them soil their own consciences.

He could see in the rear view mirror that October was eying him intently, or at least the eying the space above his empty collar—if his face had reflected, he guessed he might not have seen the older man at all. Aurea was keeping her eyes on the road, but clearly listening with both ears.

"The Sharmas are there," Clement said shakily. "Dr. and Professor Sharma. It turns out that they're…deathguards. From one of the Indian Kali Camps."

The car slowed. Didn't stop. Slowed.

"And…?" October said noncommittally.

"I…only… There are FIDO people in town to arrest them. I only thought…maybe…someone should warn them. Before the FIDO men find them."

The car speeded up again. Going, maybe a little faster than before, in the same direction.

October said, "And that would be why they had you locked in down there? And tied up, if I understand what you hinted about the blood on your wrists."

Clement nodded, remembered the older man might not be able to see his nod so well from back there, and said, "Yes."

"Glad I sensed your call," the shopkeeper replied simply.

"It's like a miracle! Are you people angels? Or something?"

They seemed to exchange glances via the rear view mirror, and both of them chuckled a little. "Hardly angels!" said Aurea. "No, I wouldn't call us angels. Would you, Octie?"

"Just a couple of imperfect floaters who know all too well what it is to be flawed," her husband agreed. "Badly flawed. Are we getting close?"

"This is Traut Road now."

In front of 278, she pulled to the curb and stopped.

"Thanks again," Clement told them gratefully. "You don't have to come in. Or even wait." Trying not to sound rude, just offering them a chance to bow out.

"We'll wait," said October. "We still have those long stories to tell each other, you and me."

* * * *

Dr. al Shammari and M. Wanamaker answered the door chime together. They looked as though they had been crying. Clement wondered whether they had been able to announce their engagement yet.

"M. Czarny?" said Clement's doctor.

"You're too late," said the nurse. "They're gone."

"Gone?" Clement repeated. He seemed to feel his heart thudding in his stomach.

"Carl was here," M. Wanamaker explained. "He warned them. In gratitude for Dr. Sharma saving Milly and the baby last year."

"The FIDO men and your fraternity brothers," said Dr. al Shammari, "have not yet come. I think that for a time they must have suspected me, also. Or why would Carl be so careful to assure us they know that I am who I have always said I am?"

Clement breathed more easily. Carl must have slipped out when he took the puppy upstairs. Maybe Ramon had even covered for him, said something like, Let him stay out of it now, brothers. This physician saved his wife and son, after all. "Where have they gone?" the vampire asked. "Do you know?"

"They said," Dr. al Shammari answered soberly, "that suicides can be most easily and quickly arranged at Hellmouth Amusement Park. For a high fee, but they would have no more use for the money in this life."

* * * *

"Hellmouth Park!" Aurea's voice sounded…white.

"Can you…" Clement went on. "Could you just take me back to the Pi Rho house? Or I can walk there from here, and maybe borrow a car from one of the brothers who doesn't know what's going on."

"No," October said firmly. "We're taking you there. All the way. Inside, if we have to. If it comes to that."

"Oh, October…" said his wife. "Do you really think…?"

"Maybe it isn't quite so bad since they rebuilt it."

"I was there in 1948," said Clement. "The year I turned sixteen. It was pretty bad then, and that was years after it'd been rebuilt. But I've got to try and stop them from committing suicide. If I can."

"I agree," said October. "Clement, get in."

"But…" said Aurea.

"Honey. Remember Rodney? Jason James? Poor Skipper? Cassandra?"

"You're right." Aurea nodded. "*No one* deserves to die in *there*. We've got to try to stop them, if we can. We've just got to make one stop first."

"Why?"

"For a new fuel cell. It's about an hour's drive, isn't it?"

"We'd better do it faster than that," said October. "If we can."

"We still can't do it without fuel."

They stopped at the Shale station at the west edge of town. October went in for the fuel cell and finally came out again with it and a large canvas bag. Also several receipt coupons for Aurea.

"I hope we'll still be around to use them," she said. "After tonight."

"That's why I made sure to get them. It's like a promise to ourselves, Aurie, that we *will* still be around to someday own that lamp you're saving these up for. Here, Clement. Maybe we'd both better get in the back seat."

Once there, October pulled an old Penguins jacket out of the canvas bag. "They have a rummage bin in there, and I thought you'd probably want to get out of or cover up as much vampire costume as you can. But first, let me see your wrists. I also got some bandages."

Once Clement's wrists were bandaged, and they were well out of town, October said, "Well, maybe we'd better trade those long stories before things get too much rougher. Clement, you go first."

Clement didn't really want to, so he told it as simply and briefly as he could, skipping blow-by-blow descriptions of the scuffling and all of his tied-up-alone meditations except for the few minutes he had wondered who he could even consider calling on for help.

"That must have been it," said Aurea.

"Yes," October agreed.

"'It,' how?" asked Clement. "That doesn't really answer anything for me. Is it time for your long story now?"

October sighed. "Well...I'm afraid it may go back to our experience in the old Hellmouth Park, the one that burned down. I don't think I've ever told this before, not even to my therapists except as if it had been dream squibbets...maybe it was...but I've been trying too hard to forget it all—"

"If it was a dream," said Aurea, "it was one we both had together, at the same time, detail for detail as far as we can tell. And the sooner told, the sooner done with for tonight."

"Yes. Well, Clement, you already know we were there that night, Aurea and I, the night it burned. At a party in one of the subbasement so-called party rooms..."

"It was supposed to have been a costume party," Aurea said into her husband's long pause.

"Yes. Anyway. I think I told you that I had on a vampire costume. A really cheap one. And...at midnight...our costumes sort of...*imprinted* on us, somehow."

"Imprinted?" Clement asked.

"For our sins." October gave a sheepish, shaky grin. "For about six hours or so of my life, I was a vampire, too. Not one like you. Your trick of coping with crosses and things by keeping your conscience clear—I wish I'd known it then. Even the X's in the door numbers hit me."

"He finally had to lie down and let me pull him past those doors," said Aurea. "He had the super-strength and almost supernatural powers of recovery and all that, though. He really was your stereotypical movie Dracula."

"Maybe because we were in Hellmouth. And back then, I didn't know there was any other kind. Of course, the good conscience trick would've been a little late for me, anyway. My conscience already having that big one on it—"

"Not so very big," Aurea objected. "Yours was human weakness."

"And fantasizing about yanking people's heads off to lap up the gushers?"

"That was only after your costume imprinted, and it made you all the more heroic for keeping it from anything more than fantasizing," she said definitively. "My sin was avarice and deliberate malice."

"Don't be too hard on yourself, love. 'Be to yourself as you would to others,' as Shakespeare or the Bible or someone like that says somewhere. Maybe it was Dante."

Clement put in, awed, "*You* were the ones in all those tales? The angels in ragged costumes or whoever it was who got all those people out to safety?"

"Could have been, I guess," October admitted, more like a forced confession than anything else. "Don't let it get any farther than us three."

Aurea said, "I'd been wearing an old sequined green dress and a ton or so of jewelry, and it turned me into a kind of small dragon. Thank God, we changed back at dawn!"

"And those others you mentioned? Skipper and Jason James and…"

"Weren't so lucky," October replied in a way that said, Let's just stop talking about it. "That's why we've got to try to get the Sharmas out of there. Whether they thank us or not. Any kind of human War Crimes Trial justice has to be better than what happened to the other people at our so-called party." He sighed again, shook his head, and asked, "What happened to you, in there? Or do you mind telling us?"

"Oh. They tried to recruit me as an employee. They seemed to want a real vampire on their payroll…if they have anything as mundane as a payroll. They even tried to convince me I'd already made some kind of verbal contract with them. Their…efforts at persuasion involved a Dante's Devil kind of head rising out of an underground lake of blood that smelled…really sickening, even for a vampire like me. Fortunately, I was still almost two weeks shy of sixteen, so they finally had to throw me back. Or, it could all have been a nightmare," Clement finished. "I mean, a dream kind of nightmare."

"Or maybe not," said October. "No, it doesn't sound like rebuilding changed the place too much, after all."

Aurea said, "I think there's a car following us. Should I pull over and see if it passes?"

"No!" said October. "If they *are* following us, we want to get there first."

Clement risked turning around for a look out the back window. His overworked heart plummeted again. It looked like Ramon's Chevrolet Victory, and it was speeding up. He hunched down in his seat, doing his best to hide behind October and not be seen.

The dark Buick overtook the Rockne, passed, sped on.

"Well, it wasn't following us," Aurea observed.

"Let's hope it isn't headed for the same place we are," October said grimly.

Clement feared it had to be. Hadn't there been a dark car parked a short distance away from Dr. al Shammari's house on Traut Road? That he hadn't even looked at twice, at the time? Why hadn't he? He thought he should probably say something to October and Aurea about his fears.

But he didn't, not yet, even though his doubt seemed to make his earring pinch a little. He could have been wrong about whose car it was. And it had to be his doubts that made his earring pinch, regardless of whether or not it really was Ramon's Chevy.

* * * *

Dolores Wanamaker sighed and leaned back heavily on her future husband's arm. "Oh, Rabar! Do you think that could possibly be the last of them?"

He began counting on his fingers. "First, there was Carl. He warned us that others would surely come. As many, perhaps, as three cars. Then came young M. Czarny, my own patient, in whom my interest is so great. There were two, I think, who waited in the car which brought him. Then soon after him came M. Mendoza, but where the car which brought him was, I did not see."

"I saw a dark one, parked pretty far down the block. I don't know if there were any other people in it."

"Well! Then some minutes later, come these four people together, the two men from FIDO and two students, who ask the same questions over again, but repeat their assurances that they know who I am and do not any longer suspect me."

"Thank God for that!" Dolores sighed again.

"M. Czarny, M. Mendoza, and the FIDO men, three cars. And then at last came a fourth, whom we did not any longer expect, the good Professor Fairchild with two frosh under his wing and a young man, I think perhaps an older student, waiting behind the wheel of his car. So that is four cars, one more than the three Carl promised us. Yes, now we should at last be safe."

"Oh, I hope so! Rabar, is it going to be like this all the rest of our lives?"

"For the rest of our lives, I think we should have only the worries of medicine and of the hospital. Which are small next to these."

"And worries that we're used to." The nurse sat subdued in the doctor's arm a few moments longer. Then, all at once, she began to sob. "How? Rabar, they seemed like such *good* people! *How?*"

"What I regret the most," he answered slowly, "is that way I argued with him, how much I wished that all the records of those experiments which were done in the Eugenics Farms and Kali Camps should be opened for the medical research of the world. Always he cried no, it would be wrong, unforgivable, almost as wicked as those experiments themselves. Dolores, my Dolores, how I must have opened old wounds in him! How I must have hurt him with my thoughtless philosophy talk!

My trusting that our being almost sent to one ourselves, my poor dear Fariza and I, gave me a right to talk this philosophy."

* * * *

The first car to reach Hellmouth Park was the 1946 Chevrolet Victory. Ramon scrutinized the area with his superb night vision, circling the car park with special care to make sure his was indeed the first. In parking, he so angled his vehicle as to give himself alone a clear view of the lolling artificial tongue that made a pathway to the entrance.

In any case, it was not long before his two sophomore charges napped. In Ramon's observation of life, too much excitement could sometimes have that effect, the more so on the young, as soon as activity eased for any length of time. Besides, he was humming them a lullaby.

His little frat brother had been too quick to shrug off the power of suggestion as only another Lurid Legend of the vampire. True, Clement's own chosen way of coping offered limited scope for the power to bend and direct the human mind...

And so Clement had escaped both his bonds and his makeshift dungeon cell in the Pi Rho basement. And, somehow, gathered a pair of helpers to his cause. Ramon had seen those two around town and at assorted school shows and games, but never closely enough to know them by name. They appeared to be good people, and probably reasonably competent. Someday, soon perhaps, when tonight's business was safely put behind them all, he thought that he would tell Clement he had already been quite aware he was in that dark Rockne when the Chevrolet Victory passed it. He would share with him what pride, what satisfaction, he—Ramon—took in his little brother's courage and resourcefulness.

Meanwhile, in addition to everything else, Ramon had two soph brothers to safeguard. Sophomores were still very young. Fairchild believed Carl to be with them—probably, in fact, considered Ramon more Carl's assistant than otherwise.

Fairchild and John Rogers had already been gone, their white Buick the second car to leave the Pi Rho house after that of the FIDO agents, when Carl whispered to Ramon that he could not allow the man who had saved his son Carl, Jr., and perhaps his wife as well, to be taken this way by surprise; that he happened to know where the Sharmas really were this evening, he was going to warn them, and would Ramon cover for him? Ramon would, in return for the secret of where they really were and the promise not to use this knowledge until after Carl had had his chance to warn them.

So that when, eventually, he and the sophomores reached the Sharmas' home and found no one there—even the earlier hunters had clearly given up and continued their search elsewhere—Ramon covered his lack of surprise, and proposed trying the Hindu physician's friend, the Muslim physician. Where, humming the sophs into a drowse, he parked some distance down the block and indulged in that ironically named exercise, a stakeout. And, having seen Clement consult with the newly engaged medical couple and take his departure, had gone up in his turn to learn what his little brother had learned.

And now, an hour's drive later, he sat in his second stakeout of that night, watching, waiting, and from time to time humming lullabies. Sleep, sophomores, sleep...

Here came the dark Rockne now. It pulled into a space a dozen cars distant from Ramon's old Victory. The driver got out—a plumpish, tallish older woman with rather dark skin and silvering red hair. And her backseat rider, a man about her own age, balding on top, potbelly perhaps a little larger, proportionately, than that of Lance Hartwick's senior FIDO partner. A pleasant enough looking couple, this woman and man. Clement should be emerging on the other side of the Rockne... Ah! Here he came now, atypically dressed in a blue Penguins jacket, looking sharply around, looking... Let your gaze slide right over this car, little brother...

Apparently, it did. After a hushed exchange with his new friends, none of them sparing another glance in Ramon's direction, the three proceeded to the red tongue walkway.

Ramon sat back to continue his wait. He had yet to be inside Hellmouth "Amusement" Park, but despite the rumors, as sterling a young man as Clement could be in little more danger there, especially with so staid and respectable-seeming an older couple at his side, than he had been when bound and alone in the locked basement Meeting Room of the Pi Rho house.

And neither Clement Czarny nor the deathguards themselves constituted Ramon Mendoza's first and foremost concern this night. So, he waited.

* * * *

"I don't think they've rebuilt it *exactly* the way it was before the fire," said Aurea. "Shouldn't there have been a ticket booth at the door?"

"I think that was somewhere farther inside," October answered. "In the middle of those flames. Or just past them. Darnit, I never thought I'd have any reason to try and remember details like that!"

"Clement," Aurea went on, "you're the one who's been here since the new park was opened."

"There's a thing in the middle of these fake flames," Clement remembered, "where you feed your money into a statue of Cerberus before going on. It's supposed to be honor system, more or less. But no one under sixteen years old is allowed inside the main building—"

"Supposedly," said Aurea.

"Supposedly. Well, I wasn't sixteen yet, and I'd already been a vampire for several years, so the 'Not Invited In' taboo kept me from getting any farther."

"Some of the old vampire lore applies to you," October observed.

"When there are that many legends," said Clement, "a few of them almost have to have some basis in fact. I've been figuring out which ones since I was thirteen."

The "flames" of the entrance maze were a combination of movie projections and distorting mirrors that reflected back the screen images. The effect was supposed to make visitors feel like lost souls seeing crowds of other lost souls bumbling around. It was a good special effect. One part of Clement's mind wondered whether it could be adapted to the stage. Meanwhile, he was morbidly fascinated by the way that, to his eyes, one of the "lost souls" was an empty but animated set of clothes bouncing around through distortion after distortion. Not really a vampire uniform any longer. His cape was still in the Pi Rho basement, where they'd stripped it off when they tied him up. Every accessory he could easily and decently remove, he had, except his jewelry—*that* hardly fit the vampire stereotype anyway. The blue and white Penguins jacket covered his white dress shirt, and black trousers were always pretty anonymous by themselves. Still, he'd been in mufti that earlier time, too…

"Aurie," October asked anxiously, "and Clement. Can you see my reflection?"

"Just a minute," Clement replied. "It's all… Yes! Yes, there are you are!" He pointed to one of the mirrors.

"I see us, all three!" Aurea added on a note of triumph.

"That's good." October sighed in relief. "I don't."

"Do you see mine?" Clement wanted to know.

"I see your clothes," said October. "Just your clothes, not you. I can't even see my own clothes, so naturally I was afraid…"

"Then yours has got to be a psychomystical trick," Clement said. "About yourself. As for me, you're seeing my clothes the way I'm seeing them."

"I think I see the coin machine," said Aurea. "Over there—no, it's gone again."

"Blame mazes," said October.

"But there was someone," she insisted, "back in 1940. Not just an honor-system coin machine—some real demon or person in a demon suit, standing there to look at our costumes and choose who they'd give those special-party passes to…"

"Maybe that was only on certain nights," said October. "We were there near Hallowe'en."

"I was there on Walpurgis," said Clement. "The end of April." April. He thought this was the first time she'd come into his thoughts since he had Noble the puppy out for a little walk, when things still seemed normal.

Aurea said, "But somehow I can't see coming in this way when it's a question of buying the park's suicide services."

"You chimed?" said a deep bass voice.

Where had *she* come from? A bearded but obviously female demon in stretchy, clinging, luridly glittery crimson skintights stood before them, twirling her pitchfork and puffing away on a blood-red cigar.

Giving Clement a nudge, October held his left hand up behind his back so the younger man could see his crossed fingers, and asked the demon, "Did I say the magic words?"

The demon touched one of her horns and nodded. "We always have to interpret any call on our suicide services as an intention to make a deal with the Devil."

October was clutching hands with Aurea—Clement hadn't seen which of them reached for the other first—but he turned around and looked at Clement. "Still sure you want to go through with this, son?"

Clement guessed what the older man was doing: seizing the chance to learn right away where the Sharmas might be in this huge building. They had worried over the problem most of the way here. At least nine subbasement levels' worth, at least two hundred and thirty-four rooms, access probably limited or even restricted to certain "privileged" guests, and the last known suicide here had been in one of the restaurants above ground in the demon's head itself. "If there's any lying to be done," October had made Clement promise, "leave it to Aurea and me. We've probably got a little more wiggle room that way. At least, assuming we stay ourselves."

So far, Clement had seen no change in either of his friends. And his earring and fraternity ring were still pinching a little from—he guessed—his keeping quiet in the car about maybe recognizing Ramon's Chevy following and passing them. Under the circumstances, wasn't not speaking out to your allies about any and every possible danger, as good as duplicity?

"A deal with the Devil," October was repeating. "All right, take us where we can bargain."

The demon giggled. For so deep a speaking voice, she had an astonishingly high-pitched giggle. "Like you'll have any more use for tridollars?"

"You accept cash?" Aurea sounded surprised.

"Hellmouth Park operates on the bad old temporal plane, M. Lostsoul. Sure, we can always use a little more root of all evil for our day-to-day operating expenses. But you, once you've shuffled off this mortal coil…" Another high-pitched, grating giggle.

October said, "There are always heirs. Now. Do we have to deal directly with *you?*"

"I like your attitude, M. Lostsoul. Come on. Lemme take you to our leader."

October and Aurea had said that, during their ordeal here the night of the fire, they'd been told on strong authority that most of the Hellmouth Park employees were simple, ordinary people who had no idea it was anything but a plain old job in fancy costume, and honestly thought the place was elaborately, pretentiously harmless. But a few of them seemed to be actual demons of Hell itself, the real Hell. And whether this one was human or demon, no one involved in the assisted-suicide service was exactly innocent.

But who really *was* innocent? In all the world? Clement wondered as he followed along where the demon led them, trying to memorize every turn of every corridor.

They reached a wide door between an elevator and a stairwell. A door that looked like clear glass with flames burning inside. Surely, another movie projection. And yet it looked incredibly realistic, and when the demon tabbed a button on it, her finger sizzled.

Am I dreaming again? Clement thought. Maybe we're all dreaming. Maybe it's those hallucinogenic fumes some floaters say this park pumps through the ventilation shafts. We'll have to compare notes, when we get out of here. I hope we get out of here. Let me keep my mouth shut so nobody sees my fangs.

The demon nodded. "His Infernal Majesty was elsewhere for a few moments, but he's ready to see you now." She turned the doorknob with another sizzling sound, swung the door open, and stepped inside.

Clement hardly knew what he expected, but it wasn't what he and his friends saw: a large room that could have been the comfortable office of any rich business executive in any big city. And the person who sat behind the desk could have been any rich business executive who worked out regularly at his gym. His Infernal Majesty, if that was who he really was, didn't even have horns, only two silver streaks running up through his well-combed brown hair.

"Come in, come in," he said pleasantly. Even his voice was moderate. "Zilda, feel free to close the door and wait outside."

Without a word, the demon obeyed.

For a moment, everyone seemed to be waiting for someone else to speak first. Clement wondered what October was planning to say, tried to think what he himself would say if he had to begin, with the Prince of Darkness—or chief executive demon, or whoever it was—directing that tolerant, slightly amused gaze at him. It was worse than dreaming you were onstage starring in something and didn't know your lines or what the play was or even enough of the plot to improvise. And maybe naked into the bargain.

It was Aurea who finally broke the silence. "How do you do that fiery effect with your door?"

"Like every magician, we guard the secrets of our illusions." The executive lit a cigarette in a long, blood-red holder, took a puff, and blew a smoke ring. The tobacco seemed to have a faintly sulfuric smell. "But they *are,* indeed, mere illusions. That, I promise you."

"And, of course, we can trust your promises completely." October didn't sound convinced. "And the suicides you arrange—are they illusions, too?"

The executive smiled cordially. "The deaths are quite real. Most of our ultimate clients, however, opt to avail themselves of a certain amount of illusion in the manner of their departure, or the disposal of their mortal remains, or both. It comes with the service we provide. But now for *my* question. Which, or how many of you, desire this service?"

"None of us three," October replied, to Clement's relief.

"Oh?" said the executive. "May I ask, why not?"

"If anything we said gave that impression," October went on, ignoring the executive's last question, "I'm sorry. The truth is, we learned some friends of ours came here tonight for that service, and there's something important we need to ask them before they go. Mundane business. But we need it. As long as we're still going to be sticking around a few more years in the mundane world."

The executive puffed his cigarette a moment or two in silence before saying, "I won't pretend not to know about whom you speak. We have only two here tonight for our assisted suicide service. And, yes, it was an unscheduled arrival, so they could well have left questions of mundane importance behind them in their haste.

"Nor," he went on, "will I inquire more closely as to the nature and subject matter of your particular questions. You probably do not wish to tell me, and I would probably find them boring. In our estimation, these two have even stronger reason than most to be done with all that.

We applauded their wisdom, and are doing our utmost to accommodate them."

"Are we too late?" cried Aurea.

"No, as far as I am aware, not yet. At the same time, they most expressly requested their demise to be kept strictly private." The executive finished his cigarette, stubbed it out in a ruby-red ashtray, removed the stub from the holder and dropped it in the ashes. "Well, I shall compromise this far. I shall allow you three into the subbasements. If you can find their room in good time, you may ask them whatever you wish. Here. You will need the key." He reached into his desk drawer, seemed to consult some record he had there, and finally brought out a key. It had an identifying tag, which he carefully removed before setting the naked key down on his desk for October.

"Thanks," said the games man. "We'd also like a free pass, to make sure you people let us out again afterward. A group pass will be fine."

The executive chuckled. "My, but you have a low opinion of me." He sounded greatly complimented.

"Take it any way you like, but let us have that pass. Along with the key and any other keys we may need to get back out."

"You will need only the one. Any fingerprint will tab any elevator button, and all the stair doors open freely from either side." The executive winked. "National Fire-Safety Guiderules. But I admire your precautionary wisdom, needless though it might be." Pulling a green plastic card out of his desk drawer, he laid it on top of his desk, beside the key.

"Thanks," October repeated, picking them both up, looking them over, and pocketing them. "How many tridols do we owe you?"

The executive gave October a very close, hard look. Then his eyes turned toward Aurea. Clement tried to stand as much as he could behind them, out of the way of that executive's piercing gaze.

At last the executive looked away again and waved his hand. "The clients with whom you hope to have a few parting words have already paid us very well for our services. Consider your efforts here tonight included as part of the package, and may we hope to serve you at some point in the future."

"We can't stop anybody from hoping," said October.

* * * *

Once alone in the stairwell, just the three of them, he staggered a little.

"Octie, you were wonderful!" Aurea whispered, hugging him.

He squeezed and kissed her before stepping back, running a shaky hand over his bald spot, and saying, a lot more sincerely than he ever had in the executive's office, "Thanks, Aurie. Aurea, thank you. But… let's see, over two hundred rooms to try this key in… We'd better start looking."

* * * *

Seven minutes after Ramon's protege and his duo had disappeared down the red tongue into the gaping Hellmouth, Gale Hartwick's indigo Buick Eagle pulled into the parking lot, to disgorge the four who had left before Clement was discovered: both Hartwick brothers, Theda Jones, and the older FIDO agent.

"'S up?" Doe mumbled, awakening.

"Reinforcements have arrived, bro. Wait here."

"On, no, y' don't! Hey, Al, wake up! Before they try an' get away with leavin' us out of it."

Ramon smothered a sigh. Having them sleep safely through his absence would have been expecting too much. And, once awake, he doubted very much they could have been trusted to remain in the car unsupervised. "Hurry along, then," he said aloud.

The FIDO foursome stood near their car in a cluster which, though all remained upright, otherwise reminded Ramon strongly of a football team huddling during the big game. He soon reached them, both sophomores not so much in tow as bouncing ahead.

"Mendoza!" Lancelot Hardwick sang out from his vantage of superior age—superior by approximately seven years, the classic run of the statute of limitations (save that, as Fairchild was so fond of pointing out, there was no statute of limitations on murder). "Glad you waited for us."

"More of a stakeout, watchfully awaiting developments."

"And?" asked Maklowski.

Ramon shook his head. "I saw nothing of our common quarry. Nor of any of our comrades in the chase, until your arrival."

"Where's Carl?" asked Theda.

"Avosso," Ramon answered smoothly, "begged to opt out of the actual arrest, in delicacy for the fact that Indradatt, acting as Dr. Sharma, saved his son and, perhaps, his wife. You, I take it, must have visited Dr. al Shammari soon after I did."

Maklowski nodded. "We found out the Sharmas were there when we looked for him at the hospital."

"We'd've beaten you to Shammari's place," said the elder Hartwick brother, "if Mak here hadn't insisted on stopping in the hospital coffee shop."

"Hey," the older partner parried, "a little extra quick energy never hurt anybody at times like this. Pretty big place to comb," he went on, eying Hellmouth Park.

"So it would appear." Ramon eyed it as well. "I must confess that, despite its presence almost in my backyard, figuratively speaking, I have never been inside."

"We have!" Doe piped up proudly.

"So have my partner here and I," said Maklowski. "Last month, just long enough for a look at where Blazhenov bit it."

"We witnessed that," Koby said, sounding even prouder than had his fellow sophomore.

"My first and only time," Maklowski went on. "But I think you talked about visiting the place in your student days, didn't you, Hartsie?"

"Several times." Pride was running very thick in this intrepid band of hunters.

"I've been here two or three times," Jones volunteered.

"Likewise," said the younger Hartwick.

Ramon looked at Maklowski. "We seem to be the virgins here. You less so than I, brief though your single earlier visit may have been. I was about to propose that we divide our forces so as to comb the place more quickly. Might I suggest, say…Jones, you could serve as M. Maklowski's guide, and he as your muscle of authority. Hartwick the younger, Doe, and Koby, suppose you three reconnoiter together. Leaving you, Hartwick the elder, to guide me, the complete novice."

None of them showed any sign of recognizing how Ramon had maneuvered them to his own design. Maklowski even said, "Sounds good. Any ideas where we should start?"

"Last suicide happened in the Blue Blazes Room," Doe offered brightly.

"Then why don't you three investigate the center floors?" Ramon sent a wink to Hartwick the younger, signifying that the sophomores were in his safekeeping now. "It also strikes me that carnival rides might offer suicidal possibilities in even the best amusement parks."

"So," said Jones, "we can give the devil's cranium a check-out, M. Maklowski and I."

"Where and when do we meet up and compare notes?" said Maklowski.

Watching the ear elevators, Ramon inquired, "Is the cranium level accessible from the interior?"

Several at once answered that it was.

"Then let us reassemble there in, say…"

"Half an hour?" suggested Hartwick the younger.

"Better make it forty-five minutes," said Jones. No one argued, but Maklowski said suddenly,

"Hey, what about the others? Professor Fairchild, and there are five more kids, aren't there?"

"Leaving notes for them will be best, I think, " said Ramon. "One in your windshield, one in mine. All of them know both our cars."

Both the FIDO agents had paper and pencils handy, so writing the notes and affixing them beneath the wiper blades was the work of two minutes. Then the three groups set off for the gaping red mouth.

* * * *

"Here's one obvious difference," said Aurea. "In the old park, before it burned, they had these waxwork displays mixed in with the private rooms. One here, one there, a few on every floor."

They had reached subbasement Room 1C, showing a waxwork dummy who had slashed her wrists in a warm bath.

"I'm not sure it's any improvement," said October, "this making the catalogue easier to use."

"Catalogue?" asked Clement.

"Catalogue. Of ways to suicide, with the park's kind assistance. Or ways you can hire Hellmouth Park to get rid of your enemies for you."

"Oh," said Clement. "Maybe we should just take the elevator down to Level Four right away."

October shook his head. "They weren't *all* just waxwork exhibits, back in the old park. Some of them used actual victims. In the flesh."

"I don't *think* that lady in the bathtub could be Professor Sharma," said Aurea. "Not unless they put a blond wig on her, for some strange reason."

Clement forced himself to take another look, a closer one. "No. It isn't her. But…does that mean we have to look closely at them all?"

"I think we'd probably better," the shop man replied. "Once we get past the waxworks, we'll probably find nothing but opaque doors and have to try the key in every one. And the Sharmas might as easily be hidden in these exhibits as in one of the rooms farther down."

Clement moved to 1D, looked at the arsenic victim—a man—just long enough to be sure it wasn't Dr. Sharma, and swallowed. "I've got a confession to make. That Chevy that was following us and then passed us…I think it was Ramon. Ramon Mendoza, my fraternity big brother. And some of the others."

Almost simultaneously, October asked, "The ones who left you tied up and locked in down there?" and Aurea, "Why didn't you say anything at the time?"

"I've managed to forgive them for doing that to me," Clement replied miserably. "I've got to forgive. The vampire taboos make me. And I didn't say anything because we were on the way here. I…guess I didn't want to risk having you decide to turn back. And not even try to save them."

"So," said October. "We might bump into some of your fraternity brothers looking for them? Well, we knew from the outset that could happen. This just confirms it. Did you see that Chevy out in the parking lot before we came in?"

"No. But maybe I didn't look that carefully."

"And why tell us now?" said Aurea.

"My jewelry's been pestering me about it all this time. I finally decided…it seems like a good idea to have my conscience guards as clear as possible. Down here."

To Clement's surprise, October clapped him on the shoulder. "Welcome to the human race, son. Good to know you've got at least a few clay toes."

"Like everybody else," Aurea agreed.

Clement grinned and took a few seconds to squeeze his new friends' hands gratefully. "I'm afraid the clay goes a lot farther up my legs than that."

"Doesn't everybody's?" said Aurea.

October added, "Mine goes all the way to my stomach."

"But let's not lose any more time, boys," the jeweler went on. "I'd as soon get all this behind us as quickly as we can."

* * * *

The middle floors of Hellmouth Park had five dining rooms in all—besides seven adult theaters, one dedicated to each of the classic "Seven Sins"; and a number of private rooms with locks, where at least one or two of those sins could be practiced. There had been no raids by the local law since years before the old park burned.

Gale Hartwick and the two sophomores would have liked to check all the rooms. But without some kind of official clearance, they had to settle for the restaurants and theaters. Even so, they soon saw that forty-five minutes was going to be none too long.

* * * *

Theda thoroughly enjoyed riding up in the ear elevator, watching the changing views on the devil's-head building, the picket line that had been circling the park grounds night and day all these years—with an ever-changing cast of pickets, naturally—the empty cow pasture under the night sky, the distant white shadow that was Heavengate Park, with its own circle of picketing marchers… The wise and mature FIDO man at her side…

"How much chance, really, do you think we've got of finding them in the family-fun playground?" she asked.

"Realistically? Not all that much. Realistically, if it was up to me, I'd have said, Let 'em just avail themselves of this park's suicide service and save the world another legal-circus trial."

"You don't think War Crimes Trials will put an end to all future atrocities?"

"They *may* help a little. Keep things on a smaller scale, maybe a little more carefully hidden. But as for putting an end to them…about as much chance as the last Great War has of putting a complete stop to all future squabbles and petty wars between nations."

"If you feel that way, why are you in FIDO?"

"It's a job. And, who knows? Maybe when I first joined, I believed in how much good it was going to do the world, ultimately. Yeah, maybe I believed in all that…back when I was your age."

"And why are we combing Hellmouth Park tonight?"

"Tonight? Chance for a few rides, a little fairgoing with a very lovely young lady at my side."

"Why, thank you, M. Maklowski!"

"Jason. You might as well call me Jason."

"Only if you call me Theda."

* * * *

Hartwick the elder proposed bypassing the first three subbasement levels with their waxwork museum, and taking an elevator straight to the fourth level down. Being less than sincerely interested in pursuing the deathguards of Vayalpad Kali Camp, Ramon saw no reason to reject the suggestion.

"Say," the FIDO man remarked on their ride down, "we know where the others are, but you never told 'em where *we'd* be checking."

"It should be obvious enough. Mid-earth, the stratosphere—figuratively speaking—and the depths."

"Well, we know where we'll all be meeting again in three-quarters of an hour."

"Yes. We know where we have all agreed to meet again."

The elevator came to its designated stop. Its two passengers disembarked into the famous slowly spiraling corridor of the Hellmouth Park "dungeons," opposite the door marked in blood-red figures: "4A."

The door was firmly shut. All the doors were shut, stretching down and down that long corridor. Flames done in luminescent paint covered the walls and ceiling, stiff-bristled carpeting with a pattern like charcoals smoldering in a bed of ash covered its slanting floor, and each door showed like a numeral and letter glowing starkly in the midst of a black void. Another heavy door, this one painted in flame imagery to match the walls and ceiling, closed the lower corridor off from the more public wax museum chambers of 1A to 3Z. The elevator rendered this barrier more symbolic than actual; still, it may well have been soundproofed, as all the lower doors seemed to be. Certain of the rooms presumably contained occupants engaged in activity of some sort; but throughout the corridor, silence reigned heavily.

"Well!" began Lancelot Hartwick. "Where do we start?"

"You are the return visitor. I, the novice in this place."

"Right." Hartwick rapped sharply on 4A.

No one answered. Excellent. Ramon seized the other man's arm and, combining surprise with native strength, spun him around, face to face, holding him fast against the closed door.

"Hey!" said Hartwick.

"*You* were her murderer, were you not?"

"M-murderer? I never murdered anyone!"

"*Killed,* then, if you prefer. We will even allow 'executed,' for the sake of argument. Irina Kiripovna."

"The 'Hallowe'en Hooker'?" Hartwick tried to laugh. "What makes—"

"You all but boasted of it, that night Blazhenov's suicide brought you and your partner to Fairchild's Inner Circle. Oh, spare me your posturing!" Ramon added as the other made as if to protest again. "It was transparent that this 'friend' from whom you had the story was a fiction for yourself."

"Seemed 'transparent' to *you,* maybe. Pater Fairchild—"

"Fairchild! How long did I suspect Fairchild himself, with his trifling fixation on vampires? Harmless, as it turns out. He may not really like the vampire he knows, he may never bring himself fully to trust poor Czarny, but neither would he willingly see him harmed, as he demonstrated tonight. Had Pater Fairchild discovered Irina in Greek Town, he would have informed the sheriff's office, not murdered her, unless perhaps finding her with her fangs actually in a victim's neck, which I know would not have happened. *You,* on the other hand—"

"You think I executed her for being a vampire? You think I'm as strange as Fairchild on that subject?"

"No. You killed her, I believe, because in your own strange superstition you saw an enemy spy in anyone of Russian extraction—"

"Irina Kiripovna *was* a Russian spy! Yes, I was the one who offered her secrets for sale! She *snatched* at my bait!"

"Or humored a fratty boy whom anyone would know highly unlikely to possess such secrets for sale? Were you also a client for her usual services as prostitute? A potential client? What were you to her, Lancelot Hartwick?"

"She *was* a real spy, I tell you!"

"She was a real vampire. At least Fairchild's motive would have rested in some species of fact."

"I tell you, I did the War effort a service by eliminating her!"

"And the picket fence post through her heart? Perhaps to disguise the true cause of her death? Did you already have a handgun, Hartwick? Or—"

"And what're you talking about, a 'real' vampire?"

"Irina Kiripovna," Ramon said steadily, "was to me as I am to Clement Czarny. I was a sickly child. A rich but sickly brat. Irina Kiripovna gave me the health my parents' tridollars could not."

Hartwick tried to break free. FIDO agents were not weaklings, nor did they lack training. But Ramon held him fast.

"Vampiric super-strength," said Ramon, "is a tale born of the vampire's invulnerability to disease. But I think I have worked with my own native human strength until it more than matches yours."

"If you're another vampire like Czarny, you can't hurt me. You can't do anything about me, or else the crosses and sunlight and garlic and—"

"My conscience is not quite so finely-tuned an instrument as that of my son in blood. My conscience is perfectly well satisfied with a few extraordinary good deeds and acts of heroism. Among which I number doing justice to my blood-mother's *murderer!*"

Ramon bared his fangs. Hartwick saw them, and gasped.

"Don't…don't…" he pleaded, as any other victim would under the circumstances.

"Have no fear. *You* will not become one of us. That requires the sharing of blood, and I have no intention of any such connection with *you*, Lancelot Hartwick. Nor of sedating you with my powers of suggestion. Only of sapping your will to resist. I want you to feel every pang…"

"How…will you explain it?" the victim asked weakly. "How are you going to cover this up?"

"How much grief did that problem cause you in Irina Kiripovna's case? You will be one more victim of a strange accident in Hellmouth Park, this place of strange accidents. Perhaps I will seek my own way elsewhere in the world and we will be two more of Hellmouth's never-explained disappearances." Ramon had provisions in place for continuing secretly to cover as much of Clement's expenses as the scholarship did not...

Seizing the wrist of Irina's murderer, Ramon brought it to his mouth, punctured it with one fang only, moved his lips into place, and began to suck. He disliked the flavor of the murderer's blood, not because it was in any way unwholesome to him, but because of whose it was. Nevertheless, he enjoyed the pain his sucking obviously caused the FIDO man, who gasped sharply.

"So...this... So who else have you...drained like this, Mendoza? In your 'heroics'?"

The man at least had spirit. Ramon's power of suggestion robbed his body of physical strength, but his mind continued the attempt to resist. Ramon lifted his mouth long enough to reply. "I have drained no one. Irina's sisters in the profession see to my dietary needs, as they saw to hers—animals' blood with a small admixture of human, less than engorges a wood tick. Clement and his prescribing physician deduced it for themselves, though trial and error. Occasionally I buy a rich dinner directly from one of the ladies' wrists—no more harmful to them than a donation to the Red Cross. And, for them, I render it painless. Take what comfort you may in the fact that overindulgence annoys my stomach as much as any other person's. For you, however, I will accept that discomfort. You will be the first..."

No. Lancelot Hartwick would *not* be the first. Ramon had drained Clement white, saved the boy's life only by immediate replenishment from Ramon's own veins...

He spat out his enemy's wrist. "Bandage it up," he said in disgust—disgust at *whom*, he hardly knew or even greatly cared. "You owe your life to Clement Czarny. My son in blood is a better man than I. *He* forgives."

Hartwick got out his handkerchief, unfolded it with quivering fingers, fumbled one-handedly...

Ramon, his disgust congealing into a hard lump, took the handkerchief from him and bound it firmly around the bleeding wrist. "This was an accident," he said, staring deeply into the other's eyes. "Done by a projecting nail in one of the doorframes. You will forget anything else that passed and was said here between us tonight, from the time we left the elevator until the moment I finish tying this bandage."

Lancelot Hartwick nodded.

After a few moments to rest after the encounter with the projecting nail, they continued their hunt down the corridor. Ramon wished that the congealed lump inside him were as easy to dissolve as the FIDO man's immediate memories.

They would continue the search down this corridor for as long as Ramon felt his resolution firm. As soon as he sensed it about to waver, he would maneuver his enemy to the stairwell, and they would gain the more populated areas of the park with no further delay.

At least he had conquered himself far enough to act as though he had forgiven. Thus leaving himself free to continue his own life. The Pi Rho house was not such a bad place to live, even though his whole reason for pledging, as for putting up with Fairchild's "Inner Circle" and its jejune activities, was ended now. The advanced degree he had been earning as a cover might still prove of some use to him in future life, even though his very reason for choosing the University of Minnemagantic in Hodag Crossing was finished with the discovery and permanently aborted execution of Irina's murderer.

And he could personally continue his quiet and half secret guardianship of his son in blood, as Irina had been unable to do for him.

* * * *

Rooms 3A to 3Z were entirely devoted to the cruelties and atrocities of the Last Great War, Act II. Some people said even that was far from adequate—that the park could easily have given it two levels, twenty-six showrooms *apiece* to the Stalinists and the Kali Party, and even that wouldn't have exhausted it. Other people wondered how Hellmouth Park had known back in 1941 that within five years it would want all this exhibit space.

Clement, October, and Aurea had made their painstaking way to 3F, still without reaching an exhibit of a Kali Camp itself. Through its wide show-front door, 3F showed the interior of one of the infamous cattle cars used to carry prisoners to the camps. Beneath the glass-eyed gaze of a couple of whip-wielding guards who stood at either side as if to frame the diorama, wax statues of men, women, and children stood shoulder to shoulder, hip to hip, back to stomach, crammed in like sardines, all naked. Many of them had bindi on their foreheads, but that in itself had come to make no difference, as Muslims tried to disguise themselves, and the Kali Party's net spread out over political enemies of all creeds. Human wastes puddled the floor. One man had vomited on his neighbors for lack of space to avoid them. One woman, face aghast, was trying to examine her infant baby.

Many people had died on the way, crammed into train cars like this, jolted over rough rails in freezing weather when winds blew in through the slats and the only warmth was from their own bodies, or in blazing summer when there was less than no escape from the heat. Those who died were usually counted the lucky ones.

Even the jolting of the cattle car over the rails seemed to be duplicated, though not strongly enough to endanger the wax statues. Nevertheless...

"Look!" Clement exclaimed. "That woman moved!"

"Surely another mechanical animation," Aurea guessed. "Or the way the floor is vibrating under them. *No one* could have paid to commit suicide in a scene like this."

"No! None of the others are— There! Again! And that man near her... And there! Around her neck! Isn't that her gold cross—the one you refashioned from her svastika?"

Even from that distance, it showed up—the only thing any figure in there, except the guard dummies, was wearing.

Professor Sharma looked up, seemed to catch sight of Clement, and immediately averted her eyes, trying to turn away.

"Professor! Professor Sharma! Dr. Sharma!"

There was no further movement from either. But October said, hollowly, "This time the key fits. So the Devil was honest about that much, at least."

With a rush of frigid cold, the door swung out. There would hardly have been room for it to swing in. There was hardly room for Clement to squeeze his thin self between the dummies, none of which fell over because the others were pressing so close. The cattle car was freezing. Duplicating the heat of summer would have threatened the wax, and the dummies had no body heat to give off. The wastes on the floor were probably real, but at least partly frozen, and there was no foot room to avoid them. Clement didn't try, just tried not to slip where they were icy.

"Professor Sharma! Dr. Sharma! You can't—"

"Clement," said the professor. "You are a good, brave young man, but you should not have come here. Go away now, and sing beautifully."

"We are not the Sharmas," said her husband. "We are Dharmik Indradatt and Ganesa Asan, of Vayalpad Kali Camp. And we are here for Brahman."

"To make our payment," said Professor Sharma. "To begin our next life, perhaps...not so very much soiled of this one."

"No!" Clement protested. "Not suicide! Professor, Doctor—come back and stand trial, won't that be enough payment? But don't—not suicide!"

"You good, brave boy, we suffer here what we on a time agreed that other people should suffer. This is justice. It is Brahman. And it is private. Do not ask that we go back, be made a...a spectacle for the world to hate, perhaps be sent apart to prison, never again to be husband and wife together for the rest of our lives."

"It was…a strange time," said Dr. Sharma. "They told us we must kill Muslims for the good of the whole world. They told us it was good, it was virtuous, it was noble to kill Muslims. And then, to kill others also. They told us we were brave and strong and noble when we fought against ourselves and conquered ourselves and killed these human beings who, they told us, were not truly human beings, but a kind of…evil demon. And we…we believed them. Do not ask us to explain such things to the world. Not to this sane world. Not now."

"We cannot any longer explain them to ourselves," said Professor Sharma. "Go, now, my dear, brave Clement. Clean your feet, and sing, live your life, and may you learn all the good things that we did not learn."

Dr. Sharma added, "May those who lead you be better than those who led us."

From the open doorway, October coughed as if for attention. Then he said, "All that sounds very noble, M.'s Indradatt and Asan, and if we were anywhere else in this world, you'd have convinced *me,* anyway. In that case, I'd have said, Go ahead and kill yourselves. But we're in Hellmouth. Things happen here. *Bad* things. Don't believe whatever the management may have told you when you arranged this. Believe *me.* Suicide *here,* and I'm not sure you'd ever get back on the wheel of Karma or whatever you want to call it. Trust me, if you know something about those Kali Camps of yours, I know something about Hellmouth Park, and you do *not* want to die here! Assisted suicide, victim-voluntary murder, whatever you call it, *you do* NOT *want to die down HERE!* Now come on, let us help you get back outside, and then, if you still want, I'll draw your warm bath and find you the razor blades, or whatever you like."

They looked at him.

"Here!" said Aurea. She had quietly been stripping the guard dummies of their uniforms. "Clothes," she said, holding them up in a bundle. "Not great, but better than nothing."

The Sharmas look at each other, then at Clement, Aurea, and October, each in turn. Professor Sharma sighed. "You do not plan to go away without us?"

October folded his arms across his chest and shook his head. Shivering, but they were all shivering.

Now Dr. Sharma sighed and reached for his wife's hand. They spoke together for several minutes, softly, in their native tongue. At last he turned and spoke in English to the would-be rescuers: "We will not add you very brave, very good people into our debt."

Hand in hand as best they could, they pressed behind Clement on their way out. At the door, they used the guard dummies' undershirts to wipe their feet and anything else that needed wiping. Then the Sharmas put on the rest of the guard clothing, which fit, not well, but adequately. "These terrible uniforms," said Dr. Sharma, "are what we deserve to wear."

"What happened to your own clothes?" asked Aurea. "That you wore here. Can we get to them?"

Smiling sadly, Professor Sharma shook her head. "They took them away. We did think we would need clothes again, in this life."

October said, "We'll take the stairs up. With any luck, they should lead to a Fire Safety Guiderules exit on the ground floor."

Dr. Sharma said, "We are the customers, and the park has our tridollars already for the services we have decided we will not use. I think that no one will stop us from walking out now."

In the stairwell, they encountered Ramon and the younger FIDO man, to whom the Sharmas surrendered themselves, while Clement's group, who wanted their own involvement in all this kept quiet from anyone else, slipped away to head home, October only apologizing for not supplying the warm bath and razor blades, after all.

None of them talked again until they reached the parking lot. Then October exclaimed, "We made it!" and staggered half against the side of their Rockne and half into his wife's arms. "We made it in there and got out alive again!"

"We went in for completely unselfish reasons this time," said Aurea. "Maybe that's what kept us safe."

"Kept *us* safe," Clement said sadly. "The poor Sharmas!"

CHAPTER 21

NEXT DAY: THURSDAY, NOV. 20

Once back in Hodag Crossing, they drove first to 278 Traut Road, where they found lights still on. Carl had returned to Dr. al Shammari's home, bringing his wife and son, to sit vigil through these anxious hours with his sister-in-law and her intended. Clement's news relieved their minds somewhat, and Dr. al Shammari gave Clement a sleeping preparation he had on hand in his own medicine cabinet: a capsule strong and fast-acting enough to take effect before the vampiric metabolism flushed it through.

Carl drove Clement back to the Pi Rho house, Carl volunteering to let on that after opting out of the hunt's final phase, he had been the one to return and free the vampire brother. It was a lie, but it was Carl's inspiration, and Clement felt too weary to protest, nor even to notice whether and how far his jewelry reacted.

He slept through the next day, awakening only when Ramon came into his room and tabbed on the light.

"What time's it?" Clement asked muzzily, thinking maybe almost dawn.

"Time to leave for the theater, if you plan to go on with the opera tonight."

Coming fully awake in a few heartbeats, Clement reached for the glass of supper Ramon had brought him, and quickly swallowed it down.

"Am I forgiven for last night, little brother?"

"You're forgiven," Clement answered simply, unwrapping his wrists. "All of you." His wrists already looked well enough healed that new bandaging might be more noticeable than the faint traces of last night's welts. "How...uh..." he went on, "how did it all work out?"

"Pater Fairchild's car arrived just as the rest of us were gathering to leave. I think he was secretly relieved to have kept the two frosh well and safely distant from any possible line of fire. Fletcher and Drinkwater never did make their appearance. I suspect them of seizing their opportunity to enjoy such night life as the more succulent portions of our fair town afford, but they claim to have met utter confusion at the hospital, and the pater has decided to accept their tale at face value. The Sharmas are on their way to Washington, in custody of Hartwick the elder and our own local representative of the law. Agent Maklowski offered Sheriff Nurmi a share of the glory in return for a chance to see this opera, assuming it goes on as scheduled."

This was the second time Ramon had mentioned a doubt about that. "Why shouldn't it?" Clement asked, rolling out of bed and reaching for his clothes.

"There has been idle speculation. Both the *Currents* and the *Yawp* put out special editions today, carrying reasonably accurate accounts, so far as they go, of the arrest. We have it on the authority of King Oland, our man at the *Yawp,* that for once the syndicated news services have picked the story up from *us.* Rest easy, neither your name nor those of your friends Bradley and Zimmerman are anywhere mentioned. I think, however, that very few would feel any great surprise if tonight's performance, even the entire run, were cancelled. Pending some announcement to that effect, Tallpines and most of the other Pies should be milling about Wedderburn Auditorium even as we speak."

* * * *

Clement got there twenty minutes before the scheduled show time, to find an anxious cluster gathered behind the curtain. Maybe half the performers were in their costumes and make-up, but it looked like a smaller proportion than that because the musicians as well as the stage crew were mixed in with the singers.

April stepped out to face him. She was still in her street clothes, without one dab of stage make-up. "Clement," she said, "we're all waiting for you. It all depends on you. Does this opera go on, or not?"

"I plan to go on, anyway."

"Indradatt and Asan of Vayalpad," April said in a quivering voice, "were deathguards hiding here among decent, honest people."

"What else could they do?" He'd had all the way from the Pi Rho house to the theater to think about the things Ramon had told him. "They were refugees, too, weren't they? In a way."

"*Ten million dead!*" said April. "*Ten million,* tortured to death!"

"It was… But no one deathguard killed ten million, all alone. And there was a…a kind of insanity running through those countries, India and Russia. We find other people 'Not Guilty by Reason of In—"

"Clement Czarny!" said April Greenhill. "*You* might be okay with standing up there on the stage and singing the lead all by yourself, but *I* put my conscience ahead of my career. If this opera goes on, it goes on without me!"

He looked around at the rest of them. "Do all of you feel this way?"

Keiko seemed to be struggling to keep her face neutral. Three people from the Chorus and two musicians, one of them Linda Beauchamp the oboe player, walked over to join April. Everyone else stood still.

Almost everyone else. Babs Thorvald took one step forward. She was in her Janthe costume and make-up, and she held a scorebook. "I think I could fill in for Emmy, if I can do it book in hand."

Clement nodded. "Thanks, people. Let's do this!"

April jerked Clement's pin off her blouse, almost threw it at him, stopped herself and said, "It'll be on the props table." Then she strode offstage, the three choristers and two musicians after her.

But both Keiko and Tony Tallpines were pressing up, shaking Clement's hands. "Go get into your costume and make-up, hero," Keiko told Clement. "We'll hold the curtain."

"Attaboy, bro!" said Tony. "I don't think I could've filled in for *you,* even book in hand. And they might have had to cut my great Drinking Song."

"Clement," said Babs, "will you make the indulgence announcement for me?"

"Come on, young floater," said Professor Grunewald of the Theater Department, who oversaw costumes and make-up for almost all the shows. "Let's get you dressed and ready."

He found himself very grateful, now, that he hadn't gotten the role of Figaro last year. At least it meant that nobody could accuse him of having been Professor Sharma's pet.

* * * *

The performance started almost half an hour late, but the entire audience was still waiting in a hush. When Clement stepped out on the stage in front of the closed curtains, he saw that the house was packed. M. Maklowski sat with Theda in the front row. April was sitting with Solly among the Pi brothers and sisters. October and Aurea had seats near the front in the right side section.

Clement started simply. "Gentle people. Thanks for your patience. Tonight the role of Emmy will be sung by Babs Thorvald, with book in hand. We beg your indulgence." He hesitated before going on: "I guess it's no secret what's happened this week. But everything they did here in Hodag Crossing for almost seven years—longer than Act II of the War itself lasted—everything they did here has been good. There are people alive today who wouldn't have been, without Dr. Sharma—the man we all knew as Dr. Sharma. There are three people singing with the Galop de Vache Opera, two with the Minneapolis Civic, and one with the New

York Met, who might not have been there without Professor Sharma's mentorship. And all of you have enjoyed years of good opera in the fall and good choral concerts in the spring, thanks to her.... I know it doesn't amount to very much, beside what went on…before they came here. But I think that our community at least, this one little piece of the world, should remember them for what they were all the time they lived here. With us."

April was the first to stand up—April and Solly. Then M. Maklowski, and then everybody else was on their feet. For a minute Clement thought the whole audience was about to walk out at once, following April and Solly. But no—the FIDO man was clapping. And Theda. And October and Aurea. And all the audience members except the ones who were squeezing their way to the aisles…

In the end, only about a fifth of the audience walked out. While everybody else gave Clement a standing ovation that he hoped was really for Professor and Dr. Sharma. From the wings, Keiko was beaming at him with a thumbs-up.

By the opera's second act, the house was full again, to standing room only. Either word of mouth had acted very quickly, or some of the people who'd left had come back, or both.

April and Solly did not come back. Nor did Clement ever pick her pin up from the props table. Keiko did, and kept it around until it got misplaced among the household mathoms. Many years later, she was to happen across it again, to wonder where it had come from and what it was doing in this box of oddments.

FROM THE REVIEWS, FRIDAY, NOV. 21.

Hodag Crossing Currents:

The Local Arts:

"I confess, for once in his life, this old curmudgeon was moved to tears. Those of us in the Wedderburn audience yesterday evening were privileged to hear an opening statement that for depth, sincerity, and humanity compacted into as few words as possible can best perhaps be compared to Lincoln's address at Gettysburg....

"…While respecting the questionable sentiments which clearly prompted the original performer to decamp, one could only admire Barbara Thorvald, whose book in hand actually enhanced the poignancy of the evening.... Anthony Tallpines, the other baritone of the opera, shows excellent promise; his

'Drinking Song' provided a welcome relief... Clement Czarny's singing voice has matured in expression as well as depth...

"...by the opera's conclusion, I wept almost openly for both the victims and the eponymous vampire himself, who was perhaps the chiefest victim of all...."

(This time Frank Bashaw's review took most of his regular readers and even some of his personal friends by surprise.)

John Carpenter's Quick Pick:

"Go if your conscience lets you."

The Hodag's Yawp:

"This time I have to beg off reviewing the School of Music's Fall Opera. I almost didn't go at all, after the news that staggered us Thursday about lunchtime. Nor could I in good conscience remain in the theater after Professor Sharma's, *alias* Ganesa Asan's pet baritone made his infamous opening statement, surely a worse crime than anything the character he was singing was about to perpetrate in the opera. Is our campus vampire showing his true fangs at last?"

(Again, the "Pundita" byline may have changed hands with the new school year.)

Gregory Sierramentez's "At a Gulp":

"Give it a whole line of stars. Great show! Go!"

POSTLUDE

At the 1953 Geneva War Crimes Trial, Frank Krajewski was demonstrated *not* to be Feodor Karpovsky, and freed. As in lesser legal cases, his exoneration was considered sufficient repayment in itself for the disruption to his life and grief to his family. The bride he had married after leaving Forest Green, Indiana, left him, unable to take the strain of her new husband's arrest and incarceration pending trial. Five years after being freed, unable to escape the lingering doubt and social stigma clinging to anyone so accused, even after being officially cleared by the Court, Krajewski ended his own life. Not, at least, in Hellmouth Park.

Kosya Petrovka, whose testimony was one factor in proving Krawjewski's misidentification, was sentenced to death. It was the last death sentence actually carried out in the Western World. Popular report put a grateful smile on her face both when the sentence was passed and when her head was hooded preparatory to her execution. Dmitri Garbanakov was not apprehended until 2005. The real Feodor Karpovsky never was found and brought to human justice. These were, of course, but a few of the Last Great War's all but innumerable deathguards; but they comprise all those mentioned by name in the present story.

At the trial that condemned Kosya Petrovka to the death she had chosen against at the last minute in Hellmouth Park, Dharmik Indradatt and Ganesa Asan drew sentences of life imprisonment. The two served their first thirteen years in solitary confinement, each in a different prison. Then, with the passage of time, the efforts of Amnesty Universal and numerous letter-writing campaigns (in all of which Clement Czarny participated), and a certain softening of the world's political climate, they were quietly allowed to share quarters in yet a third facility, where they were even granted a small garden plot which they could see from their cell and cultivate during their periods of outdoor exercise. Feeling unworthy to supplement their prison diet, they grew flowers, which they shared with guards and fellow inmates. He credited letters from his old colleague Rabar al Shammari, and she sound recordings from Clement and other former students of hers, with helping them maintain sanity through their thirteen years in solitary. Carrying on his work through correspondence with Dr. al Shammari, Dr. Sharma finally saw some of his work in Hodag Crossing published in the medical literature, though under Shammari's name alone—the Hindu physician himself absolutely refused to take his share of the credit under any pseudonym, lest it inadvertently be tainted with a whiff of the Kali Camp.

Dr. al Shammari and Dolores Wanamaker adoped two children, with whom Carl Avosso, Jr. played while his parents were visiting with Aunt Dolly and Uncle Rab.

Professor Matthew Fairchild retired at seventy-five from house fathering the Purple Rose, and, his zeal for hunting deathguards having at last somewhat abated, turned his hobby of mathematical artwork into a swansong career. Before his death at eighty-seven, he had seen two of his canvases hung in the Galop de Vache Museum of Fine Painting.

If Theda Jones had been ten years older, or Jason Maklowski ten years younger, a viable romance might have developed between them. As it was, after her graduation with a Bachelor's Degree, he found her a good starting position at FIDO, which she kept even after meeting and marrying another young agent there. Maklowski gave the bride away at the altar.

To general surprise, it was Maklowski who stuck with FIDO-WC until his comfortable retirement, while Lancelot Hartwick, troubled with vague dreams since arresting the two deathguards at Hellmouth, left the agency for a job with Amnesty Universal.

Although Ramon Mendoza did much volunteer work for Amnesty Universal, he never afterward encountered his old enemy. He spent his life balancing the secret of his vampiric condition with heroic efforts for various social and environmental causes. As well as his time and effort, he donated most of his inherited fortune to these causes, retaining only enough to provide himself a moderately comfortable lifestyle when at home in Hodag Crossing. He lived well past a hundred, and at his death seemed physiologically and mentally little more than a fit eighty.

Spud Bartlett went on to earn advance degrees in History, Philosophy, and Literature from the Universities of Michiana, Astoria, and Florida. He wrote philosophic novels read by almost nobody and historical philosophy that tended to top the bestseller lists, spent most of his wraparound afternoons during the football season watching the big college and professional games, and fell out of touch with his erstwhile buddies Fred Fletcher and Stallion Drinkwater.

Val Saladin eventually traded in his hero-worship for healthy self-reliance, and turned out well, as did most of those whom we have seen only in passing.

Noble lived to a ripe old doggy age and, while officially the mascot of the two Pi houses, grew to be beloved by the entire campus.

By the Saturday evening performance of *Der Vampyr,* Babs Thorvald was able to do the role of Emmy without the book. Linda Beauchamp brought her oboe back to the orchestra pit for the Friday to Sunday performances. She and Tony Tallpines decided their difference of opinion on Opening Night had been more of a starting point than otherwise for their relationship. By the spring of 1953, when the G&S Society in collaboration with the Hodag Thespians took advantage of the previous autumn's *Vampyr* to have Clement spoof his own Lord Ruthven the vampire with Gilbert and Sullivan's Sir Ruthven of Ruddigore, Linda and Tony (who were also involved, she in the orchestra and he as Sir Despard) were dating. They married a few years later, moved to Minneapolis after graduation, and sweetened mundane day jobs with rich lives in community theater and musical groups.

Unlike Linda Beauchamp, April never came back to the show and felt the difference of opinion was far too fundamental to allow any renewal of romantic feelings with Clement. A dispassionate observer might have opined that these two had never truly been compatible in any case, that it had been simply calf love for both. April eventually married Solly; and

Clement, Keiko. It was not a double wedding, although in later years the four grew to be good friends again, sometimes meeting with M.'s Bradley and Zimmerman to test some new game.

If Clement ever learned or suspected Ramon's actual earliest relationship to him, or even that Ramon was another vampire, he left no record of it. He did, however, keep up the old fraternity tie. Ramon stood godfather to each of Clement's and Keiko's three children, one conceived before the Procreational Permit system was reinstituted, and all of them healthy offspring of a happy home. After his short but satisfying career of two years with the Galop de Vache Opera, three with the Minneapolis Civic, and two auditions for the New York Metropolitan, Clement and Keiko brought their family back to Hodag Crossing, where he settled into a quiet and mundane professorship in the University of Minnemagantic School of Music, and she worked backstage with community theater once her youngest child was in high school. Clement might well have rivaled his fraternity brother's lifespan, had he not, in his early seventies, lost a surprise difference of opinion with a pickup truck that jumped a red light to speed through a crosswalk. He had obtained advance dispensation and left directives for his body to be cremated and the ashes scattered, as a simple precautionary measure, the legends of vampiric resurrection being one piece of the folklore he had never in his lifetime had means of testing. A quarter of a century after his death, the Catholic Church being in an especially inclusive and anti-bigotry mood, Clement Czarny was named a "Blessed," the penultimate step on the road to canonization as the first vampire saint in the calendar. Or, as he himself would have been quick to point out, the first one *known* to be a vampire.

October Bradley and Aurea Zimmerman enjoyed a long and uneventful latter third of life, never again going anywhere near Hellmouth Park for any reason whatever. Although he was always careful to keep the green plastic "free pass" card in a safe place in his billfold, just in case.

And still the parks brood at each other across the cow pasture. And still the picket lines encircle them in perpetual motion. And still the rumors go around that both parks, Hellmouth and Heavengate, are secretly under the same ownership and management.

AUTHOR'S NOTE

Admitting the ideal of limiting the number of characters populating any fiction to the important ones, I nevertheless found it would have rung false not to recognize that every major character would naturally know by name a host of minor ones. I believe the names listed below are the ones it might help the reader to have for ready reference. If I have succeeded in my aim, other characters are sufficiently identified each time they appear, or play their entire parts in episodes of limited duration, or are mentioned only in passing.

GOWN: THE UNIVERSITY OF MINNEMAGANTIC

Pi Rho fraternity (the "Purple Rose"):

House Father:

"Pater" Matthew Fairchild, Professor Emeritus of Mathematics

Class of 1945:

Lancelot "Lance" Hartwick, after graduation an agent of the Federal Investigative Departmental Office, War Crimes Division (FIDO, FIDO-WC)

Class of 1951:

Carl Avosso

Class of 1952:

Ramon Mendoza

Class of 1953:

Gale Hartwick, Lance Hartwick's brother
Spud Bartlett, the football star
Fred Fletcher

Class of 1954:

Clement Czarny (name pronounced "CHAR-ni," with hard "ch" as in
   "church")
Solly Goldfein, Clement's best same-gender buddy
Stallion "Stale" Drinkwater

Class of 1955:

Tony Tallpines, baritone

Pi Psi sorority (the "Purple Sigh"):

Class of 1954:

Theda Jones

Independents:

Class of 1954:

April Greenhill
Keiko "Ko-Ko" Kato

School of Music:

Professor Kastha Sharma
Babs Thorvald, Professor Sharma's student assistant

Town: Hodag Crossing, state of Minnemagantic:

Dr. Pundarit Sharma, Professor Sharma's husband, the Hindu
Dr. Rabar al Shammari, the Muslim
Dolores Wanamaker, nurse
Millicent "Milly" Wanamaker, nurse, sister of Dolores
Frank Bashaw, curmudgeonly reviewer for *Hodag Crossing Currents*
October Bradley and Aurea Zimmerman, husband and wife partners in
   B & Z shop

Irina Kiripovna, Russian prostitute and vampire, killed 1945

Based in Washington, D. C.:

Jason Maklowski, Lance Hartwick's FIDO partner

Russian deathguards still at large in 1951:

Feodor Blazhenov and Kosya Petrovka, the Demon Doktors of Novgorod
Feodor Karpovsky the Fiend of Gadansk, possibly in disguise as Frank
    Krajewski, who lived for a time near Forest Green, Ind.
Dmitri Garbanokov, the Bear of Yemtsa.

www.ingramcontent.com/pod-product-compliance
Lightning Source LLC
Chambersburg PA
CBHW022151260626
47155CB00017B/1836